They were missing something, but he couldn't quite figure it out...

Lagarde could almost see a light go on above Taylor's head.

"So, when exactly did you and Harold end your meeting?" Taylor asked.

Neal looked at Taylor, seeing him for the first time and deciding he wasn't important. "Around midnight. Harold picked up the tab at the bar." He paused and then added, in case Taylor was too dim to understand, "His credit card receipt is probably time stamped."

Taylor looked at Lagarde.

Two hours between the time they left Harold and the time he was killed were not accounted for. Lagarde made a note on his pad. A man could get in a lot of trouble in two hours. Was there a woman no one knew about? Did Harold have some really bad habits that would get him killed? No one they'd talked to so far had mentioned this time gap. The person who killed him couldn't have predicted that Harold would be on Charles Town Road at the intersection with Kearneysville Road at any precise time. He or she would have had to wait for hours and follow him. Or the killer had a heads up. They needed to find Harold's personal phone, and fast.

When it comes to murder, even brilliant scientists aren't immune...

The night Harold Munson is shot dead in his car, the primary suspect is the man's brainiac wife. But Charlotte, who has a passion for science and sex with strangers, swears all she wants is a Nobel Prize for curing brain cancer, even if that requires fudging her research and a few dead patients along the way.

When the next body drops, all signs point to Charlotte, but Detective Sam Lagarde doggedly follows the clues until he has his own Eureka moment.

Praise for the Detective Sam Lagarde mystery series

For *Cromwell's Folly*

"From the first page to the last of Ginny Fite's novel *Cromwell's Folly* I was drawn into the unfolding drama. Layer upon layer, Fite connects the dots between her well-defined and wonderfully diverse characters. The lines between good and evil, criminal and victim are decidedly blurred. The more I knew of Ben Cromwell, the sociopath with no moral compass, the more I wanted to see him die. I felt sympathy for the lives he'd destroyed, including his own family members. Cromwell's Folly is a spellbinding page turner." ~ Rochelle Wisoff-Fields, author of *Please Say Kaddish for Me*

For *No Good Deed Left Undone*

"No Good Deed Left Undone explores the life, and death, of a not very nice man…It will make you laugh, cry, and struggle to guess 'who done it.' It's one you'll want to keep on your shelf and read again and again to catch what you missed the first time." ~ Regan Murphy, The Review Team of Taylor Jones & Regan Murphy

For *Lying, Cheating, and Occasionally Murder*

"*Lying, Cheating and Occasionally Murder* is fun, clever, fast paced, and well written—an excellent addition to the series and another jewel in the crown of this talented author." ~ Regan Murphy, The Review Team of Taylor Jones & Regan Murphy

ACKNOWLEDGEMENTS

Endless thanks to the usual suspects: K.P. Rollins, Tara Bell, and Catherine Baldau for walking through this manuscript with me and finding the right words to steer me to the story. As always, deep thanks to my children for tolerating my strange research habits and odder questions. Here's a bow to neuroscientists, Dr. Bruce Brown and Dr. Valérie Doyère, for letting me pick their brains late one evening over a few glasses of wine. And, to Sam Lagarde, who has seen me through the last few years, my everlasting gratitude.

Last but not least, many thanks to the Black Opal Books staff—LP, Lauri, Faith, and Jack—and my agent Jeanie Loiacono who make my dream worlds tangible.

Lying, Cheating, and Occasionally... Murder

Ginny Fite

A Black Opal Books Publication

GENRE: MYSTERY-DETECTIVE

This is a work of fiction. Names, places, characters and incidents are either the product of the author's imagination or are used fictitiously, and any resemblance to any actual persons, living or dead, businesses, organizations, events or locales is entirely coincidental. All trademarks, service marks, registered trademarks, and registered service marks are the property of their respective owners and are used herein for identification purposes only. The publisher does not have any control over or assume any responsibility for author or third-party websites or their contents.

DEDICATION

For my darlings

"I'm sorry, we're police officers. Decisions about the future of mankind don't really feature in our job descriptions." ~ DI Robert Lewis (Inspector Lewis, "Intelligent Design")

"Something is rotten in the state of biomedical research...we know in our hearts that the majority or even the vast majority of our research claims are false." ~ Danielle Teller, physician and researcher

"It's very dangerous to believe people. I haven't for years." ~ Miss Marple, *The Sleeping Murder*

Chapter 1

March 30, 2016, 6 a.m.:

At two in the morning on a perfectly clear night, the full moon casting a beacon across western fields, and along two satin rivers unfurling between dark mountains, Harold Munson ended his perfect day by crashing right through the clapboard siding of the Weigle Insurance Company office building.

Munson's front bumper nudged the insurance agent's desk into the printer, which interpreted the jolt as an instruction to print and began beeping its out-of-paper alarm. Dave Weigle, broker and owner of the company—awakened by a newly downloaded intruder alert app on his cell phone—threw on sweat pants and a jacket, padded out to his car in slippers, and arrived first on the scene.

He peeked through the window of the car in his parking lot and saw a man slumped over the driver's side air bag, but Weigle was too preoccupied with the damage to his building to look closely. Unlocking his unscathed office door, he first examined the gaping hole caused by the front of a car ripping through the side of his building, turned off the annoying printer beeping, looked around at the mess, and called the police, just in case the new automated security system hadn't notified them.

Then he took photographs on his cell phone. He had insurance. He might as well use it. If nothing else, he could prove to his wife he really had gone to the office in the middle of the night.

Munson had been going northwest toward Martinsburg, based on the swerve marks made by his tires on the two-lane Charles Town Road, when his car rammed into the insurance building opposite the Kearneysville Post Office five miles west of Shepherdstown.

When Jefferson County Sheriff's deputies arrived ten minutes after Weigle, they bolted out of their vehicles thinking Harold was dead drunk, slumped over the airbag like that, not moving and unresponsive to their increasingly loud, shouted commands: "Hands where I can see 'em. Step out of the car. Get out of the car now."

Sheriff Harbaugh was sure he saw Munson blink as officers approached the closed window of the driver's side door, guns drawn, yelling at him to surrender. They attempted to wrench open the door to pull him out of the car and discovered it was locked. Then, in quick succession, they noticed a smear of blood and brains on the passenger seat and dashboard and two small holes in the driver's side window surrounded by rings of spider-webbed glass.

Drunk or not, Harold had been shot through the head. That might have been the cause of his leaving the road and plowing into the building. Whether he hit the building first or the bullet smashing through his brain had caused him to veer off the road would be determined by further investigation. At that point, the deputies called in the West Virginia State Police with its forensics apparatus and crime-lab personnel.

After his initial reconnoiter of the Munson crime scene, a conversation with Weigle, whose cell phone alert app had recorded the moment of impact and whose photos of the scene might prove useful, Detective Sam Lagarde, assigned to the State Police Troop 2 Command, based outside Charles Town, reminded himself he was only a short trip on winding, narrow roads up and down a few hills from his eighteenth-century farmhouse. He decided to go home and let his horses out of the barn before he went back to the office to file his initial paperwork. When he got to his house, coffee was already brewing.

Lagarde stopped describing his new case and looked down into the mug of coffee Beverly Wilson put on the kitchen table in front of him. It was the right color. He took a sip. It had the right amount of sugar. He took two gulps. It was the right temperature. He felt like Goldilocks. He still wasn't accustomed to having someone take care of him, or even give two hoots about how he liked his coffee. He marveled at his good luck. It was six in the morning, and Beverly was a tea drinker. He took a moment to savor this extraordinary gift. In a month or two, he knew, he would take it for granted.

He looked up at Beverly then out beyond the kitchen door, which he'd left open to let in the bracing spring air, and glanced toward the barn. *It was too much to ask.*

"Yes, Sam." Beverly made a face at him and then smiled and put a hand on Lagarde's shoulder. "I let the horses out and made sure they have water and a few leaves of hay. They're set for a while, unless you want to ride, in which case you're the one who'll have to catch Jake."

That was all it took, the mild pressure of her warm palm on his shoulder for him to feel completely calm and that the world was in order. The whole thing—Beverly Wilson, in his house, sleeping in his bed, making slight snoring noises that forced him to acknowledge her presence was real—was a marvel to him.

Here she was talking to him as if it was the most normal thing in the world for them to be living together. *How had this happened?* He didn't feel entitled to such a miracle. After love, women were the second most indecipherable mystery he had never solved. But then, neither had anyone else.

"Where were the bullet casings?" Beverly asked.

Lagarde wrenched himself from his reverie. "Right." He took a gulp of coffee. "They were in that pocket-sized parking lot and on the street."

"So it wasn't a random drive-by shooting." She walked around the kitchen, her hands gesturing the way she did before marking a canvas, practicing the shape in the air. "The killer fired a shot out of the driver's side window at Munson coming from the other direction."

Beverly made the classic gun-shooting gesture with her pointer finger and thumb, her right arm across her chest, pretending she was shooting out of her driver's side window. Lagarde noted she assumed the shooter was right handed.

She paced a few times around the kitchen table, generating electricity for her brain to work faster. "She must've been waiting in the post office parking lot on the other side of Charles Town Road."

Lagarde looked up, astonished, and raised his eyebrows. "She?"

"She would've had to know the make and model of Harold's car," Beverly continued as if Lagarde hadn't said anything. "She pulled out of the post office lot, zoomed up parallel with Harold's car, driver's side to driver's side, and fired. Harold would've been startled."

Lagarde certainly felt startled. He took a sip of his coffee and watched Beverly.

She walked to the kitchen door and stood looking out. "He panicked and automatically steered away from the gun. He crashed into the building, where he sat dazed and confused from the airbag exploding in his face and the whole experience of being shot at."

Beverly looked over her shoulder at Lagarde. "The killer made a U-turn, pulled her car up beside Harold in the parking lot, got out of the car, walked over to Harold's window and shot him in the head. Look for another set of skid marks that make a sharp U-turn just past the post office parking lot entrance. How many bullets?"

Lagarde blinked. "Three," he answered automatically. "That we found." He took another sip of coffee, too amazed to do anything except to answer her questions. "She?" he asked again.

Beverly again ignored his question. "Caliber?"

"Forty-five."

"So, the killer shot once to scare him, and two to get the job done. Deliberate, not random, or, what do you say? He was the target, not collateral damage." Beverly was quiet for a few minutes while she stood in front of the open refrigerator. She pulled out an eggplant and two brown eggs. "And the killer isn't a professional. She didn't pick up her shell casings."

"What have you been reading, Beverly?"

She looked over at Lagarde who gave her his quizzical look, eyebrows raised, eyes wide. She called this his "shock and awe" look caused by her doing something that took him by complete surprise. Her smile said she enjoyed surprising him.

"Are you delving into criminal justice websites these days?" Lagarde asked. He actually hated that term, an oxymoron that seemed to distort the goals of a country founded on the rule of law. Those two words side by side implied justice was criminal or only criminals, not victims, got justice. He resisted either assertion. He was a rule of law man—as in, everyone was equal under the law.

"Eggplant parmigiana, for tonight," she said, answering a question he hadn't asked. She opened the pantry door and took out a box of breadcrumbs and a large bottle of olive oil.

It briefly occurred to Lagarde that before Beverly moved into his house, he'd never had a bottle of olive oil in his pantry.

"I'll make the marinara sauce with the last of the canned tomatoes and the basil I cut from my own garden last summer. I'll have to run to the market for the mozzarella."

Lagarde thought he should pinch himself. *I'm really dreaming all of this.* It had never occurred to him that Beverly might enjoy playing detective. Maybe she was taking a forensics class online so she could understand his work. All this out-of-the-blue speculation must be a way to fit into his life. He smiled at the thought.

Beverly pulled out the cutting board from the cabinet under the counter. "Was he married?"

"Yes."

"Any kids?"

"Don't know yet. And before you ask, he was thirty-seven."

"Where do they live?"

"In one of the new developments west of Shepherd-stown along Route Four-Eighty, about ten minutes from where he was killed."

"Check the wife's alibi."

"Of course. Those closest to the victim are primary suspects." He wasn't sure whether to be amused or annoyed at Beverly's insistence that the wife was the perpetrator, but he let her play out her scenario in the way he might play out a line, standing in the river, hoping for a fish. She might help him catch something.

Beverly raised one shoulder in a half shrug. "Just a hunch she's the killer. Or she hired the killer."

"And how can you know who the killer is at this point, Miss Marple?" Lagarde preferred to plod through all the available evidence and check all alibis—putting together the puzzle pieces of motive, means and opportunity—before he started speculating about who the perpetrator was. "You haven't even been at the crime scene."

"Who else would know where Munson would be at two in the morning and what direction he'd be coming from? He could've been heavy into gambling at the casino and already bankrupted them, or he could have been cheating on his wife. She's not a sentimental woman, I think you'll find."

He grinned. "Somehow, although he's the dead guy, he sounds like the evil-doer." He changed the subject. "What time is dinner?"

She leaned over and gave him a kiss on the cheek. "When you get here." She walked back to the sink. "I guess I'm remembering one of your earlier cases—all those women who killed Ben." She looked out of the window over the sink. Her shoulders sagged a bit.

Lagarde got up off the kitchen chair, scraping the wooden legs slightly on the tile floor, stretched elaborately hoping Beverly would turn, put her arms around him, and hold him for a few minutes, which she did. *This miracle must have happened when I wasn't looking, the way all the best things happen.*

She looked up at him. "Was it at close range?"

He laughed, let her go, pulled his barn jacket off the chair back, and picked up his hat. "Gunpowder residue on the window. Close enough that it wasn't accidental. Two shots, so not random."

"He didn't roll down the window," Beverly said, almost to herself. "He must have known she wanted him dead. It was personal. She didn't care if anyone saw her standing there in the middle of the night with a gun aimed at the car. She was desperate, maybe crazy. Was anything missing from the car?"

"The doors were locked when the deputies arrived on the scene. We had to pry them open to pull out the body after we checked for fingerprints and gunpowder residue on the doors."

"She has a key to the car, so was anything missing that should have been there, or that you would expect to be there? Was the car still running?"

He looked at her—a long, steady look just in case he had never really seen her before and wanted to take inventory fast before anything else happened that changed his picture of who she was. She certainly looked like the same arty woman wearing a green sweater and yellow socks he'd met two years before. "No. The car wasn't running."

He took a gulp of coffee. It hadn't even occurred to him that someone, and certainly not the dead Harold Munson, had shut off the car before the deputies got there. He'd have to check with Harbaugh to see if his deputies turned off the vehicle. If the car was off when they got there, that was a point in favor of Beverly's assertion that someone got inside the vehicle before anyone else showed up, unless Munson had the presence of mind to turn off the engine before he was shot.

"I've got no idea right now what the killer might have been looking for. There was no briefcase or backpack in the vehicle, but I didn't think anything about that. Only images on his smart phone were photographs of buildings, and that seems odd for someone in the selfie generation. The techs are working on his phone to see what information they can retrieve."

"Maybe he had two cell phones, one for work, another for personal use."

Lagarde rocked back on his heels at that idea and thought for a minute, watching her start to peel the eggplant, long purple ribbons of skin falling gently onto the counter. It was a contemplative occupation for her, the way cleaning his horse was for him.

"Also, he's a slob. The floor of his car and the seats were littered with candy and food wrappers. There were empty drink cups, complete with straws, half-eaten sandwiches. It looks like he lived in his car."

"What kind of car was he driving?"

"A Lexus. I'd have to check my notes for what model. New, though, with leather upholstery."

"No way would he mess up the inside of that car. The killer was looking for something. She unlocked the doors with her remote key and went in through the back passenger door."

Beverly sliced the eggplant into thin rounds, scooped them up, put the slices on a plate and salted them. "Maybe she emptied his car trash bag looking for something. Whatever it was, she thought he was hiding it from her deliberately. She had to move fast. It would be something that could hold a large amount of information, although that could be as tiny as a thumb drive. Was he wearing a suit?"

Lagarde nodded. "Yes, a suit. Thumb drive?"

"You know. Flash drives. Those two-inch devices with a small metal tip you stick in the USB port on a laptop. They have a hundred times more memory than our original personal computers did."

He did know about thumb drives, but he'd never had

a reason to use one. When, he wondered, did Beverly? *Does she have a secret life I know nothing about? That wouldn't surprise me in the least.*

"When you interview her, ask to see his briefcase and see what happens."

Lagarde strode over to Beverly, wrapped his arms around her, and kissed her neck. "You are my favorite mystery, and you get better and better."

He put on his jacket, settled the tan felt Stetson Outback that he wore in all seasons on his head, and went out the kitchen door.

Beverly watched him drive off down the lane. She looked out over the fields, just starting to come up green in the early spring. Blue mountains hugged the horizon beyond them. Horses romped in the paddock. She sighed and went back to preparing the eggplant, knowing she would have to reheat it for Sam's dinner sometime around nine p.m. That was okay with her. She was, finally, right where she wanted to be, and, from where she was standing, she could see a landscape she wanted to paint.

Chapter 2

May 10, 2009, 1:15 p.m.:

Harold could not believe his luck. The woman sitting at a table for two in the window of the small French bistro in Shepherdstown looked exactly like her photo on the DateMe site where he'd found her profile.

They had exchanged the usual comments: What do you do for a living? Where do you go to relax? What's your favorite book? She was reading a review copy of *The Telomerase Revolution*, she told him, and her review would grace the front of the book. It was an eye-opening book, she said. He took her word for it. He had no idea what a telomere was and secretly didn't care.

Harold told her he'd been reading *Tipping Point*. He had, in fact, read the back cover and the first few pages. After that, he lost interest in the book except for its take-away point—that sticky messages spread like viruses by word of mouth. When he mentioned this to her, she seemed interested. He could almost hear her thinking across the digit-filled space between them.

For him, everything she said made her appear to be

the woman he had to have in his life. Permanently. Her name was Charlotte Rolle. Even her name was sexy. It occupied his mouth, rolled around on his tongue, caused friction between his tongue and palate. He couldn't wait through the recommended series of "touches" the website counseled. He had to meet her in person.

Anticipation and fear of disappointment made his breath catch in his throat as he'd walked the last ten yards to the restaurant where he paused in front of the window. Cars rolled by on the street at a pedestrian-friendly pace. Passersby regarded him briefly and walked around him.

Harold was transfixed, observing how the woman's long red hair curved over her shoulder and framed her perfect neck. She was reading the small screen on her cell phone, completely oblivious to someone staring at her from the sidewalk. Harold decided she worked out, ran or swam, or did something athletic that kept her toned.

He imagined that toned body lying on his bed, red hair spread out like the rays of the sun. He imagined her naked. His breath came faster. He gave himself a little shake, reminding himself he was looking for a wife. *But, oh, what a wife she would make.* He ran his hand over his hair, walked to the restaurant door, checked what he had always considered to be his handsome reflection in the door window—wavy blond hair, blue eyes, square chin, straight nose, full lower lip—and went in.

He took five long strides to the table, leaned over slightly in what might look like a bow to someone observing him, and murmured, "Charlotte?"

Even at that moment, he wasn't sure this was really the woman he was supposed to be meeting. He expected her to say, "Why, no, sorry, you must be looking for someone else." His face would pink, he would stutter, back away, rush out of the restaurant, and be embarrassed for life. Harold held his breath.

She looked up and smiled. "Yes," she said, dismissing his fears with a single word. "I assume you're Harold." Her hand floated in the general direction of the chair, and he sat. "I ordered a bottle of the Blanc de Blanc, to start." She blinked her green eyes. "It's my favorite white." She smiled at him again, showing her straight, white teeth. "Crisp." Her full lips pressed together on the P and his mouth imitated hers, unaware.

"Yes, yes, of course, good idea." He mentally smacked himself to stop his mouth from chattering. He had no idea what a crisp wine was. She might be too sophisticated for him. He had not been this nervous since he took the three-hour commercial real estate broker's exam to get his license. It was a good thing she didn't shake his hand. His palms were sweaty. He rubbed them against his pants, he hoped surreptitiously, under cover of the tablecloth, and then placed them on the table so that he didn't appear deceitful.

Harold's head was full of gesture and micro-expression descriptions he'd found in a book he'd been skimming that purported to tell him what his clients were thinking. He set his shoulders and presented his best smile. He wouldn't make it through the next hour in this state. He had to calm down.

He looked out of the window, observing the small shops up and down the street, the leisurely pace of pedestrians who walked, it seemed to him, in slow motion, and took a deep breath. *Might as well just tell her the truth*, he thought. His next automatic thought was, *always be closing*. He zoomed through various truths and blurted out, "You look exactly as beautiful as your profile photo." *God*, he thought, *I should just die of idiocy right now.*

But then Charlotte grinned, her face lighting as she threw her head back, exposing the lovely curve of her throat, and laughed out loud. Harold knew at that moment that his day, and perhaps the whole rest of his life, was made.

Chapter 3

March 30, 8 a.m.:

Lagarde was breaking in a new partner, Corporal Jim Taylor, and as a result, couldn't rely on the almost telepathic communication he'd enjoyed with Sergeant Larry Black, who surprised him by going into the FBI's training program just as he said he'd do after the Wodehouse case. Lagarde wished him well, but he worried Larry wouldn't fit into that huge organization.

"All you ever do is follow around politicians, journalists, and wannabe terrorists for months waiting for them to slip up," he told Black, who wasn't listening to him. "Even if you identify a network, travel patterns, or purchases that indicate someone is a potential terrorist, you can't do anything until they actually kill people. Remember San Bernardino? There are no puzzles to solve, no thinking outside the box. You'll be bored."

Black grimaced. He was intent on his vision of a future far from the tiny corner of the world called the West Virginia Eastern Panhandle. "I want to broaden my horizons."

Lagarde knew he meant he wanted to put as many

miles as possible between himself and the place where he had killed a young man in the line of duty. There were early mornings when they were both still queasy about that shooting. Quantico, Virginia was pretty far away.

Maybe distance does erase memory, Lagarde thought, but he didn't believe it. The memory of that desperate day haunted Lagarde as well, but his approach to healing was to keep doing what he did—figuring out who the next bad guy was and arresting him, or her.

It helped that Beverly had come back into his life after that miserable case. She was the magician. He was the blindfolded assistant, in more ways than one. As far as Lagarde could tell, he had nothing to do with pulling this rabbit out of the hat so late in his life. His happiness was all her doing. He did realize how tenuous his future was. What blew in the door in spring could stomp out in winter, leaving the house wide open to cold winds. That was his life-long experience with women, even when he married them.

Every human relationship, as far as he could see, was tenuous and doomed to end, one way or another. And this one with Beverly had no officially sanctioned structure to hold it together. Not, he had to admit, that a marriage certificate had any kind of power to stop a woman who wanted to leave.

Beverly, not surprisingly given her flair for independent thinking, had said no to his marriage proposal. "We're old enough to live together without tongues wagging," she told him, "or at least without caring what anyone says."

She kept her home in Falling Waters because her studio and all her painting paraphernalia were there. That's what she said. Lagarde believed she kept her home as a fallback, a place to retreat to when their new living arrangement fell apart, which meant it *would* fall apart.

Although, he was happy to see she'd moved an easel and a suitcase full of paints and brushes into the front room of his farmhouse near the windows that faced the open fields and the mountains. Maybe she'd stay with him as long as there was something she wanted to paint.

He didn't tell Beverly about that thought. When he worried about their relationship, which wasn't often, he worried he would do something so egregious that he couldn't be forgiven. He was being careful, in his own way, short of what he called walking on eggshells.

"Tiptoeing around isn't my thing," he told Beverly.

She had smiled and tipped her head to one side. "Mine either."

Lagarde tried to focus on his new case, which was always harder when he was working with someone new. He was also working on not being too cranky, something Beverly suggested. The older he got, the easier it was to be a curmudgeon—the scales of polite behavior having been shucked off with departing years revealing his true dragon self.

The fact was, he enjoyed bellyaching. He didn't tell Beverly about this discovery, although she might've figured it out herself. When he complained about how the world was run and the loonies who were running it, he experienced satisfaction in every part of his body, all its many electro-chemical interactions suddenly in glorious equilibrium.

"I'm a work in progress," he told Beverly.

"Isn't everyone," she responded, giving him the idea that she would not back off from letting him know when he'd really annoyed her.

Lagarde poured revolting office coffee into a perpetually unwashed cup that bore the words, "So? What of it?" He walked over to Taylor and clapped his new partner on the shoulder. "Hey, Taylor, let's dig into the case a little more."

Lips pressed together, face somewhat ashen, Taylor nodded, flipped open his notebook, and looked anxious. This was his first murder case. "Should I interview the wife?" He rotated in his chair to face Lagarde.

Lagarde slumped into his own chair. *The guy was so young.* He curbed his tongue. "No. I'll do that. You go over to the casino. See if they know Munson and if he's got a reputation there that might give us a motive for his murder. Talk to the waitresses in the restaurant. Stop by the pawn shop. Pick up what you can."

He paused to give Taylor time to write down every word. "If one comment leads to someone else, follow that up. See if he's got a gambling, drinking, addiction, or woman-on-the-side problem anyone knows about. Start developing a timeline of his movements as close to the time he died as possible. Take good notes—name of the person you're interviewing, date and time, where, what they say. Keep me in the loop by text, particularly if anything unexpected turns up."

Taylor looked up, the question "what's unexpected?" on his face.

"Unexpected would be, say, another dead body, or someone who claims credit for killing Munson."

Taylor nodded.

Lagarde listed a few more tasks and then watched Taylor furiously scribbling on his notepad. *At least he'll know what he forgot to do. Better than some young smart ass who's winging it.*

When the corporal raised his pen, Lagarde continued. "Then interview the folks in the house nearest the insurance office. They've got side windows that face Weigle's parking lot and a front porch that faces Charles Town Road. See if by some amazing chance, someone was standing at the window in the middle of the night, or if the car crashing through the side of a building was loud enough to wake them, and they saw the whole murder go down."

Taylor nodded and wrote down those instructions.

"Also, get a search warrant for Munson's house and any storage facility he rents, his office, bank, and phone records signed by the judge on your way back. Get the warrant to me as soon as you can. I'll be at Munson's house. After that, you get to check out what Munson's neighbors have to say."

Taylor flipped closed his pad, stood, and threw on his jacket. "No problem."

Corporal Taylor, in Lagarde's estimation so far, was meticulous, thorough and bright, but not a guesser. Taylor might have intuition, but he hadn't let Lagarde know it yet. At some point, Taylor would have to start speculating about who committed the murder, why and how, because that's what detectives did—they followed the breadcrumbs that led to where the murderer lived, sometimes deep in a forest in a tiny house covered in gumdrops that no one would ever expect harbored a criminal.

Frequently, critical breadcrumbs were missing. Unless they caught the perp standing over the body with a smoking gun, they eventually had to leap beyond the evidence if they were going to catch the killer. *It's the leap that can screw you.* Lagarde himself was careful with his leaps. They could take you right over cliffs.

Identifying the murderer was always a breathless moment for him. Riding out on his horse, connected spine to spine, alert to all the unspoken signals around him without thinking about the case—that's what worked for Lagarde. In that state, the synapses in his brain lit up everything he already knew and delivered the insight he needed. To some degree, he lived for those moments when the world's edges became crisp and clear. It wasn't a technique he could teach. Beverly's intuitive assertion aside, he'd have to see for himself who Harold Munson's killer was.

Taylor was fixed on provable facts, evidence, and where forensics took him. It was safer that way, and maybe that's the way everyone started. Even if you worked by hunches, those guesses still had to be verified with evidence, and as quickly as possible before evidence disappeared or was contaminated. Detectives didn't have the luxury of time. Everyone who watched television knew that the first forty-eight hours after a murder were crucial to solving the crime. After that, they might as well be working on a cold case. They needed to move fast.

"Head out to Charles Town now," Lagarde nudged the young detective, "get the warrants. You might have to wait around for the judge, and that's okay, because you won't find anyone at the casino until after ten a.m." Taylor gave Lagarde a half salute and walked out of the headquarters facility.

Lagarde returned the salute. *Maybe the guy has a sense of humor. That would be heartening.* He put his grimy mug down on his desk, did a quick check through his email to see if anything had come in on fingerprints, maybe on the shell casings or the car doors, but there was nothing yet.

He pondered Beverly's premise that Munson might have been a gambler. The casino didn't carry anyone. Games were pay to play, which meant if you were on a losing streak, you were getting a second mortgage on your house, pawning your wedding ring, or signing over the title to your car to get cash for your next set of bets. Pawn shops and loan sharks were spawn industries of gambling casinos.

Every gambler thought his next bet would be the one

that would square him. With just a little luck, the next spin would make him, or her, as rich as Bill Gates. All a gambler needed was that next stake. Even if Munson borrowed from less than legal sources, it was unlikely they'd bump him off while he still had something he could sell to pay off the debt, like his house.

Just in case money was the murder's proximate cause, Lagarde made a mental note to have the financial geniuses at the crime lab check Munson's bank statements and tax records as soon as they had the warrant. It was also possible that the murderer's motive was simple. Maybe Munson won big last night at the casino and flashed a wad of cash around. Someone less lucky than he could have followed him home and popped him for his winnings while he waited in his car at the intersection for the light to change. Then the murderer riffled through his car looking for that wad of cash and locked the doors before he took off into the night.

Sometimes Lagarde wished for the ubiquitous cameras that large cities had mounted on nearly all traffic lights and public buildings. Rewound video was the closest thing to time travel to the past. And then he remembered he hated cities and was glad, almost, that no one knew what anyone else was up to around here. Anonymity was an essential feature of "Wild and Wonderful."

Lagarde ticked off on his fingers a few more suspect and motive options he needed to explore. Maybe Munson cheated someone from his professional life, and they hated him enough to kill him. Something from his past may have snuck up and bitten him. Or, as Beverly said, he cheated on his wife, and she flipped. The door on suspects was still wide open, regardless of what Beverly had to say about it.

Taking the quick route to Munson's house driving northbound on Route 9, Lagarde briefly enjoyed the new

four-lane highway, speeding from Kearneysville past
views of rolling farmland, to the exit onto Leetown Road,
a more typical West Virginia winding road, running narrow with no shoulders up and down hills. He drove
through the intersection at the traffic light near the Post
Office where the road became Kearneysville Pike and
saw police tape fluttering in the breeze around his crime
scene.

The brown hilly landscape surrounded by dark
mountains still looked shell shocked from winter. Trees
hoarded spring's bright clamor just beneath their hard
bark. A gray sky in the south might harbor snow. He
thought about Beverly astride a horse slow walking
through snowy fields on a full-moon night, their breath
white veils floating in the air. He shook himself. *Enough
foolishness. Get focused.*

Parking at the curb in front of Harold Munson's
house, Lagarde took in his surroundings. It was a large,
well-kept two-story Colonial with a brick front, Mansard
roof, black shutters, double-door entrance, attached two-
car garage, and lots of large, twelve-paned windows. A
house meant to impress. Lagarde did a quick calculation
and estimated the owners had paid at least three-thousand
dollars more for those windows than if they'd gone with
what came on the model home.

The front of the home was professionally landscaped
with a paved stone walkway from the street leading to a
small patio adorned by a modern fountain before the path
meandered another ten feet to the front steps. A graceful
teak bench on the patio under two dogwoods gave the
homeowners a shady place to sit and enjoy their view of
the mountains.

Maybe, Lagarde thought, the house's occupants sat
out on that bench of a summer evening to watch the sun-
set, a chilled glass of white wine in hand. On the other

hand, the romantic landscaping might be for show.

He looked around the neighborhood—quiet street, well-kept homes, a place where covenants to deeds decreed that no rusting car hulks could be jacked up on front lawns, no farm animals could graze or defecate in backyards, and no trash would be heaped up waiting to be burned. Nothing could sully the view. The residents here, who paid extra for homes sheltered from less punctilious neighbors who had lived down the road for generations, would be shocked to learn one of their own had been killed. He was glad he had tasked Taylor with talking to them. He hated interviewing witnesses. The longer he worked as a detective, the more he shied away from talking to random observers whose perceptions were invariably wrong.

"I might hate people," he had admitted to Beverly. It wasn't that he didn't like particular people, he explained, smiling at her and chucking her under the chin, but people in the aggregate ticked him off. The more there were, the less he could stand them. She had smiled her Beverly smile at him and his annoyance at whatever it was dissipated.

He silenced his internal monologue and walked to the door. As soon as the body had a name, Mrs. Munson had been notified at approximately four a.m. by the sheriff's department that her husband was dead. She identified him from an image on the deputy's cell phone screen of her husband lying inside the body bag, a zipper under his chin.

Having to ID a loved one that way would rattle me, Lagarde thought. *I think I would insist on seeing him in person.* He wished the deputy had waited for him so he could have seen Mrs. Munson's reaction first hand, but the officer stationed outside the widow's house reported to him that she sat down on an ottoman in the living room, her face a complete blank, and said nothing.

The deputy slapped a small pad against his hand. "She was dressed, and it was four in the morning. So, either she never went to sleep, or she's a really early riser."

Lagarde closed his eyes for a second, attempting to quell his first response. "Everyone's a detective today," he said in a tone he thought was mild. "She could've slept in her clothes on the sofa because she was anxious when her husband didn't come home when he was supposed to."

He made a mental note to find out if Mrs. Munson had reported her husband missing when he didn't show up last night.

The deputy looked at Lagarde sideways, tucked his pad into his back pocket, and reported the remainder of his interaction with the widow. "She was alone in the house. I told her not to go anywhere and that you'd be here to interview her." He walked away toward his cruiser.

Lagarde sighed audibly—another youngster ticked off at him for no reason. By now, Mrs. Munson could have made several calls to cover her tracks. There was nothing to be done about that now.

He raised the brass hammer on the door and let it fall. When the new widow opened the front door, his first impression was that Charlotte Munson was tall—several inches taller than he was. She had long red hair, the new mega eyebrows that always reminded him of painter Frida Kahlo, and piercing green eyes.

Her body appeared to benefit from some physical activity that gave her muscled shoulders and upper arms, slender waist and tight thighs, all clearly visible in the clothes she was wearing—cropped yoga pants, an item of clothing he'd recently learned about from Beverly, and a halter top. *A strange outfit for the day your husband dies.*

Maybe the deputy wasn't too far afield in his suspicions after all.

Although she might be a harpy or worse, Lagarde's instant assessment of the woman was that if Mr. Munson was sneaking around on this woman, something was wrong with him. But he wouldn't be surprised if *she* was the one having an affair. There was a heat about her, waves of it shimmering off her body even from a foot away. He had an eerie feeling the hair on his arms would singe if he came into contact with her. Involuntarily, he sniffed. *Not sulfur. That's good.*

She led him into a living room that appeared to have been decorated by an interior designer down to the double draperies and fabric valances on the windows. With a wave of her hand, she indicated he should sit on the sofa. Lagarde, in whose mind the word façade was dancing around, chose to stand for a while. He offered the required, "Sorry for your loss, ma'am" and the customary presentation of his credentials, to which she merely nodded. He couldn't immediately tell if she was numb and angry, subdued and sad, or didn't give a crap that her husband was dead. She could have been all of the above.

"You don't mind if I ask you a few questions?" He didn't wait for her answer. "How long have you been married to Harold?"

She sat back in a chair upholstered in a striped silk fabric and crossed her legs. "Five years," she said, her voice barely louder than a whisper.

Lagarde watched her face."Happily?"

She looked down at her hands resting in her lap. "For the first three years, yes. After that, I thought every day about how I could get away from him." She looked squarely at Lagarde. "Is that being too honest with you?"

Lagarde shrugged and smiled slightly. He sat down on the edge of the sofa and leaned toward her. She was clever, asking him a question, enlisting him on her side of a failing marriage, playing the damsel in distress, and appearing to be completely candid. He felt shielded from her artifice by Beverly's sight-unseen assessment of the woman. He made another mental note to ask Beverly about the new eyebrow look.

Charlotte pulled her legs up under her on the seat. She seemed to need to be in motion. *Is restlessness a sign of a guilty mind?* Lagarde looked into a dining room on the opposite side of an arch from the living room and, on the other side of the foyer, he noticed an office. The house was extraordinarily neat.

"Any kids?"

Charlotte shook her head.

"Do you know why your husband was out in the middle of the night?"

"He had a big work meeting, new clients to entertain. One of the bigs, he said, some company like Amazon or Google wants to buy the empty pick and pack warehouse and adjacent twenty acres off Wiltshire near the highway, a deal worth more than ten-million dollars. They want to put something like a server farm there, I think he said. Hundreds of possible jobs might come from it. Oh, I guess you don't know. Harold sells commercial real estate."

Lagarde nodded and wrote the information on his pad with the notation: *expected him to be out late.*

Mrs. Munson seemed to be reading a script. Her voice carried no emotion, unless that was relief he was detecting. She crossed her legs in the other direction. "They were supposed to go to dinner at the casino steak house. Harold was introducing them to all the area big shots—the mayor, county council president, economic development director, even the Senator. Then they probably lost money at the roulette wheel, capped the night off with a drink in the bar, and I guess Harold headed home."

She paused for a minute and looked at him to assess the effect of her statement.

Lagarde held his pen above his pad. "Do you know anything about the folks who wanted to buy the property?"

She shrugged. "Not much. The clients are staying at the hotel near the casino. They were supposed to get together today for price negotiations and make an offer. Harold told me in advance of the meeting that it looked promising. He was excited. His commission would have been close to a million dollars. The sale would have made him, given him a national reputation."

"Do you know the names of the folks he went to dinner with? I'd like to talk to them."

"No, but the meeting will be on his calendar with their names. And their contact information, I'm guessing, will be in his contacts list." Her face said he was an idiot, and she was too polite to say so. "On his phone?" she said as she read the incomprehension on his face. "If you have his phone, you have his life." She gave him another quizzical look to say he should have thought of that.

Lagarde nodded and made himself a note to check if they had Munson's personal phone in the evidence they retrieved from his car. "Does he have a partner, or office staff, someone I could talk to about how his business was doing?"

"Yes. Edward Milliken and Randi Walker are his associates. They were probably at the dinner yesterday with him."

"Do you have their phone numbers?"

Charlotte twisted her lips to the left. His question seemed to annoy her. In one smooth movement, she stood up from the chair, strode into the office on the other side of the center hall, plucked a business card off the desk, walked back into the living room, and handed it to Lagarde. "Harold's office. You can call them."

"Do you know why he was on Charles Town Road at that hour?"

"He always comes home that way. Says it's faster than the highway and Route Two-Thirty. He grew up around here and knows all the back roads from before they were replaced by highways."

A twitch between Lagarde's shoulders acknowledged Beverly's hunch. *Maybe*, Lagarde thought, *the deputy hadn't told her how her husband died.* Even if he had, reminding her would give him an opportunity to watch her reaction, although that was a little cruel. *I might be that cruel*, he acknowledged to himself. That was one of the secrets he hoped to keep from Beverly.

"Do you think the people Harold went to dinner with had any reason to kill him?"

"No. That's absurd."

"What about his partners?"

"Also ridiculous. He was making them rich."

"Did you know your husband died of two gunshot wounds to the head?" Lagarde watched her face. Changing gears during an interrogation often tripped a suspect into accidentally telling the truth against his or her own interest. Charlotte struck him as someone who always consulted her own interest first.

Her face didn't twitch. "Do you want some coffee, detective?"

"No thanks." Lagarde changed tack. "What were *you* doing last night?"

She grabbed a filmy blue poncho off the arm of the chair and threw it over her head, then paced the thirty feet of her living room and stopped in front of him, too close for him to stand without bumping into her, forcing him to look up at her.

She must have had breast augmentation surgery, he thought, *which perhaps is what she's modeling for me with her lithe movements back and forth across the floor.*

Without answering his question, she walked toward the kitchen. Lagarde walked through the dining room and stood in the archway that led to a large kitchen equipped with stylish stainless steel appliances, white wood cabinets with glass fronts, sparkling gray tiled backsplash, and polished granite counters. *Expensive,* he noted. *Harold couldn't have been doing too badly in the money department. It must be something else that annoyed her about her husband.* She still hadn't answered his question.

"Mrs. Munson, do you have an alibi for last night?"

She turned her back to him and sauntered around the kitchen. Lagarde followed her with his eyes. Making coffee gave Charlotte more opportunities to stretch, squat, twist, and lean over from the hip to pull the French coffee maker out of a bottom cabinet, offering her trim buttocks to his view. *If she goes through all of this just to make coffee, no wonder she's in such good shape.*

"Mrs. Munson," he nudged, "my question?"

Her eyes flashed. She flicked her head, and a lock of shiny red hair flipped behind her shoulder. "I worked late and took the last MARC train back to the Duffields stop. I had a late evening yoga serenity class in town. I went to dinner around nine at Dish with friends, and then I went to my lover's place to have sex." She seared him with her green eyes. "Is that enough of an alibi for you?"

Lagarde worked hard not to blink. The trick she did with her eyes was fascinating. She was smart enough to have invented that litany of excuses on the spot. "It depends on the timing and whether anyone confirms what you said, and—" He paused as he spotted a briefcase sitting open on the kitchen desk. "—whether I believe what they say." The briefcase contents looked like they'd been tossed by a small tornado.

He asked her to write down the names and phone numbers of people who could corroborate her story. When she was finished, he pulled a glove from his pocket, took the piece of paper she handed him and placed it in a baggie he pulled from his other pocket.

She glowered at him, her hawk's wings eyebrows in an M over the bridge of her nose. "Do you think I'm infectious?"

"Not necessarily. This is a fast way to get your prints and maybe pick up traces of gunshot residue. The forensics team will be here soon to do it officially, but I like getting a jump on things." *And*, he thought, *it's a really good way to see how guilty you feel.*

Charlotte looked at him steadily for a full minute and then threw her head back and laughed. "You could've just asked for my prints," she said when her mirth subsided. "You think I shot him?" She sounded surprised anyone would suspect her of such a gross act. "Why would I do such a stupid thing? I've already started divorce proceedings against him."

Lagarde sighed. He'd hoped that Beverly was right and for once he had a simple open and shut case. Still, Beverly's intuition might turn out to be right, and the woman in front of him was a sociopath. It struck him that Charlotte used the word "stupid" and not "inhumane." He shifted subjects. "Did Mr. Munson carry life insurance?"

"No. We don't believe in betting against our own lives."

Three melodious notes repeated on her cell phone. She looked down at the screen of the device on the counter. "Do you mind?" she asked, "I have to get this."

"No, no problem," Lagarde said. His own intuition bells were ringing. He walked back into the living room and called Taylor on his mobile phone. "When you're done at the casino, check back with the prosecuting attorney and make sure the warrant gives us permission to search any and all vehicles, plus properties other than the main residence, all electronic devices including phones, computers, game stations and *whaddyacallit*, email, and those boxes in the interworld where you can store electronic documents."

"Drop Box? Google Docs? The cloud?"

"Yeah, all of that. Do it now."

Taylor said, "Yes sir," and clicked off the call. Lagarde imagined the young state trooper jumping into his vehicle and speeding back to the Charles Town court house. While she was still on her call, Lagarde walked through Charlotte's house to see whatever might be in full view. In addition to the living and dining rooms, the large kitchen, and an office, there was also a family room and morning room off the kitchen. *Lots of space for a young couple with no children. Maybe they'd planned to have them before the love ran out. Or maybe the house is their investment plan.*

Through the windows in the family room, he saw a rear lawn graced by an elegant stone patio with a covered, built-in kitchen complete with grill, small refrigerator, and sink. The Munsons presented an orderly, affluent face to the world. *But their whole world is staged.*

Her call completed, Charlotte found Lagarde in her office looking at the titles of books in her bookcase. "Do you read, detective?"

"No. I find it interferes with my sense of reality."

She had a pleasant throaty laugh. This was the second time she'd laughed this way. *Did she think exposing her throat like that made her seem vulnerable, or was it desirable she was going for?* He switched gears again. "What do you do for a living, Mrs. Munson?"

"Doctor," she corrected him. "And it's Rolle. Doctor Rolle. I'm a scientist. I didn't take my husband's name." It seemed to him she waited for the information to settle on his face. "I'm based at the National Institutes of Health, NIH. I'm working on a molecular approach to treating brain cancer. Are you interested?"

Lagarde nodded, hoping she would somehow tell him more than she should about herself, which might prove useful if she was the perp.

"In layman's terms, we're investigating whether we can eradicate a brain tumor with no invasive procedure, no surgery, no poison chemicals, and no radiation, by using an infusion of the patient's own re-jiggered T-cells."

Lagarde's highbrows went up in spite of him. "Got it," he said, even though he wasn't sure he had.

Dr. Rolle smiled and continued. "Those strengthened disease-fighting agents cross the blood-brain barrier, alert the body's natural defense systems to the presence of the cancer, attach themselves to the cancer cells, and kill them. But the best part is that the cancer cells also quit replicating. Something like waving a magic wand that results in tumor gone, no remission." She winked and wrinkled her nose.

She thinks she's Samantha from Bewitched. Lagarde's gut said something wasn't right here, but he knew nothing about medical science. He was lucky he understood each of the words she used to describe her research. *Maybe what isn't right is the way she can slip into glee about her work on the morning her husband was killed in cold blood.* He asked for the name of her supervisor and a phone number.

She reached across him to her desk, pulled a business card from a holder, leaned over and wrote a name and phone number on the back. "Do you mind if I go now? I have to stop by Harold's parents' house and talk about funeral arrangements."

She looked at his face intently. "I called them right after the officer informed me earlier this morning. They'll have had enough time to pull themselves together." She looked down at her laptop. "And I have to go to work for an important meeting. I need to put things in order there before the funeral."

Lagarde nodded and said, "How old are you?"

She looked exasperated. Women hated to be asked their age, as Beverly frequently reminded him. "What does that have to do with anything?" She huffed for a second. "I'm thirty-nine."

He would not have put her age at thirty-anything. Lagarde looked at the name she'd written on the back of her card: Dr. William Dickerson with a string of letters after his name. He turned the card over. She had a string of letters after her name also: M.D., Ph.D., a couple others. *Having lots of letters after your name must make you important at the country's top medical research organization.* Dr. Charlotte Rolle certainly didn't match the female scientist stereotype he had in his head, and she smelled like roses. She was confusing him. He didn't like being confused.

"Just a few more questions for right now, Dr. Rolle, although I may need to ask you more later. Did your husband have his briefcase with him?"

"I don't know. I don't keep track of his belongings."

"Could that be his briefcase in the kitchen?"

"Oh, maybe." She shrugged elaborately, scowled, and looked away. "Can I leave now?"

"In a minute, Dr. Rolle. Do you own a gun?"

She stared at him. "No, I don't." Her face was unreadable.

"Did your husband own a gun?"

"I don't know."

"Was your husband in trouble with anyone at the casino, or did he owe anyone money outside of normal banking and credit channels?"

"Not that I know of."

"Are there money problems? Are you in over your heads on this house or other property?"

"No. We make a decent living. Harold was licensed in three states. He did well. We cover our bills without any problem. Can I go now? I have to change into office clothes."

"Was he having any problems with colleagues or clients?"

"Not that I know of, but we weren't exactly on speaking terms this last year. We didn't see a lot of each other, and we certainly didn't confide our problems to each other."

Lagarde thought she would jump out of her skin with impatience. He sensed she wasn't accustomed to doing anything she didn't want to do. "Dr. Rolle, crime scene personnel will be searching your house in a few minutes, as soon as I have the warrant. We're going take your palm and fingerprints and test you and your clothes for gunshot residue, just to rule you out, you understand."

She made a small face and looked away from him.

"To find your husband's killer, we need to know what was going on in his life, and therefore in yours, since you lived together. That includes what's in that briefcase in the kitchen. It's evidence. Once we've gotten your prints and the clothes you're wearing, it's up to you whether you stay around for our search, but don't go farther than your work office."

He looked at the address on her business card. "Just so you understand the nature of our investigation, we'll also be checking your bank and phone records, including the call you just took, and we will probably interview your work colleagues."

"What? You can't do that. They have nothing to do with Harold. It's absurd that you would interfere with my work life this way. I'm calling my lawyer right now."

"Good idea," Lagarde said and walked out of the house to wait for Taylor and that all important warrant before he said anything she might report him for.

Something about the woman annoyed him. Maybe it was all those degrees combined with the yoga costume. Maybe it was that she didn't give a crap about her husband. She jangled up all his preconceived ideas about women, scientists, and people who took yoga classes. He didn't like having his preconceptions rearranged.

He pulled the baggie with the list of her alibi witnesses out of his pocket and looked at the names. True to stereotype, her handwriting was nearly unreadable. *Did doctors get special penmanship classes that made their scrawl indecipherable?* Taylor, he decided, could handle talking to the lover alone, face-to-face. The others they could check on by phone. *No stone unturned*, he reminded himself. Then he realized he needed to add a name to those warrants.

"Taylor," he said when the corporal answered his cell phone, "You're going to hate this. The wife calls herself Charlotte Rolle, legally. Doctor Charlotte Rolle, R-o-l-l-e. Make sure our warrants include her formal name, in case there's property or bank accounts in her name alone. And get a general background check on her, just in case. Call April at headquarters. She can help you with that." Lagarde added "thanks" before he ended the call, just in case Taylor was starting to feel put upon.

Chapter 4

The first time Harold had an inkling something was wrong in his marriage was when his ever-horny wife turned away from him in bed and said she had a headache. He knew she'd been upset over the miscarriage, but it hadn't occurred to him that meant she didn't want to have sex ever again.

The miscarriage was more than six weeks ago. Even for the five months she'd been pregnant, she always wanted to have sex. There wasn't a room in the house in which they hadn't humped like rabbits—hell, even in the garage with the door open and any neighbor driving by could see them.

Just thinking about it now made his blood thrum through his body. How were they going to make another baby if she didn't let him fuck her? He leaned over her, kissed her beautiful neck, stroked her breasts, and snuggled against her. She shrugged him off and turned onto her stomach.

"What's the deal, Charl? What's wrong with you?"

Her voice was muffled by her pillow, but Harold

thought he heard her say, "You're an idiot, Harold, that's what's wrong."

"C'mon, honey, you have to tell me what's going on. You know. Communication, the stuff you're always preaching to me about."

Charlotte raised her lovely face from her pillow, looked directly at him, and spat out, "You're disgusting. I can't stand having you touch me. Get it now?" She leaped out of bed, threw on the bathrobe she'd left lying on the chair, grabbed her pillow, and stormed out of the room. "I'm sleeping in the guest room. Leave me the hell alone."

Harold drew his fingers through his hair and lay back down. He heard the television go on in the guest bedroom. *Where on earth did her anger come from?* He tried to backtrack through his memories of what had happened in the last year, but he kept being interrupted by other thoughts. Overall, he'd thought they were doing so well. *She must have another lover.* His heart beat erratically at the thought.

Charlotte was on fire at work. If she got another award, she'd grow wings. At the last cocktail party he'd attended with her department a year before, her colleagues were saying that her work had Nobel Prize written all over it—although it was early, they qualified, at least ten years too early to tell. The results of her trials would have to be replicated. Scores of post docs were lining up to work with her. Even Harold was excited by the idea that she was going to be famous, although he had no idea what she was doing.

But even if he didn't understand the science at all, the Nobel Prize, he'd heard, came with some nice money. He watched his wife flitting around the rooms of Dr. Whatshisname's Bethesda home as if she'd already won the biggest prize in medicine, that gleam in her eye, a slight blush across her cheeks, and thought about fucking her in the guy's bathroom. What *was* that guy's name? Oh, right, Dickerson, doctor, lawyer, Indian-chief Dickerson.

The doc looked to Harold like he also wanted to put it to Charlotte in the worst way. But then, Harold thought that about all men. That constant knife-edge of jealousy kept him primed. He enjoyed being the husband of the woman everyone craved. He reveled in their envy. He was the man.

The only fly in Charlotte's work ointment, as far as he could tell, was that strange Dr. Liu, Charlotte's new post-doctoral fellow, chosen from a list of fifty prospects. He assumed she was brilliant, because why not? Charlotte only chose the smartest people she could find. Apparently, Liu was now challenging Charlotte about everything, and his wife, as he knew, didn't do well with obstructionists. It was Charlotte's way, or it was nothing at all, that much he had learned from his marriage.

But Liu was a stunner, all right. The night of Dickerson's party, he watched her watching his wife. Her face was on fire with hate, or maybe that was envy. Or was it lust? She could hardly drag her eyes away from Charlotte to look at anything else.

To his surprise, Liu worked her way through the crowded room to him, put a cool hand on his, and leaned forward so he could hear her whisper through her perfectly shaped, pink lips. "She's quite something, isn't she?"

Harold didn't know how to take Liu's comment. In her own way, Dr. Liu was as beautiful as Charlotte. Her black cap of hair glimmered in the light. Her skin was perfect, and she was showing a fair amount of it in a little black satin dress that was hardly more than a slip.

Without thinking, he whispered back, "You are also." When her eyebrows scrunched together, he changed his approach. "To be in this company, I mean." He expected her to smile at the compliment.

Instead, she fired a look at him that would shrivel most men. "Please don't condescend to me. I know who I am and I am not fooled by you or your wife."

She turned and walked away from him. Harold wiped his face with his hand. *These scientific women were tricky. You never knew what would set them off. And what did she mean by being fooled by Charlotte?*

Harold had made his first million dollars that year and thought of himself as a big man in his own right. He was only thirty-five, and although he hadn't hit the target set by the internet entrepreneurs, he was doing quite well for his little neck of the woods. They celebrated the sale that put him over the top by having dinner at the Bavarian Inn with his parents. As a couple, they were going places, he told himself.

When Charlotte announced at dinner that she was pregnant, Harold was thrilled. That she hadn't told him privately didn't strike him as odd. She liked a big fuss, and his parents would provide that. The idea of having a baby with his amazingly brilliant wife capped his year. His mother, her face wreathed in a smile, immediately declared she would start crocheting baby things. Even his father grinned at him without being nudged in the ribs by his mother.

"Continuity, son," the elder Munson said, "that's what conveys immortality." Harold laughed and patted his father's shoulder but thought the old guy had missed the point. This was *his* baby they were talking about. Just the idea that he was going to be a father made him feel like a real man for the first time in his life. He'd won the biggest lottery jackpot and taken the cash payout. His baby, his son, colored in all the pictures he had ever drawn for a perfect life.

A baby would cement them. Even if Charlotte became world-famous, she wouldn't leave him if they had a child together. She would need him. He would be her rock, the earth she had to put her feet back down on from time to time. He loved the idea of being a father, teaching his kid how to fish and throw a ball.

Now he thought back on it, he must have known something was wrong with their relationship if he'd been considering the possibility that she would leave him. Perhaps that thought was always in the back of his mind, but he had a kind of blindness where Charlotte was concerned. Even now, years after their wedding, when she came into a room, he forgot everything he was thinking. He even forgot *how* to think.

The miscarriage happened in the middle of the day. Charlotte was at work. She called him from a bathroom stall in her office building, sobbing into the phone. It took him five long minutes to figure out what was happening. He'd jumped into the Lexus and flew down the highway to get her. By the time he got there, she was already at the hospital, D&C complete, already calm. *Too calm*, he thought. *Of course, the doctor must have given her something. Nothing to worry about.*

"There was something wrong with the fetus," she told him. "It wasn't viable. Better to have this happen than to carry it to full term and then…" Her voice trailed off, and she looked away from him. "Maybe it's just as well."

Harold had no idea what to say. His heart had prepared for a child, and now there wouldn't be one. A void formed in his body where warmth had been. A chill shook him. He wracked his brain for the right thing to say. "You were working too hard, honey. Next time, you'll ease up, maybe take a break."

"I don't want a next time. I should have stayed focused on my work. My work is what's important." She closed her eyes. Her hand was limp in his. "I should stick to what I know how to do."

"Honey, you'll get over this. You'll be okay."

Her eyes flashed at him. He felt electricity flare through all his nerve endings. His brain screamed "DANGER." He knew instantly he had said the wrong thing but there was no taking it back and he had no idea what the right thing to say might be. He leaned over to kiss her, and she slapped him. He backed off the hospital bed and looked around the room for a flak-jacket and a helmet somewhere that he could put on.

"Did you bring me clothes?"

"What? Clothes? No. I just came right away..."

"Never mind. I'll have Susan bring me the workout clothes I have in my locker at the lab." She picked her cell phone up from the table and made the call. When she clicked off, she said to him, "You can go. I've got my own car today. Susan will take me to it. I'll see you back at the house."

"Should you be driving?" His voice froze at her look. He waved helplessly from the door of her room and left, all his hopes for a happy future gathered in a lump in his throat.

That was almost two months ago. He was sure she'd gotten over her annoyance with him by now, but apparently not. Harold rolled over on his side, thinking he would figure this all out in time, and fell asleep.

Chapter 5

Nick Waters slept nude. It was faster if he was going to get lucky in the morning, and if not, it was quicker getting into the shower. Sleeping nude was an efficient practice. He liked the idea that he was efficient. He was all about efficiency. The fact was, he was more comfortable out of his clothes than in them.

He rolled out of bed, the five-hundred-thread-count Egyptian cotton sheets he'd purchased online from Neiman Marcus slipping off his lean body like silk. He stood in front of the mirror for a few seconds checking out his torso.

He admired his own trim core. Nick checked himself out in every reflective surface he passed. It was something he'd done since he was a teenager. He considered what he saw in the mirror. *Not bad for someone pushing twenty-eight.*

He turned his face to a right profile and then the left. Maybe he'd keep this morning shadow stubble going. Satisfied, he strode into the bathroom, turned on the shower, and stood under the steaming water to revive.

Charlotte had left in the middle of the night while he slept. That was normal for her.

"I'm not a cuddler," she told him on their first meet-up at the Dish bar, setting the rules before she even let him sample the goods. "I like to wake up in the morning in my own bed."

He wasn't exactly sure when she'd left last night, but the sex had seared him to the bone. She was particularly hot, demanding, and experimental and suddenly liberated, although in his estimation she'd been a free woman for a long time. The only thing he didn't like about sex with Charlotte was that she issued step-by-step instructions— "Lick me, suck my nipple, two fingers, three, oh God, turn me over"—and she left cash on his night stand.

The money made him feel like a whore, and he didn't like that feeling. He *did* like what the money could buy. At five-hundred dollars a pop, the money added up. It never occurred to him that he could have asked for more. She also never offered more.

He and Charlotte had found each other on an online hook-up site and quickly realized they wanted the same thing—sex without strings. She winked, and they clicked. Then she rolled out her rules. She didn't want to be seen in public with him, even though she told him he was handsome and sexy, usually in that breathless voice just before he came. "Oh, God, you're so sexy, oh, God, so handsome. Give it to me, baby, let me have it, oh, now, now." *Verbal fellatio*, he thought, *worked every time.*

She told him the rest of the rules: he could never come to her house; she never stayed overnight; they did not do weekends, even in another state. This arrangement had no future, only a now. Charlotte's money made it clear that sex had nothing to do with feelings. That hurt a little because Nick always hoped his ladies would fall a little in love with him, but it didn't hurt enough to change anything. He'd already bought that sweet electric blue BMW i8 he wanted and they'd only been seeing each other a year. If he could keep up with her, he could quit his day job as a physician's assistant in a busy urgent care office and just chill all day, every day. He was thinking about taking up kayaking and cross-country skiing. He couldn't understand why women always complained about being kept. This was the life.

Nick stepped out of the shower, wrapped a towel around his waist, and called Charlotte. Maybe she'd be good for a second round tonight. She whispered over the phone, "I can't talk right now. I'll come over later. But listen, I didn't leave your place until three-thirty in the morning."

"Okay, no problem."

"Did you hear what I said? I left at three-thirty, you got that?"

"Yeah, yeah, I got that. What's the deal?"

"It's important that you remember. I'll talk to you later. Must go."

Nick didn't like it when Charlotte was mysterious. He got confused and felt left behind. Confusion made him feel that he had to do something to put her in her place. She was the woman, after all. He was supposed to be in charge. Then he shrugged and remembered her tits and thighs, her ass. His body shivered with memories. Too bad she wasn't here right now, he thought. He'd show her he knew how to be top dog. He fondled himself to let off the head of steam he'd built up thinking about her.

When the doorbell rang, interrupting him, Nick jumped, then wrapped a towel around his waist, ran down the stairs, and opened the door. A clean-shaven black man about his own age with close-cropped hair wearing a nice leather jacket over a black t-shirt, gray slacks, and running shoes stood on the small cement porch of Nick's townhouse holding out West Virginia State Police credentials in his hand.

"Are you Nick Waters?" the man asked him.

For a second, Nick didn't understand what he was seeing. He thought the guy might be a Jehovah's witness or the police benevolent association collecting money for wounded officers and he was about to apologize for being undressed. Then he realized the guy was a cop. "Oh, okay, wait a minute, I'll get some clothes on," he said and closed the door, leaving the officer outside.

He ran upstairs to his bedroom, pulled on a t-shirt and a pair of cotton shorts, and then rummaged in the bed table drawers, scooped up the various illicit drugs he and Charlotte used to enhance their pleasure, dumped it all in the toilet and flushed. On the way back to the door, he wondered who'd ratted on him. The doorbell rang twice while he was tidying up. He opened the door. The cop was still there.

"Let's start over," the cop said. "I'm Corporal Taylor of the West Virginia State Police. I want to talk to you about Charlotte Rolle's whereabouts last night."

"Oh, yeah, sure. She was here."

"Could I come in, Mr. Waters?"

"Oh, yeah." Nick stepped aside and let the officer into the narrow foyer but didn't move into any of the rooms that opened off the hallway. He wondered how the cop knew his name and where he lived but didn't ask.

"Okay if we go into the living room?" Taylor edged by him and started down the short hall, looking to his right and left as he walked.

"Yeah, that's fine." Nick watched the cop scope out his place as they moved into the living room at the back of the townhouse. It wasn't a big house, but it was his and not a gift from his sleazoid lawyer father, which was fortunate because the guy was currently doing four years in a federal pen for defrauding the government.

Being the owner of his own house meant he was an adult. He *was* an adult. Sometimes he had to remind himself of that fact. At twenty-eight years old he had a job, owned a house and a BMW. He was a success, as far as he was concerned. *And really, who else's opinion mattered?* Not his father's, that was for sure. Nick checked his image in the hall mirror, squared his shoulders, walked into the living room, and sat down on his couch. The officer remained standing.

A two-seat black-leather sofa; a sixty-inch television; his X-box game console; an imitation wood-grained coffee table to put his pizza, beer, and feet on; and a chair he took from his mother's spare room in case he had company were all the furniture in the room. Vertical blinds on the sliding glass doors in the dining area and mini-blinds on the two windows facing the woods out back were always open. It never occurred to him to close them. Who was going to look in? He was out in the middle of nowhere. The room had a motel look about it, but Nick figured that someday he'd marry the right girl and she would make his house look homey, the way it was supposed to.

The officer interrupted his reverie. "So you said Charlotte Rolle was here last night?"

"Yeah, she was, until around three-thirty. Then she went home."

"Were you awake when she left, then?"

"Nah, I was sleeping, but that's the time she said she left."

"When did she tell you that?"

"Maybe half an hour ago when I called her."

The cop wrote something in his notebook. "How long have you known Charlotte?"

"About a year. She's really hot," Nick touched the tip of his pointer finger to his buttock, jerked it away, and blew on his finger. "Whoo! I'm one lucky guy."

"How old are you, Mr. Waters?"

"Twenty-eight."

"And what do you do for a living?"

"I'm a physician's assistant at the Harpers Ferry urgent care. I'm also in the West Virginia Air National Guard, the One-Sixty-Seventh Airlift Wing, Medical Group, based out of Martinsburg. I make a decent salary, and I help people." Nick sat straighter, proud of his work and his service to his country. Between work, his gym routine, the gun club, his National Guard buds, and Charlotte, of course, he was pretty well fixed up.

"Were you in Iraq?"

Nick stared at his blank television screen. "Nah. I joined after. I got lucky, I think. A few guys in my unit got purple hearts but—" Unexpected sorrow tugged on his face. His feelings surprised him.

Taylor changed subjects. "Do you know what Charlotte does for a living?"

"Some medical research thing for the government." Nick wasn't really interested in what she did all day. *The cop doesn't get it. It's what Charlotte and I do together that makes me cream my pants even when she isn't here.* He shifted his position on the couch, stretched his arms along the cushions.

"What time did you meet Charlotte last night?"

"She got here around eleven, I guess. I finished my shift at eight, hit the gym, had a pizza and a couple of beers. Fox News at ten was over. I was just kicking back, scrolling through channels, looking for something to watch while I had my last beer."

"So you watch the news?"

"Yeah, well, you gotta stay on top of things, right?"

"Are you aware that Charlotte's husband, Harold, was shot in the early morning hours today?"

"What? Whoa. No way that I had anything to do with that." Nick jumped up from the sofa, ran both hands through his thick, wavy hair and then held his hands, palms out, away from his sides, showing Taylor that he had nothing up his sleeves.

"Do you own a gun, Mr. Waters?"

"Yeah, I do. Got a carry permit even though I don't have to. Practice at the gun club in Millville a few times a week. What about it?"

"Could you show me the gun, please, if you don't mind?"

Nick walked into the kitchen, opened the top cabinet to the right of the sink and felt around on the first shelf. The gun wasn't there. His heart tripped and banged in his chest. He ran upstairs into his bedroom and went through every drawer in his dresser. He checked under the bed, threw open his closet doors, rummaging under stuff on the shelf. Just in case he had taken precautions he'd forgotten about, he went into the bathroom and lifted the toilet lid. Nothing. He stood still trying to remember where he might have put the gun. The last place he saw it was in the kitchen cabinet, in its holster.

"Shit." His mouth dry, he ran back downstairs and into the living room. "I must've been robbed," he said. "It's not here, the gun's not here."

"What kind of gun is it?"

"A Smith & Wesson thirty-eight special."

"That's an expensive gun. How about you show me your license?"

Nick took three strides into the hallway, picked up his wallet from the table by the door, pulled out his carry permit and handed it to Taylor, who'd followed him into the hall. The corporal looked at the permit, jotted down the number in his notebook, and handed it back. Nick Waters' background check would be on file in the hand-gun database.

"Don't worry, Mr. Waters, We'll find your gun," Taylor said and then sucked in his breath.

Nick realized, from expertise gleaned from television cop shows, that Corporal Taylor had just made the rookie mistake of promising any kind of investigative out-come—and of assuming Nick wasn't the killer he was looking for. It took some effort to suppress a smile.

Taylor regained his authoritative demeanor. "Mean-while, don't make any plans to leave the area. We may want to talk to you again."

Nick walked the cop to the door. Outside, at the bot-tom of three cement steps, Corporal Taylor turned around. From the look on his face, Nick guessed the cop had thought of a new angle.

"You know what," Taylor said, "why don't you come with me right now and we'll get your statement and fingerprints on the record. That way we'll have every-thing ship shape."

Nick shrugged. It wasn't exactly a request, but he had nothing to lose. He didn't kill anyone. "Okay."

He slipped on the flip-flops lying on the floor near the door, picked up his keys and wallet from the hall table and went with Taylor in the police cruiser to Command headquarters in Kearneysville.

Chapter 6

March 30, 11 a.m.:

Williiam Dickerson, MD, PhD, MPH, JD stood in front of the window of the large departmental conference room of the new cancer research building—the one he had made the case for and won, the physical monument to his leadership, determination, and power. He gazed out at the meticulously landscaped campus of the nation's largest health research facility in Bethesda, Maryland. He was proud to be here. His position was the culmination of years of effort, not a title he fell into or didn't deserve. He took his role in guiding the geniuses who conducted medical research seriously.

His protégé, Charlotte Rolle, had informed him four hours ago that her husband had been killed in the middle of the night. Her voice was terribly calm. He was sure she was in shock. Life, as he knew from personal experience, didn't conform to expectations. You couldn't prepare a plan for it, couldn't test the outliers and determine probabilities. Grief was never expected.

"Take some time off, Charlotte," he told her on the phone when she called to let him know. "No one expects you to be here. You have ample leave available."

"But," she said into the ear which he pressed to the phone so intently that his fingertips turned white, "I want to work. I'm just finishing up the analysis on my latest trial, and the data looks promising, I don't want to stop."

When Charlotte was in a room with him, Dickerson had difficulty looking at anything but her breasts. It didn't help that she often wore tight sweaters or blouses that gave a clear view of the sumptuous swell of those breasts. A man with a restless intellect always needing to consume more information, Dickerson felt his brain switch to primal setting when Charlotte was around. All he could think about was tearing off her clothes and wrapping his mouth around her nipples, both of them at once. He tore his mind away and paced up and down the conference room, trying to regain his composure.

Within months of her coming to work in his department, he realized that communicating with Charlotte by phone or email was safer. Once, in a one-on-one supervisory meeting with her, he embarrassed himself by whispering "breasts" out loud as she was reporting on her research. He had wanted to die on the spot.

She hadn't seemed perturbed by the complete non sequitur, but he was in a dither for months over his politically incorrect utterance, waiting for her to go to Human Resources and report him for workplace sexual abuse. He was, after all, the director of the National Center for Cancer Research and she was a lab chief working under him.

He had attained this lofty position not just by being brilliant but by being utterly scrupulous in every way from his personal to his professional life. He engaged problems as a battlefield general, constructing three-dimensional strategies in his head, examining every angle, discarding solutions that failed and moving on to win in the fewest possible skirmishes. He even hummed the theme from Tchaikovsky's *1812 Overture* as he walked through the corridors of his building.

Charlotte Rolle, he worried, was his Waterloo. Whenever he met with her in person, Dickerson could barely hear Charlotte's words over the buzzing of desire in his ears. *I'm really too old for this*, he would berate himself. He had to take off his rimless glasses, rub his forehead, and smooth the few hairs remaining over the top of his balding head to focus his attention on what she was saying.

He went back to the window and stood looking out, his hands clasped behind his back. Charlotte's research now had a big pharmaceutical backer, one of the early entrants into what they hoped would be the trillion-dollar business of individually bio-engineered immunological treatments for dire diseases. Dickerson could feel the hot breath of the pharma company's greed flicking across the back of his neck every time Charlotte said she had to hurry and get to stage three trials. She had been showered with grants from private companies eager to get in on a ground-breaking cure early on in its development.

It didn't surprise him that she had commercial backing for her research at this point in her career. After all, she was a rising star, graduating at the top of her University of California class at the astonishing age of eighteen. She came to NIH with a New Innovator award worth over two-million dollars. There was nothing to stop her rising to the height of her profession. Dickerson knew it would be hard to keep her working in a government lab for long unless he could help her snag the field's most prestigious awards for research.

Her theory was ground breaking, and she was driven. They were lucky to have her, but her research strained resources. The welcomed outside revenue was a double-edged sword that also put pressure on her to try to fast-track her treatment scheme, bypassing what he thought of as essential early reviews. Dickerson was sure it was far too early for full-blown clinical trials, and certainly FDA fast-track authority was out of the question. He wanted her to slow down, to have time to review and think about her results.

It wasn't enough to have published articles on her research to great interest and acclaim. She'd moved too fast from theoretical work to Petri dishes to animal studies. Most recently, she had administered her special T-cell sauce to a small sample of seven human subjects dying of brain cancer. They had nothing to lose. After her treatment, three subjects died immediately, three lived three to five months longer than expected at their stage of the disease. One was still alive a year later, although the quality of life wasn't high. Charlotte was right, or she was lucky. The results could be a complete accident. The experiment would have to be conducted again using the same methodology to see if those results could be repeated.

But something felt off to him. Her results were too perfect. He was still painstakingly reading through her data from that small sample trial and her last animal study, and he had questions. Numbers that were far too precise repeated in different subject outcomes. In other instances, it appeared she had fabricated data. *That couldn't be.* He couldn't imagine she had lied. She needed to walk him through the results so that he was comfortable signing off on the next step.

Dickerson had time to rectify these problems. He wasn't anxious. Only two days ago, as he was reviewing her latest paper she was eager to send off to *Nature*, he'd sent her an email asking specific questions about her research and latest claims. She hadn't answered him yet. Now that her husband was dead, he couldn't bear to bring up the subject. Except that it nagged at him. Scientific fraud was at an all time high, and the last thing he wanted was for his lab to be caught up in a scandal that would destroy everyone's reputations.

Lying about research results was a professional disaster. If she was lying, journals that had published her papers would be embarrassed. All his investigators would be second guessed for years to come. Last year, over five-hundred papers were retracted, almost half due to fraud, their authors shamed. He hoped Charlotte had not been desperate enough for immediate success to take that path.

He wouldn't be able to broach the subject today, especially since the man was killed in such a horrible way, and he found he was happy to put off that conversation. Her work was obviously the only thing that would keep her sane. He'd felt a deep surge of empathy for her when she told him about Harold's death and, surprising even himself, invited her to have lunch with him if she came to work.

To his amazement, Charlotte gratefully accepted. Any other thoughts Dickerson might have had were chased out of his head by lust. It was too much to hope that she would think of him the way he thought of her. It struck him suddenly that she was no longer married. His heart trembled. He was a widower and, now, she was a widow. What could be more appropriate than two brilliant colleagues joining forces?

He imagined himself applauding her as she gave her acceptance speech at the Nobel awards ceremony in ten years. With a great effort, Dickerson snapped himself back to the present. At lunch, he would be sitting less than a foot from her. He worried that in his nervousness at her proximity he would drop his food, spill his drink, and knock utensils off the table. He was mentally rehearsing control over his extremities when Charlotte walked into the conference room.

"Oh, William, I'm so glad I found you." She sighed and touched his arm. "You're right. I can't concentrate on anything. I should go home." She shook her head, her hair a flag rippling in the sunlight. She leaned into him. Her breast touched his arm. "Do you think we could do dinner, instead, at my house? Tomorrow? That would be easier for me."

The alphabet jumbled in his throat. Dickerson nodded vigorously, a whole new world of possibilities opening to him. Had he been a younger man, he would have leaped into the air and clicked his heels.

She touched his arm again, one finger brushing his bare wrist, her hand lingering a minute longer than before. "Tomorrow, then." She turned to leave the room. "Six o'clock. Don't forget," she said, looking back over her shoulder.

He watched her hips go out the door and down the corridor, checked his watch, and began a countdown in his head.

Chapter 7

February 28, 6:30 a.m.:

Harold snuck down the stairs, careful to avoid any of the spots that creaked. Charlotte was in the shower, water running. He had half an hour. She wouldn't hear him, but he wanted to be sure. He opened the briefcase he kept on the kitchen desk, fished through it until his hands found the thumb drive, and walked into her office.

Waking her laptop, he thought for a moment about what she might have changed her security password to and typed in her birth date. *The woman's a total narcissist*, he reasoned, *all she thinks about is herself.*

The laptop screen came to life. Harold listened to the house. Water was still running in the shower. He had no idea where to find the file he'd seen open on her laptop a few days before, the one he'd read over her shoulder and in which he'd seen something just a little bit off in her data analysis. *Not that I know anything about it. She's right about that.* He scanned through her documents. She had her own file naming convention that didn't give anyone an idea of what the content might be.

He sighed and opened a folder on the desktop titled "Recent Results." That file name should indicate she kept recent data files in it. A dozen separate files rolled out, each with her own idiosyncratic naming convention. *Shit. This is impossible.* He opened, scanned, and closed several files before he thought to look at the file dates. Then he had it. He clicked open the file dated the day he had spotted the math error—or whatever it was—and there it was, a formula in which the variables weren't quite right. He looked through the document again. *This is it. This is all I need.* He closed the file, stuck his thumb drive in the USB port, and waited for the folder to load.

When the portable drive opened, he decided to upload Charlotte's entire Recent Results folder. *Why not? There might be something else useful in there I can use to get what I want.* While the files loaded, Harold looked around at his wife's organized office and felt a slight pang of remorse. *Maybe I'm making a mistake.* He shook himself. *Trust your gut, man,* he reminded himself. *Just like Dad taught you.* Without intending to, he remembered a time in his childhood when he hadn't.

෴෴෴

The light was failing. At the far end of the harvested cornfield where he and his friends played every afternoon after school, Harold spotted the Epsom brothers slouching toward them. The sight of them made his breath catch. They never meant any good.

"Hey, guys," Harold called to his friends, "I think it's time to go in now."

"Just a little longer," Ralph urged. "We've got it going now."

Harold wanted to oblige his friends even though the approach of the older boys made him uneasy. His father had been teaching him to "trust his gut," as he called it, but Harold wasn't always sure when his gut was telling him the truth or when it was telling him he was a coward. He hated the idea that he was a coward. It took him forever to sort out the difference on each occasion when danger presented itself. *But when all the hairs on the back of my neck are standing up, isn't that time to run?* Even asking himself the question made him feel he was a yellow-bellied chicken.

The Epsom boys lived about half a mile away, around a bend in the road in a falling-down house that had seen better years. Will and Harry weren't his friends, but they weren't strangers either. If they rode their bikes by Harold's house and he was out on the porch, they would wave.

At sixteen they'd dropped out of school and spent their days shooting holes in signs and killing small things, often with their bare hands. Frequently they dropped by Harold's porch to show off their trophies. When they stood on his porch steps holding up the dead animal, Harold always felt vaguely threatened, as if they were hinting, "See, this is what we're going to do to you."

They smoked and drank beer snuck from their mother's refrigerator—which should have made them exciting but somehow had the opposite effect on Harold. Their dirty blond hair stuck out in greasy hanks from their heads, and their fingernails were always dirty. Harold thought they never washed. He always kept five feet away from them, at least.

He tried telling his mother how the sight of their beady gray eyes and narrow lips made his stomach lurch. He leaned on the table while she was slicing apples for pie, her hands already dusted with flour from the piecrust that sat in a plump ball on the wood board. "Mom."

She glanced over at him then went back to her slicing.

"Mom, those Epsom brothers are creepy."

She put a gentle, apple-scented hand on his mouth. "Let's try to think the best of everyone, Harold."

"But Mom…"

"Now, Harold, that family's lived here for three generations, same as us in our house. Be neighborly."

The exchange left him more confused than ever. *How could he think the best of someone his gut was telling him to run away from as fast as he could?* When Will Epsom wanted Harold to go hunting with them, Harold felt vaguely honored but also wary. In a moment of what he later thought of as brilliance, he ran inside the house and asked his father if he could go with them.

His father looked up from his newspaper, took his pipe out of his mouth, and studied Harold. "You're too young to handle a gun," his father said. "You're only ten. When it's time for you to learn, I'll take you out myself." He was adamant.

Harold was relieved. He could blame his father to save himself embarrassment. He ran out onto the porch to tell the Epsom brothers no. "Can't go. My dad says. Sorry guys." He stared at the rifles they had laid casually across their bike handlebars. Those weren't BB guns. "Maybe next time," he lied.

"Chicken," they jeered at him as they sped away on their bikes down the dirt road that fronted Harold's family farm, "Momma's boy, itty bitty wiener." Even when they were out of sight, he could still hear them shaming him, "jerk-off, dirt farmer, yellow belly."

He could endure name-calling to be released from their snare. If he'd gone with them, he was sure he'd be the one they hunted. Knowing that, he told himself, was the gut thing his father was talking about.

This afternoon, Lizzie, Ann, Ralph, and he had been constructing a small fort from scrap wood they gathered from around their various houses and dragged to a corner of the field near a grove of oak trees. Harold had been friends with them since first grade when they discovered they took the school bus at the same corner and wore the same brand of jeans. The jeans clinched their solidarity. They were cool.

As they fit boards together and hammered nails, Harold could see their construction of an elaborate forest lodge, designed from their collective memory of a Robin Hood movie, wasn't going to come out the way they imagined. That didn't matter. It was the effort, his father said. His father approved of this project, and that alone made it worth doing.

Ann cupped the long nails he'd found in his father's basement workshop, and Harold pounded away, trying to drive a nail through the board into the one behind it. Ralph held the planks together, recoiling with each whack against the nail.

"You're doing it all wrong. My dad says you're supposed to do one hard hit instead of a bunch of small taps."

Harold, who'd been trying to avoid smacking the fingers holding the nail in place, lowered the hammer. He wiped the sweat off his forehead with his arm. "You do it then."

He handed Ralph the hammer and looked around for Lizzie, who always seemed to be able to comfort his hurt feelings without words.

She was standing ten feet away squinting into the setting sun at the Epsom brothers walking toward her. The sun gathered in a halo above braids pinned to the top of her head.

She turned around, looked at Harold, and wordlessly

pointed to the rifles the Epsom brothers carried.

"Ann, get help," Harold managed to get out of a throat suddenly twisted into a knot.

Ann, clutching the nails, took off like a shot to Harold's house. Harold ran to Lizzie and took her hand, intending to run back to his house with her, but she didn't move when he tugged. Ralph stood where he was, as rooted as field grass.

Will Epsom walked closer, dead corn stalks crunching under his boots, and called out "Hey, Harold, how come you play with these half-breed freaks and not us?"

Harold opened his mouth to say something, but no sounds emerged. His face flamed. An agony of speechlessness seared his skin.

Lizzie looked at him, squeezed his hand, and said in an utterly calm voice, "We're friends."

Will Epsom brought his rifle up to his shoulder, closed one eye, and aimed it at Lizzie. "White boy can't be no friend of yours. Ain't natural."

All the breath in Harold's body gathered in his chest, enough breath to blow the Epsom brothers to kingdom come, and yet he couldn't speak. He began to shake, not from fear but from fury, from words that burned to escape his chest and leap out of his mouth, scorching them, melting the skin off their faces. His eyes burned.

Finally, he managed a whisper. "Get out of here. You aren't good enough to even talk to her."

Will Epsom sighed dramatically, seeming to be sorry Harold's remark forced him to act. He sighted in on his quarry and shot.

The bullet went through Lizzie's left shoulder, grazed Harold's right arm, and made a hole in the board Ralph was holding.

The Epsom brothers took off running across the field, laughing and squawking, "Did you see her face?

Gawd, what a sight. Knocked the shit out of that little ho."

Lizzie moaned and collapsed on the ground. Harold sank to his knees next to her. "I'm so sorry, Lizzie, I'm so sorry. I didn't know what to do."

She closed her eyes, and he watched her tears slip from under her lids and crisscross her cheeks. The blood stain on her shirt spread across her chest. In the next minute, Harold's mother was there, scooping up the girl, running toward the house, yelling over her shoulder, "Come on, Harold, come on. You can make it, son. You'll be all right."

Her tone—hard and soft at the same time—made Harold wonder what was wrong with him. Then he looked at his arm and realized blood dripped from his fingers. He shuddered, and tears spurted from his eyes. He wiped at his tears with his bloody hand and ran after her.

"Ralph, you go home," Harold's mother shouted over her shoulder at Ralph who was on his knees bawling for his mother.

Inside the house, she laid Lizzie on the kitchen table and pressed a clean dishtowel against the girl's shoulder. "Harold, call nine-one-one." Her hands gloved in Lizzie's blood, she turned to him, eyes wide, and whispered, "What were you thinking, honey?"

Harold looked down at his shoes, found only misery, and shook his head. "I don't know, Mom. I couldn't think. I couldn't move. I wanted to be anywhere else but here."

ღღღ

Harold snapped himself back to the present. *No point in crying over spilled milk.* Download complete, he ejected the thumb drive and pulled it out. He needed a safe place to keep it, but for the time being, his pocket would work. Charlotte wouldn't know he had this information until he wanted her to know, until he could use it to his best advantage and blow her to smithereens.

He shuddered a bit at his own ferocity and went into the kitchen to make himself some breakfast.

Chapter 8

March 30, 2 p.m.:

They weren't going to find anything particularly incriminating at Munson's house, Lagarde decided halfway through the search, although they did bag up the briefcase in the kitchen, Harold's laptop, and his checkbook.

It appeared that Harold and Charlotte may have shared the house but slept in separate rooms. That was interesting and might indicate some kind of motive but on its own didn't prove anything. If something here was useful to his case—like the gun that killed Harold—it would have already been found. Lagarde was mildly disappointed, but smart, thorough people would go through the contents of the briefcase, Harold's laptop, and his finances, and let him know if anything important popped up.

That image pinged a memory of a Jack in the Box that terrified him as a child. By the third time his mother cranked the handle on the new toy, he already knew what was coming. The horrible mechanical music, "All around the mulberry bush," the click of the handle in its final turn, Jack's head lurching out of the box, that garish face leering up at him from its gyrating neck. He would put his hands over his eyes. The memory had never left him.

Something about this case made him feel he was going to be eerily surprised. He wasn't happy about that. He didn't like surprises, and murder was always surprise enough. He told Taylor he would meet him at headquarters and went back to the spot on Charles Town Road where Munson's car went off the road.

He parked in the post office lot and looked back from there toward the spot where Harold was shot. It was always good to get a different perspective. Across the street, Weigle, the agency's owner/broker, his white shirt sleeves rolled up, his red tie flapping in the wind, was struggling to get a blue tarp stretched across the opening in the wall of his building, which appeared to have been struck by a missile. He seemed to be a one-man operation. Lagarde felt no obligation to help him, even though Weigle looked hopefully in his direction.

Few cars were on the road, even in the middle of the day. One other car besides his was parked in the post office lot. At the one-story bank branch in the next lot over, one car idled in the drive-through ATM lane. Lagarde noticed that bank employees apparently parked behind the building. Across the road, a nineteenth-century white-clapboard church with a classic steeple might have had room for fifty in its pews on a holiday. Opposite the church on the other side of Charles Town Road was a permanently closed and shuttered gas station, all its branding signs and pumps removed. *This is the crossroads where the twentieth century died*, Lagarde thought.

At two in the morning, the intersection would have been deserted. The lone street light on the corner by the bank had been shot out. Except for the moon and the dim traffic light, someone standing here would be a mere shadow. Unless the few people whose houses flanked the businesses at this intersection walked outside in the middle of the night, they couldn't be sure what they saw, if they saw anything.

Taking advantage of the absence of traffic, Lagarde walked to the center of the road and paced twenty feet in both directions. Beverly, it turned out, was right. A second set of skid marks circled back toward the intersection with Kearneysville Road and then swerved into the insurance agency parking lot. By itself, that didn't prove anything. Anyone could have turned their car around in the last two days. But he called the crime lab to have personnel come out and pull a tire print, just in case he needed to know what make and vehicle model produced those tracks.

Lagarde got back into his car, drove across the road, and parked on the side of the battered insurance office. He worked a grid search back and forth across the asphalt parking lot, looking for whatever was there for him to find. It wasn't that the police weren't thorough. It was that it was damned dark out here at night and, even in the morning, when they were all exhausted from being hauled out of bed without enough sleep, they might have missed something, what with all the vehicles and personnel extracting the body and towing Harold's car.

'*Something big could be inside something very small.*' Wasn't that what Beverly said this morning?

On the fourth pass, he spotted it: a thumb drive—literally the length of his thumb—lay on the asphalt. *Amazing it hasn't been smashed by police vehicles.* He pulled out a glove to pick it up, walked into the insurance office, and asked Weigle if the memory stick belonged to him.

Weigle reacted as if Lagarde had asked him whether he kept pet snakes. His shoulders reared back, he shook his head. His face went red. "God, no, never use the things. Never take client data out of the office, not on paper, not by computer file. I'm too careful for that. You never know when an identity thief is going to strike."

Lagarde thanked him and went back outside. He didn't point out the obvious to the man: that anyone could drive his car right through the office wall in the middle of the night and take all the pieces of paper he wanted. Lagarde put the thumb drive in a baggie, marked on the bag what it was, where he found it, and when. Back in the office, he gave the thumb drive to techs who would sort through what was on it.

He always asked the crime lab scientists for the short version when they started to explain the intricacies of their methods for extracting data. "Bottom-line it, guys," he said, trying not to roll his eyes or fall into an instant coma. He didn't want any more information than he could swallow in one lump. "Old brain," he said to those clever young folks, "low tolerance for techno-speak. Just give me the skinny."

They were happy to oblige. Lagarde had a reputation among them for being something of an idiot savant, arriving at correct conclusions without benefit of their technological wizardry.

Next, he conferred with Taylor, who handed him Nick Waters' statement. Lagarde read it, shook his head, and whistled. "What did you think of him?"

"He didn't do it."

"Good guess." Lagarde wondered if Taylor's intuition had recently been activated by his interview with Waters. "Tell me why."

"He has no reason to kill Munson. He was already getting the milk. Besides, Munson's wife being with him at his house alibis him as well as her for the time of the murder."

It took Lagarde a second to understand the milk metaphor. "Right. His life is working fine as far as he's concerned so why should he mess it up with a murder. Makes sense. Of course, they both might be lying about the alibi. Maybe they did it together."

"Yeah, well." Taylor leaned back against his desk, crossed his arms and consulted his impression of Nick Waters again. "I don't think he wants to marry Mrs. Munson or even have something long-term. I mean, Dr. Rolle. Also, he seems too placid. He's not psychologically constituted to commit murder."

Lagarde grinned. "That's a strong assertion. You don't think Charlotte Rolle could convince him to do murder to save her from a misery of a husband?"

Taylor laughed. "I don't think anyone could nudge Waters out of his comfort zone. But we've got his prints to match against those we find on the gun, whenever we find it."

Lagarde looked at the statement again. "Waters' gun didn't kill Munson. He's got a thirty-eight. Those are forty-five caliber bullets that went through Munson's head. So, if Waters killed Munson, he didn't do it with the gun he registered."

"Oh, yeah, that too." Taylor walked over to the coffee pot. "Want a cup?"

Lagarde shook his head no. "Now that I know what real coffee tastes like, I can't drink that rotgut more than once a day." He walked into the hallway, put his coins in the slot, waited a few seconds, gave the soda machine a solid whack, and brought the can back into the office. He peeled back the top of the can and resumed the conversation. "Our prime suspects—the wife and her lover—have corroborating alibis, which means, we're going to have to be smarter than they are. What did you learn at the casino?"

"Munson wasn't enough of a player that anyone in

casino management or any of the guys in security knew him. A few of the waitresses in the steak house restaurant said he was a big tipper—which is why they remember him—and a little grabby when he's drunk but that they'd only see him from time to time. I'd say, gambling isn't the motive."

"Did you get anything from Munson's neighbors?"

"I don't think any of those people ever go outside except to grill a steak in the backyard or get in their cars to go somewhere else. They didn't even know Munson's name, much less what he was up to."

Lagarde nodded. "What about the folks who live next to the insurance company."

"The homeowner closest to the parking lot, Stanley Weatherall, said he heard the crash and looked out his bedroom window. He saw the car half through the wall, watched Mr. Weigle arrive and then the police. But he didn't see anything before the sound of the crash, which he described as 'being like a helicopter plowing into the street' and he didn't call in the crash himself. Claimed he didn't see any other cars or people, didn't see a shooting. Didn't want to get involved, he said. He had the look of a guy who might have tied one on last night and wasn't sure what he was seeing."

"Thanks." Lagarde swiveled around in his chair and pulled up his email. "Get on those calls to Dr. Rolle's other alibi witnesses. Let's try to nail down her timeline. And then we'll head out to talk to Munson's associates. Maybe they know something."

Lagarde flipped through his contacts and found Sheriff Dennis Harbaugh's number. "Hey, Dennis, Sam Lagarde here." He listened for a few seconds. "Yeah, yeah, we're making our way through the case. Hey, do you recall if Munson's vehicle was still on when your boys got the door open?" Lagarde held the phone away from his ear while Harbaugh yelled at someone, seemingly down the hall from his office by the decibels employed, and got the shouted reply. "No. You're sure the car was turned off? Thanks. Yeah, that's it for now."

He turned around in his chair. "Taylor." Taylor swiveled and looked at him. "Someone, and probably the shooter, got inside the car before Weigle or the deputies arrived at the scene." Taylor nodded his head to say he understood the import of that fact and went back to his calls. Lagarde put another check on the mental list he was keeping of Beverly's guesses.

Two emails in Lagarde's in-box interested him. The first told him there was no gunshot residue on Charlotte Rolle's hands, face, or clothes. He sighed and knocked a point off Beverly's list. The second email said forensics was sending the prints from the shell casings they'd found in the parking lot to the feds for identification, in addition to comparing them to the ones they took from Rolle and Nick Waters.

If the shooter was anywhere in the system, either from a prior arrest or from having worked in government, they'd have a name in twenty-four hours. Of course, it was possible the shooter hadn't loaded the gun, or the gun could have been stolen. Or a clever murderer had someone else load the clip or wore gloves. Sam wondered if Charlotte of the many degrees was that clever.

Chapter 9

The sixty-mile drive from NIH to her home in the Eastern Panhandle gave Charlotte lots of time to think. Cruising at seventy-miles-an-hour, her mind rolled out the scene of the brief staff meeting she convened before she left to assure her research team that their work was not going to stop because her husband had died. Tension zinged around the lab.

Her team was uneasy, and it wasn't because Harold had died or they felt sympathy for her. An undertone of revolt had surfaced among them over the last six months, a steady drum beat of obstinate glares and negativity. She needed to quell the revolt before it got out of hand.

She looked around at their wary faces. "I want a ninety-eight percent cure rate." A few scientists sighed loudly and looked down at the table.

This was her whole world—rows of workstations with white metal shelves holding bulging folders of data, beakers of chemicals, and desks with flat screen monitors. White coated scientists staring into microscopes intent on solving one of the universe's riddles. She could say out loud here what she hoped to achieve. She didn't have to keep it a secret.

"I want no recurrence of tumors. That's our goal."

Some of her team looked away, chins pointing over shoulders, showing their disdain for her.

Charlotte didn't think her demand for near perfection was arrogance. It was simply what was required to meet the challenge of the disease. *If you don't have big goals, you can't accomplish anything.*

Her team squirmed, but such an outcome was no longer unheard of. It was the claim made for the new Hepatitis C treatment: a twelve-week treatment that cured ninety-eight percent of people with the right genotype, people who were almost certainly going to die of cirrhosis of the liver or cancer. It was a miracle.

Sometimes, similar miracles even happened with cancer—Jimmy Carter's melanoma, for instance. When the usual cut, burn, and poison treatment failed, his cancer disappeared after treatment with an experimental drug in Phase I trials that harnessed his own immune system to fight the disease.

That's what Charlotte was after—a miracle cure—but they had a long way to go to achieve that level of success. "We're on our way." She waved her hand in the air, holding an invisible victory flag. "Sixty-percent of our subjects live longer on our treatment than with any other modality," she reminded them. "We beat placebo, chemo, and no treatment."

Her team shook their heads and gazed into their coffee cups, seeming to see their future written there. They had heard this recruitment speech from her before. Some, the ones her ambitious post-doc, Betty Liu, claimed had drunk the Kool-Aid, still jotted notes on their tablets.

Charlotte knew in her bones that she was on the right track. To get to her goal, and the Nobel Prize she craved, she had to keep going. "I want cancer-free patients," she told them. "I want people who would have died to get up from their beds and get on with their lives."

Her staff had reservations. "Post-infusion systemic inflammation in every patient is too great," Dr. Liu asserted three months before. "Patients are suffering horribly even if they live longer. The fevers, hallucinations, there's zero quality of life. You can't rate a treatment simply on longevity." Liu had stood and put both fists on the table in a declaration of war with Charlotte. "We're doctors first. We can no longer look into dying faces and calm families' fears. What happened to first do no harm?"

"This is your job," Charlotte countered, maintaining her extreme calm, her teeth grating together. "Subjects are going to die anyway. Families know that going in. Right now what we're doing is designed to find the approach that forces cancer cell death without killing surrounding tissue. Since that is likely different for each individual, we're also looking for the formula that will enable us to calibrate what each individual needs to eliminate his or her cancer. If we get anything beyond that, like longer life for a subject, it's all to the good."

Dr. Liz Brown, as she had done in previous staff meetings, reminded them of the hideous results of a Phase 1 clinical trial in Northwestern France where previously healthy subjects suffered irreversible brain damage.

She was a broken record as far as Charlotte was concerned. "Experimental disasters appear to be Brown's thing these days." Charlotte worked hard to keep her face from scowling, but she couldn't repress the words. "You're becoming tedious. If you can't deal with the death of your subjects, this is not your field. Go become a pediatrician."

The stricken look on the research associate's face as she fled the room told Charlotte that Dr. Brown would leave her team as soon as another post was available. She would no doubt begin emailing her resume immediately to her network of well-placed colleagues.

Outcomes like the one in France did scare everyone. Charlotte admitted that, but only to herself. Bad press, payouts to families, and maybe starting over from scratch if the project wasn't scrapped entirely would make all the other companies working on treatments directly affecting the brain take a step back and evaluate their research methods, not the least because of insurance costs.

As Charlotte saw it, these news stories were scare tactics toted out by smaller minds to slow her down. Timid people got in the way of the solution. She was thinking about having all the objectors on her team, as she thought of them, moved to other labs. Her real problem was that their results with actual humans didn't match the animal research outcomes. System-wide inflammation after treatment as their own immune systems attacked everything in sight was literally killing them. Liu was right about that.

She had to find the treatment spectrum that killed the cancer and left the human alive. Liu had the nerve to suggest that they go back to animal studies again and redo preliminary tests to see where they had gone wrong. *Little, careful minds,* Charlotte told herself, *get nowhere in this world.*

"Did Marie Curie complain?" Charlotte asked her staff. *She didn't have time for the timid. Was it Liu who got Dickerson's panties in a twist? She would see about that.* Perhaps Liu needed some personal hand holding to shore up her confidence. Handling her hadn't been too unpleasant the last time. Maybe Liu needed a booster shot.

Today, she wanted to stir up the team, make them feel they were all important. "Look," she said, "Ebulon Pharmaceutical Company invested two million dollars in this work because of its potential. We're not simply titrating doses of the same known chemical cocktail. We're doing the opposite of 'one size fits all' chemotherapy. Our work is groundbreaking." She stared into each scientist's eyes, daring them to disagree. "We have proved the hypothesis. We're just tweaking and testing to find the algorithm that will yield the best outcome for each patient."

Charlotte wished she could travel forward in time and see what happened when her treatment was applied before surgery and body-poisoning chemotherapy. *Would outcomes be improved by earlier application?*

Stirring herself from her thoughts, Charlotte looked around. She'd forgotten she was driving. It was only seven miles to her home. She turned right onto Route 230 at the intersection in Halltown that, in her estimation, should be erased from the planet. On one side of the road was a post office so old that the wooden building leaned and had no indoor plumbing. A Porto-potty stood steadfastly next to the entrance door. Opposite the post office, a rickety assortment of cinderblock, tin, wood, and cement slapped together formed a paper recycling plant that belched hydrogen sulfide and black particles into the air while flushing toxic effluent into a small creek that ran out to the Potomac River. She held her breath and zoomed through the intersection.

Halltown was one of those places that reminded Charlotte what happens when legislators don't believe in science. *I'm not just fighting with smart people in the lab. I'm at odds with the entire world.* She fought the impulse to close her eyes. *I'll be back at my beautiful home in fifteen minutes. I can breathe there.*

For the next ten miles, she pondered the insurgency among her research associates. In the first small trial with human subjects, two people died instantly from toxic shock reaction while being infused. A moment of doubt had run through her, chilling her to the core.

Nevertheless, when it came time to publish, she found a way to make the numbers prove her treatment was a success. Statistics were plastic. They could be manipulated to say what you wanted. *Explaining research results is an art form.*

Later, when data manipulation failed, she had no problem fudging the numbers. Her idea was right. She was sure of that. Going in the right direction was what mattered. Everything else was simply running in place, distractions she had to ignore to continue.

But after the latest small group study of seven terminally ill patients, it got trickier to demonstrate effectiveness and downplay the frequency of the worst side effect: death of the patient. Even the subject who lived a year after treatment had finally died. Charlotte preferred not to think of that as a failure. The woman had been able to attend her grandson's wedding.

Today, she had made one last attempt to rouse her staff. "We've developed a once-a-week infusion that harnesses the patient's own defense system to fight tumors using modified T cells. Our treatment engages the immune system as a whole to explicitly treat a specific disease. If we can test the agent on more people, we can extend life expectancy after a brain cancer diagnosis to two years." She'd looked at them triumphantly.

They looked down at their hands, the table, out of the door, anywhere but at her.

She didn't remind them that the gold standard was a cure. Maybe that was just too much to ask for. If there was a God of scientific endeavor, Charlotte wasn't certain he was on her side anymore. But when she left the building, she was sure she had at least five brilliant people with her. She didn't need the rest of them.

ﻉﭏﻉﭏ

At home, Charlotte's house crawled with uniformed personnel, turning over every piece of paper, looking under every cup, seat cushion, and piece of furniture. She shook her head, repulsed. *It's a cockroach invasion!*

"This isn't even where Harold was killed!" she sputtered to the first person she saw in the hallway pawing through the small hand-painted bureau where she kept winter gloves, hats, and scarves.

The policeman shrugged. "Orders, ma'am."

Everywhere she looked, cops scuttled through her drawers. She shuddered at her own imagination. Then she squared her shoulders, dropped her briefcase in her office—*let them look inside that also, like they'll understand a single word on a single page*—and marched into the kitchen to fix a cup of coffee.

Well, she remembered, *during a post-doctoral fellowship with Dr. Bennett, I once glued tiny microchips to the backs of extremely large roaches to study their foraging patterns. I can survive my revulsion now also.*

There was nothing for them to find, she was sure of that. Right now, she was more worried about Dickerson than anyone else. The email he sent her a few days ago frightened her. She guessed that he had never before looked carefully at her data analyses. He read her papers and just took her word that her results were scientifically significant.

She kept Dickerson apprised of her competition: the brilliant team at Duke University using the polio virus to infect a brain tumor, tricking the body's natural defense system into attacking the cancer. They were getting enormous support for their effort. There were others investigating this immunological approach also, of course. Immunotherapy was the new "in" thing in medical research.

That morning, on the way in to Bethesda, she'd listened to a news story about a neurosurgeon who had tried direct application of bacteria to the brain to cure a tumor when nothing else had worked. It was groundbreaking, the newscaster said. That's what she wanted the world to think about her treatment: groundbreaking. She wanted everyone to know she was a genius. That she was right—about everything.

In particular, she wanted her father to know. He had always told her that her thinking was second rate, fuzzy, derivative, that she would never rise above the level of a competent technician. "You simply don't have the mental equipment to be a brilliant scientist, my dear," he would say to her in front of one of his colleagues. "Be happy to be a better-than-adequate physician, like your mother."

Her mother, accustomed to these assaults, simply looked at the floor or the drink in her hand.

Charlotte had decided long ago that she would never settle for her father's assessment of her, even if it took her entire life to prove him wrong. *I am proving him wrong*, she reminded herself. She delighted in sending him links to her most recent publications and the glowing editorials in big journals that often accompanied them. He never sent her a congratulatory email in reply.

She wanted to stuff the editor's words, "groundbreaking work," down her father's throat. An image of him sprang into her mind: he was duct-taped into a chair, his head pulled back, his mouth forced open, and wads of paper, with the word "groundbreaking" written on them, filled his mouth.

She took a sip of her coffee. Everything would have been fine if Harold hadn't sneaked up behind her at the end of February as she was working on her latest paper for the *Journal of Medical Breakthroughs in Cancer*. The editor had contacted her by email asking for a paper for the twenty-fifth anniversary issue. He reminded her they'd met at the last conference at the Hyatt bar in Bethesda. She could hear the husky sound of lust in his voice. He said peer review would be a snap. No worries. "Your work is all the buzz." His words made Charlotte glow.

Harold was too nosy for his own good, and he wasn't a slouch in the math department. He'd leaned over her shoulder, slipped his hands over her breasts as if she was a trophy he could fondle any time he wanted, and said, "Hey, hon, I think you might have this number wrong right here." He pointed at the formula on her screen.

"No, you're wrong, Harold. Go away. You don't know what you're talking about."

"Really, Charl, look. That number can't be right. You can't claim that you have an eighty percent survival rate or that your survival rate is fifty percent higher than the control group. Matter of fact," he leaned over and put his chin on her shoulder, "it looks like all your subjects died."

She wrested her body away from him. "You have no idea what you're talking about."

Charlotte had wanted to ignore him but worried he might report her somehow. Not that he knew anyone at all in the scientific world, except Dickerson. William wouldn't have listened to Harold. But her work was searchable online. Harold could have found the names of journal editors and their email addresses. He could have written to them directly. He might, at the least, have made them uneasy about accepting her papers.

She'd had nothing to hold over Harold's head. She had already started divorce proceedings. There wasn't much else she could do to shut him up. She'd had him served with divorce papers while he was lunching with a client at the Mediterranean, a Charles Town restaurant with salads they liked. He'd been pissed about that. In her estimation, he wasn't sad to see the marriage end, but he thought she was being petty to make a scene about it. She had embarrassed him.

He texted her: *You suck.*

When he got home that evening, he stood in the doorway and ranted, "I want half of what we own." Their entire neighborhood would know their business. "Half includes the condo on Hilton Head and the house in Key West. Half is what West Virginia law guarantees. I haven't done anything horrible, or at any rate, more heinous than you have."

His face turned red, making his eyelashes appear painfully blond against his skin when he blinked. She wondered what he'd done that would make him blush at the memory of it. For a split second, she regretted that he hadn't done it with her. *How did we get to such an appalling place?* It wasn't regret she felt, but tired and disappointed. Her idea about them had been so different from the outcome. This experiment, certainly, had failed.

Harold had made this argument for a simple, equitable split of their assets earlier, before she filed for divorce, hoping to save money on outrageous lawyer fees. He was pushing for a no fault divorce. To no avail. Charlotte wanted it all, everything.

She didn't question her motives or feel she was being unfair. He wouldn't be where he was without her. He had failed her somehow, even if she couldn't put her finger on exactly what his fault was. He should be grateful she wasn't demanding half of all his future income. Of course, she wasn't willing to give him half of hers, either. Embarrassing him in front of a client was a ploy to get him to surrender.

His challenging her on a matter of science was simply too much. "What do you know about anything?"

"I know when you're cheating and lying, I certainly do, and I think some of your colleagues would like to know it too."

"You know nothing!" She'd screamed at him, jumped up from her chair, put her hands on his chest and pushed him out of her office. "I shouldn't have let you stay here. Pack your stuff and go find somewhere else to live."

"No way, bitch. You don't own this house. My name's on the deed too. Until we have a divorce contract signed by a judge, I'm staying right here."

Harold stomped upstairs, flipped the television to wrestling, and turned the sound up to a humanly unbearable level. Charlotte saved her document, moved a copy into the Cloud, threw on a sweater and drove to Nick's house where at least she got some satisfaction.

It was hard to believe that was barely more than a month ago. Charlotte sighed and took another sip of coffee. With Harold dead, at least she had the house to herself, with the exception of the police, but they wouldn't be there that long. There was nothing incriminating here. What they found on her computer would be incomprehensible to them and had nothing to do with Harold's murder. She was blameless.

She walked into the kitchen, opened the refrigerator, noticed that even her food had been moved around on the shelves, and wondered what the police thought they were looking for. Did they think she would hide a gun in the pickle jar? She laughed to herself and pulled out one of the already assembled salads for a late lunch.

Chapter 10

Lagarde dialed Dr. William Dickerson's number and was surprised that the man answered his own phone. "Oh, ah, Dr. Dickerson," he said to regain his composure, having expected to speak to a female assistant, "This is Detective Sam Lagarde, West Virginia State Police. We're investigating the murder of Harold Munson. I understand you are Dr. Charlotte Rolle's supervisor at NIH."

"Yes, well, I don't think of myself as her supervisor. We're colleagues. I head the center in which her lab is based."

Lagarde chewed on this sophisticated humble-brag as Dickerson shared a few glowing assessments of Charlotte's work. He heard an undertone of anxiety and, perhaps, shame in the man's voice. Had Charlotte enlisted this scientist in killing her husband? Beverly might think so. But by voice alone, Lagarde estimated Dickerson was in his late sixties, maybe early seventies, and may have smoked for a fair portion of his youth. Lagarde waited a few seconds after Dickerson stopped talking, an amount of time that would have seemed like hours to Dickerson, before he asked, "Have you known her for a while?"

"Oh, no. She only came to NIH five years ago. We've never worked together on a project. She came here with grant funding because of the enormous potential of her research. We were delighted to have her. She did postdoctoral work with Dr. Samuel Bennett before she came here. She's highly regarded. Many publications…"

Dickerson droned on. Lagarde listened for the place where Dickerson would break off and accidentally tell him some fact that would be useful in the investigation of Harold Munson's murder. Even that Charlotte had recently dyed her hair that astonishing red, that she was routinely late to work, or that she ate other people's lunches out of the lab refrigerator and didn't admit it would make her seem humanly fallible.

He had already Googled her and found mention of all her degrees, postdoctoral fellowships, awards, and the long list of indecipherable titles of her many papers. He'd read several of the short abstracts of those papers and was glad she had given him the layman's bottom line on her research. He didn't think any of that information would help him find out if she was Harold's killer. He needed to know about her as a person, as Harold's wife.

So far, no one they'd interviewed seemed to know her beyond her degrees and professional activities, or, he corrected himself, her active sex life. The yoga folks knew her from yoga, and that was all. "She's flexible," her yoga instructor said, "and dedicated to her practice," she added as an afterthought. *No intimacy there.*

"She's a laugh-riot," said one of the friends she'd gone to dinner with a few hours before Harold died. "She says the most unexpected things."

And her sex slave, Nick Waters, who would normally be expected to have known her most intimately, knew nothing about her, except the amazing positions she invented, which he was happy to share in great detail during his interview with Taylor.

"There was this one time," he confided to Taylor in a voice rasping with lust, "when she hooked her right leg over my neck, arched her back, and..."

Taylor immediately stopped telling Lagarde the anecdote when he saw his senior officer's face had twisted itself into a knot of distaste.

Lagarde figured that Charlotte's yoga practice helped her get into positions that required great flexibility. All of this—the yoga, the boy-toy, the so-called friends, maybe even the devotion to science—were a smoke screen, he thought, for the real person, who was, what? An empty shell? A stage for the performances of whatever character she was playing at that moment? Maybe just a projection of what they wanted to see.

She was almost like the Wizard of Oz. He would have to get behind the curtain of all the many perceptions Charlotte had created of herself for the benefit of various audiences to the real person before he could either rule her out as a suspect or concentrate on figuring out how she committed the murder.

"She did take a week off after her miscarriage two years ago," Dickerson said.

Lagarde sat up. "She was pregnant and had a miscarriage? Two years ago?"

"Yes, it was sad. She'd been so excited about being pregnant. She even stopped working twelve-hour days when she learned she was going to have a baby. She seemed happier for a while. But she's back to being herself now, you know, driven, highly capable, competitive."

Could Charlotte blame Harold for her miscarriage? Was that a motive for killing him? "Was her husband supportive of her pregnancy, do you know?"

"You know, I've only met the man at departmental parties, I'm sorry to say. Just to say hello. And Charlotte hardly talked about him. She said he was absorbed in his business. Of course, I'll go to his funeral. We all will. Everyone here is devastated for her."

There was that strange thrill in the man's voice again. *Maybe he was hoping to be the next Mr. Dr. Charlotte Rolle.* "Perhaps I'll see you at the funeral, Dr. Dickerson," Lagarde said. "Thank you for talking with me. If I have other questions, I'll contact you again."

"Why, of course, anything I can do to help Charlotte."

"Oh, I do have one more question."

"Yes?"

"Did anyone in Dr. Rolle's lab, any of her colleagues, have a grudge against Harold? Did something happen at one of those departmental parties that might have triggered a desire for revenge? Anyone there have an affair with Dr. Rolle that might spur them to eliminate the competition?" Lagarde wondered if he'd struck a chord with the last question.

Dickerson was quiet for a few seconds, consulting a possible catalog of responses and choosing the best one. "I don't believe anyone here knew Harold well enough to have any thoughts about him at all. The only colleague who appears to feel animosity toward Charlotte is Dr. Liu, Dr. Elizabeth Liu, but that, as far as I can see, derives from an intellectual dispute over methods and has nothing to do with poor Harold. As for affairs, I believe Charlotte kept her work and private worlds completely separate."

"To your chagrin, I'll bet," Lagarde said out loud after he hung up.

Chapter 11

"Mommy, look what I'm making." Charlotte spread her arms apart to emphasize the immensity of her project and grinned at her mother. The Pacific Ocean beat out its whoosh and wham behind her.

Her mother looked over the top of her magazine. "That's nice, dear." She returned to her reading.

Charlotte went back to her industrious digging. It was rare that her parents were together with her at the beach. Their schedules barely permitted weekend family dinners together. Charlotte had grown to the observant age of ten knowing her parents were important, busy people. She didn't expect them to play with her. She had learned to manage for herself, as her mother was always urging her to do.

At the club, the hospital, even at her private day school, people deferred to her parents in small, almost indefinable ways, allowing her mother to walk through a door first, tilting their heads to the side, their faces composed in awe-filled silence while her father pontificated about something. The first time Charlotte had seen the word "pontificate" in a sentence, she knew that's what her father did around other people. Her father thought he was the pope, pronouncing on the word of God.

Her parents' importance added to her sense of being special, of being born for something important herself. Her importance was inevitable. It was meant to happen, like the divine right of kings she'd read about. In the stories she made up in her head, she was always the chosen one. Her exaltedness was a given, something she didn't have to earn, or even prove, except when her father deliberately stripped it from her, pointing out she was nothing but a pebble in the road to be crushed to sand under his shoe. By ten years old, she'd already learned to navigate carefully between her natural exaltedness and her father's bone-crushing disdain.

Charlotte carefully emptied the wet sand from her bucket onto the small hill intended to be the second turret in the castle she was constructing and patted it in place. Once the turrets were solid, she would dig a tunnel through them. Next, she would dig the moat around the structure, and then build the castle wall. Her plan, as far as she could tell, was perfect.

Her skin prickled from a combination of sun, salt, and blowing sand, but she was a California child brought up not to care about mild physical discomfort. The ocean was fifty steps away, less than ten seconds if she ran, dashing into the spray, the white foam, and the blessing of cool water tumbling over her head. She loved the beach. She could romp in the waves until she was pickled.

Her mother was reading the latest issue of the *Journal of the American Medical Association*. Charlotte looked around. Other mothers were reading novels or magazines with beautiful models or elegant rooms on the

covers. Her mother's beach reading material was a statement, asserting that even on a gloriously sunny day with
light glinting off blue waves sending the message "come
in, come in, come in," she was still professional, absorbed in her subject and rigorously disciplining her
mind.

Charlotte had taught herself to pay attention to such
small details. These were the values her parents wanted to
instill. This was what was important. There were patterns
here that mattered. She brushed a golden strand of hair
away from her mouth with the back of her hand and
watched her father emerge from the ocean.

He shook his head and droplets of water sprayed
around him. Droplets clung to the matted hair on his
chest giving him silver armor. All he was missing was the
trident. She smiled tentatively at her father, never sure
whether he would stroke or strike her, not with his hands
but with words. A few cruel words, she had discovered,
could rip her heart out of her chest and leave her breathless for days.

His erratic responses seemed to have nothing to do
with what she had done. She had stopped trying to calibrate her behavior. She never knew how he would react
to her. He might praise her for a clever turn of phrase
when debating with her mother about being allowed to
read in bed after her curfew. But with his next sentence,
he could berate her to tears if she mispronounced "deny,"
a word she had only read in a book but never heard used
in conversation. Her parents, of course, never denied anything. Her father's scorn was something to avoid. Yet the
hope of praise made her look up at him as he approached,
refreshed by his swim.

He strode toward them, calling out to her mother,
"Janine, the water's wonderful. You should go in, at least
for a few minutes." Charlotte looked at him expectantly.

Perhaps he would take her into the ocean with him. She stood up, her arms and legs crusted with sand, waiting for him to take her hand. She smiled.

Her father glanced at her and looked at her castle. "What is this mess? You're never going to be an architect, that's certain. You simply don't have the spatial reasoning skills." With two swift kicks, he demolished her castle, turned his back on her, and sank into his chair.

Charlotte's lungs depleted themselves of oxygen in one breath. In her mind, she could see two useless, limp sacks hanging inside her body. Sharp pain sliced her chest. Her face froze. Carefully she inhaled, a test to see if her lungs could still inflate.

Her mother looked up from her journal. "Oh, Magnus, you didn't need to do that. She was happy."

"Blithering idiots are happy. You should want more for her. Life is tough. She needs to learn discipline."

Her mother pulled the top of her swimsuit higher, turned her face away from him without a word, and went back to reading the article. Her father leaned his head back and closed his eyes.

Seconds ticked by. Charlotte felt control of her limbs return. She walked down to the ocean and sat where the waves could lick her legs. Blood returned to her brain. *I'll show him,* she thought. *I'll be smarter than him in every way possible.*

Chapter 12

March 30, 4:00 p.m.:

Lagarde assessed the store-front offices of Munson, Milliken & Walker LLC, a restored two-story, brick-front building on Washington Street in the heart of Charles Town, the 230-year-old town that became the county seat of the newly made Jefferson County in 1801.

The brick had been re-pointed, the wood trim around the door and windows painted a glossy black. The windows were clean. Munson's business wasn't failing. Neatly presented images of properties for sale or lease were arrayed on professional-looking displays in the windows. A black sign with gold lettering, presumably adhering to the town's many restrictions about signs in the four-block historic area, was neatly done.

Charles Town, Lagarde knew, was torn by two competing impulses: preserve the past and thrive in the present. Year to year, it was impossible to predict whether it would become a ghost town or suddenly burst into new life. A new pawn shop, bodega, empty store fronts, and ever changing eateries did not bode well.

He was rooting for this town, but it didn't seem to benefit from the population boom in the panhandle. Since he'd lived in the area, more than two decades now, the county's population had nearly doubled, but few newcomers ever ventured downtown. He thought about Middleburg, Virginia—horsey high-brow with overpriced shops—and Ellicott City in Maryland with its many restaurants, art galleries, and jewelry shops—both within a fifty minute drive from where he stood and about the same size in terms of population—and wondered how those councils had revived their towns. The trick couldn't just be cobblestone streets.

He looked down the street in both directions to see how the Munson building fit into the historic district. Across the street was Needful Things, the antique-thrift-store-luncheonette that served a tuna fish sandwich on wheat toast that wouldn't kill you. On one side of Munson's building was the lone upscale restaurant in town, the one Charlotte Rolle favored, and on the other side was a building that was constantly leased out every four months to different enterprises since the Wodehouse-Waters law partnership had gone belly up. It was tricky being in business in the Eastern Panhandle, although a block away the Mediterranean restaurant had held its own for more than ten years. Good food counted for something, Lagarde thought. And people had to eat.

"What do you think?" Lagarde asked Taylor, who was intently reading property descriptions on the display in the window.

Taylor shrugged slightly. "They've been doing okay, looks like." He pointed to one of the property cards. "When they don't have prices, does that mean they're really expensive?"

Lagarde snorted. "You catch on fast." He leaned forward, pushed on the brass door handle, walked inside and looked around. Wide-planked wood floors, restored brick walls, well-done black and white photographs—someone had taste, that was his first take. His second take was a sense of lassitude, a laid-back quality that belied the crispness of the photographs. *Mixed messages. Does that confuse potential commercial property buyers or put them at ease?*

A young man in a suit, blue button-down shirt, but no tie was sitting in the swivel chair behind the receptionist's desk looking at the screen on his mobile device. Lagarde nodded at him and asked for Edward Milliken or Randi Walker.

"That's me," the young man said, "I'm Milliken." He stood and held out his hand. "Are you looking for commercial property?" He gave Lagarde a once over, probably trying to gauge how much this prospect was willing to spend, and how much time and effort should, therefore, be spent on him.

Lagarde showed his credentials and introduced himself and Taylor. Milliken led them to a seating group in the back of the office space—black leather sofa, a square glass-top coffee table, and two 'seventies-era fabric chairs with tapered wooden legs Lagarde thought might have been picked up across the street from Needful Things. Milliken slouched down in one of the chairs and gestured toward the sofa indicating they could sit if they wanted to.

"We'd like to ask you some questions about Harold Munson."

"I saw it on Facebook this morning," Milliken said. "The death, I mean. I thought I'd better come in. We're waiting to hear from prospects on a major deal. I texted them saying we were still up to the deal."

"Saw what?"

"The thing about Harold dying in a car crash last

night. It happened after he left us."

Lagarde nearly rolled his head around on his shoulders. They were interviewing a guy who was an expert on the obvious. "So, what do you think happened?"

"You know, I don't know. Harold wasn't that drunk. We had some big steaks, potatoes, the whole thing. Dessert. Sure, he put back some brews, a couple of shots, but he just couldn't have been that drunk. He was playing the clients like a chess master and looking for that ultimate win-win moment."

Lagarde made a note on his pad and wondered if the kid always talked this way, half joking, half serious. "Facebook said Harold Munson was drunk?"

Lagarde wasn't sure how Facebook worked, whether it was like a newspaper with headlines on a front page, or an email sent to lots of people at once, or that old game of telephone where the message was garbled by the time the third person told it. He had never seen a Facebook page and, frankly, didn't want to. When Beverly prodded him about setting up his own page, he said, "I've got nothing I want to share with anyone who isn't standing right in front of me where I can see 'em."

Beverly had laughed. He really loved her laugh.

"It was from the local weekly newspaper's feed," Taylor said. "I saw it too. Mr. Milliken here must follow them. The paper probably picked up the information from the police scanner that there was a crash—suspected drunk-driving accident is how it first went out—plus the dead guy's name when we identified him and put it up on their Facebook page."

Lagarde rolled his eyes. He hated how democratic the news had become. No one had any control anymore. And everyone thought he was a reporter, no verification of actual facts needed. He turned to Milliken. "Mr. Munson was shot in the head, twice, deliberately. He was murdered." He waited for the man to react.

Milliken leaned back in his chair, ran one slender hand over his suddenly gray face, and let out a small whoosh of air—he'd been punched in the gut. "Jesus. Shot? Holy shit. Does his wife know? Oh, crap. This will screw our deal."

Lagarde nodded. Edward Milliken wasn't the killer. He'd made it immediately clear that he benefited by Munson staying alive. "Is Randi Walker here today?"

"Yeah, she's in her office. Upstairs."

She. Lagarde's head rocked back on his neck. Was Beverly right about the killer's gender after all? "Taylor, would you get her, please? Be good if they were both in this conversation at this point."

Milliken lifted his phone and starting typing with his thumbs. Lagarde held up his hand. "Mr. Milliken, would you hold up on letting the world know that Munson was murdered, please? We've got more folks to interview, and I'd rather keep the element of surprise on my side for as long as possible."

"Oh, yeah, sure. No problem." Milliken slipped the phone into his inside jacket pocket, but Lagarde could see his fingers were itching to be the one who updated Facebook-world with the new information.

"Was Munson your boss? Can you fill me in on the details of your business arrangement?"

"Oh, yeah. No, not my boss exactly. More like a colleague. Harold is the agency's broker. He takes a share of all commissions on sales regardless of who generates the lead. I'm an associate. Randi is a full partner. Basically, this all affects how shares of commissions are split. I'm the newest member of the firm, so I get less. But if I bring in the client then I get more. The money works out best for me if I get the property listing and bring in a client to buy it. But day to day, nobody tells me what to do.

I generate my own leads and clients. You get that, right?"

Lagarde nodded. *Milliken, bottom of the totem pole, no real motive*, he wrote on his pad. When he looked up, he found a stunning woman in her forties, by the faint horizontal lines across her long neck, short brunette hair cut in one of those modern peacock-feather styles and swept away from her still unwrinkled face, wearing an expensive plum-colored gabardine pants suit and a startling orange-colored silk scarf. *Beverly would be happy with my choice of color adjectives*, he thought.

The woman held out her hand for a business-like shake. "Randi Walker."

Lagarde shook her hand, said "Detective Lagarde," and added to his list of details about Ms. Walker. *Eyes like a lion*, he noted. *No wedding ring, expensive gold necklace and earrings.* Their business was doing well. Was she Munson's lover? "Corporal Taylor told you about Mr. Munson?"

"Yes." She sat on the sofa in a way that made it clear no one should sit next to her. Milliken got up and then sat down again in the chair he'd been sitting in. *She makes him uncomfortable*, Lagarde observed. He and Taylor stood.

"Eddie texted me first thing this morning that Harold was dead. I've been on the phone with the clients we've been wooing for the Wiltshire Road property. It's too soon to tell if the deal will fall through or not."

This woman is cold, Lagarde thought. *No love lost here.* "Where were you after you all parted after dinner last night?"

Randi Walker seemed to blush. The blush made her seem more human. "I went home with one of the prospects, Neal Beatty. You can check that with him."

"Where's your home?"

"I have a house in Mission Ridge, overlooking the river."

An image of the large, stone mini-mansions on Mission Ridge sprang into Lagarde's mind. He recalibrated his idea of their business doing well. They were highly successful. Mission Ridge was also in the opposite direction from where Munson had been heading. "Whose car did you go in?"

"He followed me in his car."

"When did he leave you?"

"We had breakfast together this morning in my kitchen."

There was that charming blush again. Lagarde irrationally hoped Randi Walker going above and beyond the call of duty would get her the deal. Pre-Beverly, she would have been exactly the kind of woman who made him lose his balance. "Is that normal for you, taking your clients home?"

She turned her face toward him. "Who I sleep with and when is none of your business, is it? But, if you must know, they represent a multi-billion-dollar international company that's always scouting for property, and this might, incidentally, be a good time for me to make a change to a position with a high six-figure salary plus bonuses. Particularly long term, for pension benefits and so on. I think of relationship-building as part of the job interview."

Lagarde nodded. *Puts me in my place. She's no victim, knows what she wants.* "I'd like Mr. Beatty's phone number, and the names and contact information for others in your dinner party yesterday." He signaled for Taylor to hand Randi his notepad and pen. "Do either of you know anyone, clients, prospects, sellers, who might want Harold dead?"

Milliken and Walker shook their heads no in unison. "No one," Milliken muttered.

"No," Randi said. "Except maybe his wife."

Lagarde looked up. "Why is that?"

"She's suing him for divorce, and she wants everything. She wasn't willing to follow the state's community property laws and give him half of what they owned." She put her lips together, knowing she'd said too much and stared at Lagarde.

"He was fighting her about the divorce?"

"Not about the marriage ending, he'd had enough of her. You should hear the stories. They were fighting about the property division. They have places on Hilton Head and in the Florida Keys, in addition to the Shepherdstown house. And there's money, a stock portfolio. I guess she gets it all now."

"Did you and Harold Munson have a relationship?" Lagarde instantly felt he should duck.

Randi Walker glared at him. "Let's say, we were friends with occasional benefits. He was a handsome guy, smart, fun to be around, and generous. I liked him. He was making us rich. So, I'll miss him." She turned her face away from Lagarde's gaze.

So, she has no obvious motive and a semi-solid alibi, Lagarde thought and handed them both his card. "If you think of anything, please give me a call. I may be back in touch with you."

Back on the sidewalk, Lagarde turned to Taylor. "Let's call over to the hotel where Beatty is staying and set up an interview with those folks. I want to see if he corroborates Walker's statement."

"She does seem a little slicker than most women around here," Taylor volunteered.

"You haven't met the women who kill," Lagarde said. "They can be very slick."

Chapter 13

Armed with another soda from the office machine, the smell and taste of eggplant parmigiana wafting through his memory making him long to go home for dinner, Lagarde opened his email to see if anything new had come from the forensics techs.

An email from Dave Weigle, broker of the insurance company with a car-sized hole through the wall, had the tantalizing subject: "Some guy in the photo."

Lagarde opened the email and clicked on the attached photos. The images were date and time stamped and included shots of Munson slumped over the air bag, the front of his car smashed through the wood building, the mess the crash made on the office inside, and then, like a ghost, the shadowy figure of a man standing across the street on the grass between the Post Office and the bank parking lot, peering back at Weigle. The man was gone in the next frame.

"Taylor, take a look at these."

Corporal Taylor scooted his chair over to Lagarde's desk and leaned over to scrutinize the screen. "Make it bigger." Lagarde rolled his mouse around. Nothing happened. "Enlarge the photo," Taylor said in the tone a man uses when he's patiently teaching his son to pee inside the toilet. Lagarde looked at him quizzically. Taylor put his hands on the keyboard and magically the man in the distance was larger, if somewhat fuzzier looking. "He's definitely looking right at the scene."

Lagarde huffed, exasperated. He hated technology. "So we've got a witness, at least. Looks to be Caucasian, medium height, middle aged..." He noticed the smirk on Taylor's face. "Okay, so maybe he's in his early sixties, out in the middle of the night on foot, looking at what appears from his side of the road to be an accident. No excuse to be out in the middle of the night. I don't see a vehicle, bike, or a dog, nearby. He wasn't playing Good Samaritan. He didn't run across the street to help. No excuse to be there except rubbernecking. What's that in his hand?"

Taylor moved in to take a closer look at the image. "It's a cell phone. He's taking photos of the crash."

"He was gone before the deputies arrived and he wasn't one of the neighbors you interviewed. Right?"

Taylor nodded. "Yep."

"Well, we've got a rubbernecker with a camera. We have to find him. At least, we might have an eye-witness with images to prove what happened."

"We might have a shot at figuring out who he is." Taylor tapped a few more keys, closing the image and forwarding the email. "I sent the photo to forensics. They can clean it up and run it through facial recognition software, see if this guy shows up in the FBI's new data set, either as a past offender or government employee."

Lagarde nodded. "Right. Why didn't I think of that?"

Taylor grinned and shrugged. "Too much on your mind, perhaps."

"Yeah, like dinner. But let's talk to Munson's million dollar clients first. I'll follow you in my car."

Chapter 14

May 15, 1994, 3 p.m.:

Charlotte stood next to her parents in the reception area of their club waiting to be seated for dinner. Her father was happily pontificating on some subject about which he claimed brilliance. The friends dining with them were nodding and smiling. She had stopped listening to him years ago.

No matter what the subject, the subtext was always that he was smarter than anyone else. He brooked no discussion, no arbitrary dissent. He interrupted, his hand slashing away at anyone else's arguments. His was the only accurate point of view about everything. The minute his pointer finger went up, her hearing went off. Recently, she had begun to realize there were limits to his expertise. Watching her mother's face closely, Charlotte realized she also had stopped listening to her husband.

Her mother pulled the strap on Charlotte's summer dress back onto her shoulder and smiled at her. "You look lovely, darling."

Charlotte nodded and looked out of the windows at the sun going down at the horizon-edge of the Pacific

Ocean—yellow, red, and orange melting into the water. *Anywhere but here*, she thought, *if I could be anywhere but here*.

Her classes at the university weren't onerous. She breezed through textbooks, read every book on the optional list for each of her classes, delved deeply into the subjects presented to her in labs, and happily engaged in classroom discussion. Her professors were kind and encouraging. Her classmates were admiring, if a little careful of befriending her.

That was all right with her. She was several years younger than they were. She was used to being alone, and there were other smart kids around she sometimes met unexpectedly in the library or in the dining hall, eating while deep in some esoteric text. She found herself checking the titles of books as she walked by people as a way to assess whether they might be someone she could talk to but mostly she kept to herself. It was easier that way. She wouldn't get her hopes up and her heart broken by someone who turned to her in a group and said, "Why are you standing here?"

She enjoyed her physical freedom, riding her bike across the airy campus, going to sleep when she wanted, eating when she wanted. No one here demeaned her. It was coming home she dreaded—home was a recurring malaria with sweats, uncontrollable chills, and fever. At home, she waited for the moment her father would suddenly turn on her and tell her she was completely witless. No matter how much she anticipated it, she was always struck dumb when he did it.

"Charlotte is already at the university," she heard her father say. She looked over at him as a chill formed in the center of her back. When her father bragged about her to his friends, there was a special danger. At any minute, he might destroy her in front of strangers. "Tell the Howards what Dr. Battersy said about epigenetics this week, Charlotte."

There was a sneer in his voice. It was her warning. She had to find the correct, narrow path to walk from where she was to safety. If she tripped, she could fall into a swamp of scorn on one side or the fire of total intellectual annihilation on the other. She could almost smell the fetid mash of rotting matter and hear the first snap of fire igniting.

A perfect puppet, Charlotte said, "Dr. Battersy said that environmental factors can influence genetic expression that may be passed down to subsequent generations. For instance, a starvation diet suffered by a father as a teenager can cause changes to genes that are passed down through generations to his sons and their sons, and these alterations can affect susceptibility to certain diseases."

Dr. Howard leaned toward her. "Do you think that's true?"

"I think," Charlotte said, feeling she had won a point in a tennis match and then immediately suppressing her glee, "that it remains to be proven. Also, before we can deliberately employ epigenetic methods to mitigate disease processes, we need to address the issue that triggering certain cellular behaviors could lead to new cancers or other unwanted outcomes. But certainly, it's an approach that should be investigated."

Howard looked over at her father and smiled. "Smart kid you've got there. How old did you say she is? Fifteen? You're going to have your hands full."

First, her father preened at the compliment. After all, she was the fruit of his loins. Then his smile stiffened. "I expect that Charlotte will do what all women do. She'll dabble in the intellectual arts for a while and then succumb to the tides of her already-quite-ripe body." He

paused and let his eyes rove across her. "She'll most likely marry, leave school, and breed."

Charlotte's breath fled her chest. Her neck stiffened.
Her eyes sought out her mother, begging for help, but her
mother turned her face in the opposite direction, her jaw
rigid. The men laughed. Dr. Howard's wife looked for-
lorn. She put out a hand and lightly touched Charlotte's
arm.

Charlotte's face burned. She turned to look out the
window. She could feel her entire body shutting down,
system by system, until all that was left was her ability to
observe life moving swiftly around her, outside the window.

Chapter 15

Ted Norge, Oliver Stone, and Neal Beatty of Datapile had arrayed themselves in the dove gray leather club chairs in the hotel lobby. Each was deep into his own mobile phone.

Lagarde had called ahead and arranged to meet them there. He spotted them the moment he breezed through the automatic door. Somehow, the t-shirt plus expensive sports jacket over worn jeans fashion they sported made him think of spoiled brats. He gave himself a mental shake to tamp down his prejudices against the young and obscenely rich and looked sideways at Taylor, who seemed to be having the same reaction. The feeling on Lagarde's skin was similar to the first contact with poison ivy. He would need a shower with strong soap.

Lagarde walked up to the group, pulled out his credentials, flashed his badge, and introduced himself. The men nodded but didn't rise from their chairs or offer handshakes. Clearly, they didn't care what kind of impression they made on him. He might take that as a sign they were not guilty, or he might not. *Depends on wheth-*

er they are sociopaths or not, he thought.

"Gentlemen, let's move into one of the small meeting rooms." He looked over and saw the concierge signaling him toward a door in the wide corridor to the left of the reception desk. "We'll have more privacy there."

The men rose without comment and followed him to the room where a shiny wood conference table and ten black resin and chrome chairs took up most of the space. Lagarde looked out of the large window at the golf course illuminated by well-placed lamps and wondered briefly about people who could spend their days hitting a small ball across hills and dales in the middle of the week. He thought about his horse, Jake, and wished he was riding him instead of doing this interview.

When he looked back at the Datapile executives, they seemed to be as casually comfortable seated in these straight-backed chairs as they were before. *Perhaps that's another benefit of wealth, or maybe it was youth—you're comfortable in your own skin anywhere you are.*

He pulled out his pad and pen. "You already know that Harold Munson, with whom you met yesterday, was killed around two a.m. this morning."

The men glanced at each other and nodded, each in his own way.

They weren't, Lagarde noted, complete automatons. "I'd like to know where each of you was between one and three a.m. this morning."

The sandy haired man identified himself as Neal Beatty. "I was with Randi Walker at her house on Mission Ridge."

Lagarde's mind flashed him a quick image—long bare legs, a breast, a head tilted back. He blinked and focused on Beatty. The guy wasn't blushing. Perhaps he had women in every location he spotted for his company. Lagarde wondered if Ms. Walker understood that about her new conquest. "When did you leave Ms. Walker's house?"

"I was there until eight this morning, but you don't seriously think any of us has a motive for killing Harold, do you? Frankly, he was practically giving away that facility on Wiltshire. It's way undervalued. We were ready to close tomorrow if the seller accepted our offer today and Harold could pull the papers together. We'd like to get this business done and move on to refitting the space."

"I'm Ted Norge," said another tanned, trim, expensively groomed executive. "Oliver and I came back here after our night cap at the casino bar to put together our offer. Took us a few hours, several emails, a few phone calls back to headquarters. We were in the hotel business services office running copies around two a.m. The bill might show the time it was charged to my suite."

"I made a call to Portland, to my wife at eleven p.m. her time, so that's two a.m. Eastern time," Oliver said. "You can probably check my phone records." He shrugged. "We were better off with Harold alive, frankly. We'd have gotten this deal done faster. This whole murder thing throws a real kink in our schedule."

Lagarde and Taylor exchanged a look that said, *Man, what a shithead, but not involved in our murder.* Lagarde changed tactics. "What do you think of Harold, did you notice anyone at the casino or restaurant yesterday evening who might have had a beef with him? Did you see anyone threaten him?"

The men shook their heads, no. "Nothing like that," Neal said. "He seemed to be universally liked. We took that as a good sign. His murder does give us some pause about this environment." He looked over at his partners, who shook their heads.

"Yeah," Oliver followed up, "in all of our contacts

with him, he seemed to be a straight shooter, knew what he was talking about, didn't waste our time." He gave a one-shoulder shrug. "It's sort of unbelievable that this," he floundered around for a second looking for the right word to use instead of murder and settled on, "this thing happened."

Lagarde could almost see a light go on above Taylor's head. "So, when exactly did you and Harold end your meeting?"

Neal looked at Taylor, seeing him for the first time and deciding he wasn't important. "Around midnight. Harold picked up the tab at the bar." He paused and then added, in case Taylor was too dim to understand, "His credit card receipt is probably time stamped."

Taylor looked at Lagarde. Two hours between the time they left Harold and the time he was killed were not accounted for. Lagarde made a note on his pad. A man could get in a lot of trouble in two hours. Was there a woman no one knew about? Did Harold have some really bad habits that would get him killed? No one they'd talked to so far had mentioned this time gap. The person who killed him couldn't have predicted Harold would be on Charles Town Road at the intersection with Kearneysville Road at any precise time. He or she would have had to wait for hours and follow him. Or the killer had a heads up. They needed to find Harold's personal phone, and fast.

They thanked the men for their cooperation and walked out of the hotel. "We need a dinner break," Lagarde said, to which Taylor raised his eyebrows in relief. "After that, go through Munson's whole life again, examine every piece of paper in that briefcase we took from the house, see if you can find out if he had a woman on the side or a drug habit. I'll be at home. Call me if you find anything."

Taylor saluted and walked off to his unmarked car. Lagarde, walking to his own car, thought he might just get used to the guy.

Chapter 16

March 30, 8 p.m.:

Dinner was as delicious as Lagarde had anticipated all day it would be. Beverly poured him another glass of the Valpolicella she bought at the wine store in Shepherdstown. He took a long sip and savored the rich, multi-layered taste of the red wine before swallowing. She'd already brought the horses into the barn, fed, and watered them. Before Beverly, dinner would have been a cheese steak sandwich from the gas station quick foods section, a bag of chips, and a soda consumed at his desk in the office. She was spoiling him.

Beverly leaned back in her chair. "Any headway in the case?"

Lagarde grimaced. At least she'd waited until he finished eating. "So, the wife, Charlotte Rolle, with doctor before her name and a string of other letters after it, has a lover who's her alibi for the time of the shooting, was suing Munson for divorce, had a miscarriage a while back, and is pretty well known in her field—which is developing a cure for brain cancer, by the way. She's smart, feisty, and uncomfortably seductive but so far, my dear

Beverly, she seems to have no motive to kill her husband. She was getting rid of him anyway."

"What makes you think divorce is sufficient? Maybe she wanted to obliterate all traces of him on the earth, in the old Greek tragedy way."

Lagarde's head reared back the way his horse's did when he galloped up on his own shadow. "Wow! Remind me not to get on your bad side. It doesn't look like she's the one who was scorned. There's no cause for fury. If anything, he's the one with the complaint. What do you mean?"

"Did you find anything at the scene?" Beverly got up and pulled strawberry shortcake from the refrigerator, set it down on the table, and cut him a huge slice. She put the dessert in a bowl in front of him with a clean spoon.

"Oh, yes. A thumb drive." He smiled at the strawberry shortcake. It was his favorite dessert. "Like you said, something small that could hold a lot of information. The tech guys are sorting through it for me."

"There'll be a clue in that information. I'll bet my life on it."

Lagarde made sure each bite he took had cake, strawberry and whipped cream, licked his lips when it was gone, got up from the table, picked up his plate, flatware, and glass and brought them over to the sink. He wrapped his arms around Beverly. "I don't want you to bet your life on anything. But you're making me think you're a little clairvoyant, or something."

She smiled at him and snuggled against him. "It's not clairvoyance. It's just logic. Did Munson have any other enemies?"

"Not that we've found so far, but we have a two-hour gap in his timeline. The folks he met for dinner left him around midnight. He wasn't killed until around two a.m. So where did he go in those two hours?"

"Did *he* have a lover?"

"Don't know. That's the question we got to." He lifted her face and kissed her. All this talk was warming him up.

"Two hours," she murmured against his chest. "So, he goes to see his lady friend for a little sex, texts his wife when he's leaving there, so she thinks he's being thoughtful, just to keep up appearances, and she jumps in her car and races over to the intersection she knows he'll drive through on the way home."

Lagarde shook his head. "Her lover swears she was with him until three-thirty a.m., although I think that's what she told him to say. But there was no trace of gunpowder on her hands or clothing, no record that she owns a gun, and we didn't find one at the house. The second set of tire tracks from a swerve on the road—yes, you were right about that too—don't match the tires of her car."

"Or—" Beverly tugged on his hand, leading him toward the back steps up to their bedroom, "Dr. Charlotte Rolle had an accomplice she called or a hired killer who *she* texted to say Harold was on his way."

They got as far as the bed when Lagarde's phone rang. He looked at her with regret. "The tech guys," he explained. "They never sleep."

He listened to the forensic technician tell him they'd found a hoard of information on the thumb drive. "Apparently, Mr. Munson was in a disagreement with the IRS about tax fraud, in a dispute with a Randi Walker over a commission he claimed she was not supposed to get, and there's a stash of documents that appear to be statistical analyses of some esoteric data we don't understand. We're going to send those documents over to a professor of statistics at West Virginia University to sort through. He'll let us know what that's about."

"Thanks, man," Lagarde said. "You guys are amazing. Can you shoot me the original documents as an attachment to an email? Tag the thumb drive for evidence when you're done."

"Will do. Glad we could help."

Lagarde turned back to Beverly, who while he was preoccupied on the phone, had changed into a beguiling peach negligee. He widened his eyes and grinned. "Harold Munson was apparently not Mr. Clean." He unbuttoned his shirt. "Was this some special date I've forgotten?"

"It's the anniversary of the day we met." She held out her arms to him, and they forgot all about murder for a while.

Chapter 17

April 17, 2001, 8:30 a.m.:

She told herself it wasn't the gush, the waterfall of blood from the surgical wound that made her dizzy, that made her step back, away from the table. It was the close proximity of so many bodies in surgical garb, the intensity of the lights, the way oxygen barely filtered through her mask that made her dizzy. Charlotte's mind grayed. She couldn't concentrate. Her face felt cold and sweaty at the same time. She struggled against fainting.

It was a simple procedure, her first on surgical rounds during her internship. She would not be asked to do anything difficult, at most to close the wound, she guessed. But something had gone wrong. The surgeon had clipped an artery. Hands rushed to stem the flow of blood, to reconnect essential pieces of this boy's body together so that it worked again. The team did what it was supposed to, the anesthetist calling off the patient's dropping vital signs in a steady rhythm that indicated doom.

In her head, all Charlotte could hear was her father's voice whispering "You're losing him, you're losing him.

If you weren't so inept at everything, this patient would live. You're not meant to do this." Her father had warned her that surgery was not her field when she excitedly reported by telephone that she would start her surgical rounds today. She should have known better than to tell him anything.

Her mother had tried to salve the sting of her father's comments. "It's just exposure to a specialty, part of your training. You don't have to choose it. Just make a display of competence."

Charlotte took a second step back from the operating table. Behind her, the chief surgical resident said, "If you can't cope, Rolle, get out of the way."

She looked up and caught the sneer in his eyes, took a deep breath to conceal her sob, and fled the operating room.

She changed in time to watch from a respectful distance as the chief surgeon told the family that they'd lost the patient on the table. At no time did he admit it was his error, or anyone else's on the surgical team, or that their mistakes caused the patient's death. He was calm and grave, and then he walked away from them as they collapsed in grief. All sound muted, Charlotte saw the mother's arms fly up, the father step forward to catch her, the daughter reach for her mother. Charlotte turned her head away.

She waited in the corridor for the surgical resident to ask him about why the surgeon hadn't explained to the family what happened in the operating room. He looked at her quizzically when he emerged from the locker room, showered, in clean scrubs. "Well, Rolle, what's your problem?"

He was the first man Charlotte had a crush on. She was twenty-four. He was thirty-something. The elegance of his hands made her swoon. He seemed to have nothing but contempt for her. Her heart broke every day he threw a snide remark her way and turned his back on her. Being book smart wasn't enough for this man. Her *fingers* had to be smart, and she didn't seem to have the dexterity for surgery. This was her first experience with failure.

"I want to understand what happened."

He stopped and turned to her, seeming astonished. "Who are you to ask about what happened? You're the intern. You know less than nothing about anything."

Blood stopped in her veins. Her mouth opened. Tears leaked from her eyes. She looked at him, wordless. He stepped toward her, put his hands on her shoulders, pushed her back against the wall, took her face in his hand and possessed her mouth. When he drew back, inhaling deeply, she sobbed.

"You should stick with what you're good at," he said. With one finger, he flicked her nipple, turned on his heel, and strode away.

When she could move, Charlotte looked left and right. No one was watching her. No one knew, except her. Her mind offered a solution: *Destroy him.*

Chapter 18

Lagarde called his friendly neighborhood tax accountant, Sarah Parker, CPA, about Harold Munson's dispute with the IRS over failure to report a few hundred-thousand dollars in income the previous year. The dispute was one of the new pieces of information about Harold that came from the thumb drive Lagarde found in the insurance agency parking lot. He knew he was only dotting Is, but he had to check the box, just in case.

"This isn't a big deal," Sarah told him. "He negotiates this down to a few thousand in taxes and a relatively small penalty. Easy peasy. Certainly not worth being killed over. Or killing himself about. He's running a business. He must have an accountant."

Lagarde had to smile at Sarah's idea that an accountant would save you from suicide or murder. But Sarah wouldn't lead him astray. He wondered what it would be like to have an extra hundred-thousand dollars coming in over the course of one year. He really couldn't imagine it. Munson obviously lived in a different world from his even if they resided in the same geographic locale. *Moving on*, he thought before he spotted Taylor on his way to the coffee maker.

"Hey, Taylor, let's go visit Randi Walker again. There's a little detail she left out when we talked to her before, like Harold Munson was trying to swindle her out of a commission."

Taylor's eyebrows shot up. He got his coffee, brought the cup back to his desk, took a sip. "Is that worth killing him over? Wouldn't that be like killing the goose that laid the golden egg?"

Lagarde turned his head and looked at Taylor out of the corner of his eye. "So you think she wouldn't kill him over ten-thousand dollars?"

"No way. She's too smart for that. She's making six figures every year out of that partnership, easy. He's the rainmaker. Why would she give that up to get a tenth the value one time?"

Lagarde smiled at his apprentice's sharpening analytic skills. "She is the remaining partner now. She gets *all* the business and says who gets what percentage."

"Nah, not enough motive, I think. Compared to life in prison, anyway. Cost-benefit analysis says no, it's not her."

Lagarde nodded. "Let's go see her anyway. Maybe she knows what Munson was doing during those two missing hours. You drive."

They drove down Wiltshire Road and stopped for two cups of real coffee from Black Dog café, a fresh-roasted-coffee place plus farmer's market that had caught on as a farmer-hippie hangout. Inside, they inhaled the aroma, shook hands and traded comments about the weather with the regulars.

When they got back into their four-wheel-drive vehicle, Taylor took the new highway into Charles Town. As always, Lagarde wished coffee tasted as good as it smelled.

They arrived at Munson's office just as Randi was unlocking the door. *A little surprise always helps with candor*, Lagarde thought. She momentarily looked like someone who woke up from a nightmare and realized she really was out on the street naked.

"Sorry to bother you this early in the morning, Ms. Walker." Lagarde watched her walk around the office, turn on lights, check the phone for messages, and turn on the computer. "We want to ask you about the commission Harold owed you."

Randi stopped moving for the tiniest flick of a second, waved her hand in front of her face, took off her jacket, and put it on the back of the chair. She sat down in the receptionist's seat and didn't motion for them to pull up chairs. "Oh, that. It's nothing. We would have straightened that out in time. Harold was just being a little extra greedy. I had paperwork proving the client and the property were mine."

"So Harold trying to cheat you is not something that happened routinely between the two of you?"

"No, no. He just got it in his head that he had brought in that client instead of me." She shrugged. "Anyway, it's moot now, isn't it?"

Taylor turned around from a photograph he'd been studying. "I'm just going to take a look in Harold's office. Our warrant covers any and all locations—"

Randi nodded. "Of course."

Lagarde rolled a chair over to the desk and sat down. He rested his hands on the arms. "Was Harold having an affair, Ms. Walker?"

Randi's well-rouged lips formed a perfect O. She looked down at her lap. "I guess that doesn't make any difference now either." She raised her eyebrows, blinked, pressed her lips together. "He had a casual thing going with the catering manager at the hotel."

"Casual as in, nobody was jealous of anyone ever?"

"Well, casual as in they met up whenever he called her. No preliminaries, no dates, you know. Maintenance sex."

"Is there a term of art for this kind of relationship, like the one you had with Harold, friends with benefits?"

"Oh, I don't think they were friends. They had nothing in common. She wasn't his mistress in the strict definition of that term—he didn't give her money or pay for her living expenses—if that's what you're implying, and I don't think she had any designs on being his wife. They just liked to have sex together, the way some people like Dairy Queen milk shakes or McDonald's fries. Do you know what I mean?"

"You didn't approve?"

She shrugged. "I thought it was a mistake. She wasn't discreet. Harold was becoming an important man in the county." She turned her head and stared out the display window at the front of the office.

The world is tilting right under my feet without my knowing anything at all about it. Randi's objection to Harold's affair wasn't based on morality but on some measure of social utility. True, Sam had had affairs in his day, but he always felt vaguely guilty about them, the way people are supposed to. Something about this woman disturbed him. If this was what the younger generation was up to, no wonder he sometimes felt like he was losing his balance. *Maybe the problem with humanity is that people don't have only one season a year they are in heat. They are in heat every damn day. And of course, there is the problem with greed. Greed never goes out of fashion.*

"So, Harold's wife knew about this milk shake and

fries craving of his, and she wasn't jealous?"

"I don't think she cared what Harold did. Didn't she have someone on the side also?"

"Harold knew about that?"

"Oh, yes. He hired some private detective to find out. They were duking it out in the divorce. He said he needed ammunition. He showed me some of the photos. Steamy. And the guy is way younger than her." Randi winked at him. "Gave me ideas."

Lagarde shook his head to clear it. *Was this woman coming on to him?* "Do you have Harold's girlfriend's name? Contact information?"

Randi opened a drawer in the desk, pulled out a business card, and handed it to Lagarde. *Barbara Benson, Catering Manager*, was printed on the card along with a phone number, address, and email. Lagarde had everything he needed. He stood and rolled the chair back to where he'd found it.

"One more thing," he said as Taylor walked out of Harold's office with his hands spread in a gesture that meant *no joy*, "Do you know where Harold went after your meeting ended?"

"He might have gone to see Barbara. He texted someone."

"Thanks." Lagarde gave her a slight nod, Taylor held open the door, and they left the office. On the walk to the car, Taylor told Lagarde there was no cell phone in Munson's office.

"Okay," Lagarde said. "Let's head to the casino hotel, have a little chat with Ms. Barbara Benson."

Chapter 19

March 31, 8:30 a.m.:

Lagarde's phone bleeped as he got into the car. He glanced at the screen. "Message from the tech guys," he told Taylor. "They've figured out who the guy is in the photograph Weigle took after Munson's shooting."

He looked at the text again. "His name is Mark Wiseman. He's a retired Baltimore City cop. He lives right here in Jefferson County, over by the Shenandoah River. I think we'll pay a visit to Ms. Benson another time. Let's check out Wiseman's story. Maybe we'll get an eyewitness account of the Munson murder out of it."

Taylor nodded, punched the address Lagarde gave him into the GPS and made a sharp right hand turn onto Jefferson Street to head out toward the river. "He was pretty far from home to be out on foot across from the insurance office in the middle of the night."

"Right." Lagarde looked out of his window, his mind following the same logical pathway Taylor was taking. "He might be more than a casual witness."

"We might need a warrant."

"Right again. But at this moment we've got no probable cause to get one. Let's talk to the guy as a witness first and see what he tells us."

They drove south on Charles Town Road for fifteen minutes and, instantly, they were transported one-hundred years into the past as West Virginia's rolling hills and open fields glistened in the early spring morning as they had for centuries. Taylor turned left on Millville Road, the Shenandoah River rolling wide and quiet on their right, and pulled left into a long lane that led from the road to a log cabin.

Built fairly recently, in Lagarde's assessment, the house had a wide veranda that wrapped around the front to face the river. It was a fairly expensive house, well-tended. No vehicles sat in the gravel drive. Lagarde walked up onto the porch and knocked on the door. Taylor walked around to the back of the house. No one answered their knocks, no dogs barked.

Taylor bounded up onto the porch and looked around at the view. "Nice location. He's uphill and has at least a half-mile between the house and the river. Even a fifty-year flood shouldn't hurt him, although the road would be washed out. Great view, quiet, easy fishing. In the summer, when the trees are leafed out, his neighbors won't be able to see him."

Lagarde nodded. Taylor had just provided a shorthand version of his own values. He agreed with the kid. "Right. His biggest problem is getting Lyme disease from deer ticks. So what is a retired cop who's got this nice house, and obviously a generous pension, doing fifteen miles away in Kearneysville in the middle of the night right across from a murder?" He shook his head. "Hard to see what his motive could be for standing there taking photographs."

He walked along the porch and peered into the large

windows. "There's nothing obvious. If he is our perp, we've got to surprise him. It appears he's got the resources to run. Maybe he's done that already."

"Maybe the photo of him at the scene in the middle of the night is enough for a search warrant for his house," Taylor said.

"Good idea. Drop me off at headquarters, and I'll talk to Ms. Benson on the phone while you talk to the prosecutor into a warrant."

Chapter 20

February 20, 4 p.m.:

Standing in line at the in-store Subway, waiting for the thinly gloved woman on the other side of the glass case to slop lettuce, tomatoes, pickles, mushrooms, and peppers on toasted buns, the redhead in front of Mark Wiseman commented out loud, "What makes them think those gloves keep any bacteria off that food?"

Something in his gut jumped. It was the unexpectedness of her talking to him. "It's all about perception," Mark replied.

She turned and looked at him with those green eyes in a way he'd figured no woman would ever look at him again, sizing him up, evaluating his manhood, his juice, and smiled at him.

At the time, he'd thought it was lust, and all the youth left in him leaped for joy.

They sat on the metal bench at the front of the Bigmart waiting for a fierce rain to let up, eating the sandwiches they'd just purchased—his a meatball, hers a veggie. "Charlotte Rolle," she said, licking her fingers clean and holding out her hand for a shake.

"Mark Wiseman," he responded, taking her sticky hand and holding it as long as she let him.

She laughed at something he said—God knows, he couldn't remember what—and suddenly there were her long fingers slipping across his thigh, putting mild pressure on his adductor muscle. Heat radiated from her touch. He was suddenly forty-five again. He sucked in air and sat up straighter. Life was not over.

Before the rain stopped, he told her he was a retired Baltimore cop moved out to West Virginia's Eastern Panhandle because house prices were cheap, and the crime rate, except for people killing themselves for illicit drugs, was low.

She told him about her miserable excuse for a husband, not physically abusive but emotionally a vampire, draining her of her initiative, dampening her joy in her work—which was terribly important and would save millions of lives—blowing away her ability to concentrate. He listened intently. He was convinced Harold Munson was a demonic manipulator who was abusing this beautiful, intelligent woman who had chosen to confide in him.

How long had it been since a woman talked to him this way, leaning into his shoulder, whispering, her mouth moving, her tongue swishing over her lips? He imagined her lips under his. He breathed deeply. *To hell with morals*, he thought. *How many chances will I get? I'm sixty. This is probably it.*

He leaped. "Would you like to see my cabin? I'm right off the river. It's kind of beautiful there." He waited, one breath, two. Time stopped in his mouth.

She said yes, and the sky cleared, the rain stopped. She followed him out through the parking lot to his aging Honda pickup truck and hopped up inside it. She might have been riding in vehicles like his all her life, although he could tell by her expensive shoes that she hadn't.

He drove her out the old, narrow roads along the Shenandoah River, the road rising slightly into the hills and then flattening out near the wide bank. Sun broke through the clouds and laid a bright hand on the water just as he pulled into his graveled driveway. She jumped out of the truck and strode up onto the wide porch. She stood facing the river for a minute, taking in the view, then turned toward him, unsnapped her vest, unbuttoned her shirt, her abundant breasts tumbling out from the constraining fabric, and looked at him.

Smiling slowly, she leaned back against the wooden railing. "Well, do you need more invitation than this?"

He didn't. He strode to her, turned her to face the river, embraced her from behind, unbuttoned her designer jeans, and slid his hand under her thong. Her moans, echoing across the water, made him feel he could do anything. She leaned her head back against his shoulder and guided his other hand to her breast.

"I think I can walk on water," Mark whispered.

All week, he waited to see if she would contact him. Parked near the tracks, he watched her get off the train and into her car every evening. He went to Bigmart, pacing near the Subway, all hunger except for her gone, hoping to meet her accidentally. Thoughts of her drove him crazy. He couldn't sit out on the porch without her smell embracing him. Twice he caught himself groaning out loud. The following Saturday, she called him and said she needed to meet. His breath was a balloon in his chest, swelling. Her voice on the phone was a taste of the drug to come.

In half an hour she was at his door, removing a piece of clothing with each step into the front room. When she was naked, she hopped up onto his kitchen counter and opened her legs. "Almost heaven," he whispered to himself, burying his face between her breasts.

Later, lying on the floor, sweat cooling, she said, "I need you to do something for me."

"Of course," he said then. "Anything. Tell me what you need."

Now, he thought that initial jolt had been a danger signal, his gut telling him to keep away. He should have known. He had enough evidence that she was dangerous. But it was too late. He was in too deep.

Chapter 21

March 31, 9 a.m.:

The phone interview with Barbara Benson was, in Lagarde's estimation, a waste of time. If she was emotionally affected by Munson's death, she didn't show it. Of course, she'd had a day to recover any composure she might have lost when she learned her lover was killed. She did confirm that Munson had texted her shortly after midnight on March thirtieth.

As far as Lagarde could tell, she had no motive to kill him, if murder was the end result of caring too much about something—love, money, power, honor—or too little.

"For the last two months," Ms. Benson complained, "he just talked about the big deal he was about to close. He was excited about it. 'Biggest deal I ever made,' he said. He promised to take me to Paris after he drew his commission."

That was the only moment Lagarde sensed any regret in the woman's voice. She wouldn't have Paris. He was beginning to feel sorry for his victim. No one seemed to give a damn about Harold Munson. Of course, he hadn't talked to the man's parents yet, and he wasn't looking forward to that conversation. Shock waves of grief had a way of reverberating off people, upsetting his equilibrium.

"But you didn't see him that night?" he pressed.

"No. I thought he was coming. That's why he texted. I waited up for him. But he never showed."

Ms. Benson confirmed she kept a room at the hotel for their trysts—off the books, of course. Their affair, if it could be called that, seemed no more exciting than a slot machine gambling habit. *At least once every few pulls he gets a little ka-ching.*

By the time Lagarde hung up the phone, he was thoroughly depressed. When he was a young man, pseudo-sophisticated kids at his college declared God was dead. The early part of the twenty-first century, Lagarde thought, would go down as the "Love is dead" phase of human history. He consoled himself with the fact that he had started filling in the gap in his timeline. But he was still left with a one-and-a-half-hour hole through which all kinds of doubt could be driven in a court room. Where had Harold gone before he headed home and to his death?

Against his better judgment, Lagarde poured office coffee into his mug, looked at the slimy film floating on the brown surface of the liquid, and thought better of it. Now that Beverly was in his life, maybe his gut was worth protecting. He walked into the bathroom and tossed the contents into the sink. Looking at his image in the mirror, he realized he needed to take Jake out for a ride. He looked like hell. He needed the easy rhythm of Jake's canter across a field, the sense of being in balance with the earth, of oxygen being abundant. The walls of this job were closing in on him, constricting his breathing.

What he really wanted was to spend time with his

horse, and Beverly. More time with Beverly would do him a world of good.

And then it hit him. He and Wiseman were practically the same age. Wiseman thought that Charlotte Rolle was his Beverly, that she was his last chance to have something that mattered in his life and he would do anything to get it. Wiseman was Munson's killer, and maybe Beverly was half right—Charlotte was Wiseman's motive. That had to be it, but he was a long way from proving his hypothesis.

Back at his desk, Lagarde routinely checked his email, not expecting anything useful at this point. There in the incoming email list was a bold subject line that got his attention: "Data from Munson thumb drive analyzed." Lagarde clicked open the email.

From Professor Norton at WVU, the email read. Lagarde sighed and scanned the email, hoping it would not take him the rest of his life to decipher academic jargon that might prove useless.

A portion of the material sent to me appears to be raw data from clinical trials tracking the use of a new treatment for end-stage brain cancer patients. The analyses of the data from this clinical trial, however, appear to be hugely flawed with compound mathematical errors, misinterpretation, or deliberate manipulation of data intended to put experimental results in a more positive light.

Below that paragraph was a note from the tech saying there was a more specific line-by-line analysis of the data from Dr. Norton but he figured the bottom line was all Lagarde needed.

Lagarde chuckled. The kid was right. This was all he needed. The brilliant Charlotte Rolle was cheating on the results of her human trials and lying about the outcomes. The question was whether she would kill to keep other people, particularly the people who were paying for her research, from knowing that. It seemed unlikely. More probably, she was a skillful liar and manipulator in the service of her career and had nothing to do with her husband's death. But there was a chance she hired Wiseman to do her dirty work for her, and he had to follow that line of inquiry to its conclusion.

"Great job," he typed in reply. "Print off and save the professor's response with a date stamp and preserve the document with the thumb drive as evidence." A few seconds clicked by as he thought about what this information really told them about their killer.

"Do we have fingerprints on the thumb drive?" Lagarde typed in a new email. He waited.

Before a minute had passed, there was a reply. "Prints on the thumb drive are Munson's."

Lagarde typed, "Thanks, you're a genius," hit send, and turned to see Taylor walk into the office waving a warrant to search Wiseman's house. He was starting to enjoy Taylor's enthusiasm.

"Hey, Jim, you're right on time." He watched Taylor react to the use of his familiar name, his face showing, first, shock and then pleasure. "Harold Munson had the goods on his wife. Now we've got them, and they might give her a motive."

Taylor pocketed the warrant and sat forward in his chair. "You mean he had a way to force her into giving him what he wanted in the divorce settlement?" Taylor looked up at the ceiling and Lagarde thought he could see electricity flashing between synapses in his partner's brain. "What's the evidence?"

"Remember that thumb drive I found? It's a gold mine of data, now analyzed by a statistical wizard at

WVU—an expert who could testify in court, no less. And Munson's prints are on the thumb drive. It was in his possession the night he was murdered." Lagarde had to admit that from time to time the job had its small rewards.

Taylor leaned back in his chair. "How did we get the thumb drive, again?"

"I found it in the parking lot outside the insurance agency." Lagarde grinned. "Beverly told me to look for it."

"Do you think that's why there was all that mess in Munson's car? The killer was looking for the thumb drive? And how did it wind up on the ground?"

"I'm guessing that it dropped out of Munson's pocket when he was pulled out of the wreck. Only his prints were on it. The killer never found the thumb drive. We don't know if he, or she, was looking for it."

"You don't think it was planted there for us to find?"

Lagarde groaned. "You've been watching too many movies. People around here aren't as clever as Hollywood script writers."

"Did Charlotte know he had the data? Did Munson know what the data meant? If the answer to either of those questions is no, then we don't have a motive."

Taylor was asking the right questions. Lagarde grimaced. "We don't know the answers to either of those questions yet. My next call is to Dr. Dickerson at NIH. Let's find out whether he knows that Dr. Rolle is fudging her data and lying about the effectiveness of her magic potion."

Chapter 22

D r. Betty Liu was a pain in the ass. She second-guessed Charlotte in staff meetings and fomented discontent about her research methods in conversations behind her back. She belittled everyone's statistical analyses and bullied younger fellows into following her lead. At staff meetings, she had to be smarter than anyone on the team. Liu had surely gone to Dickerson with her complaints about Charlotte. It was time to do something about her.

Charlotte considered her options. She could find something wrong with Liu's performance and force her out by humiliating her. She hated that option. A long history of being humiliated by her father and other men with power made her loathe the idea of using that method against any other woman. She could quietly lobby Dickerson to move Liu to another lab without diminishing her future prospects. She might be able to entice another lab chief to ask Liu to join his team, if the work was interesting enough. Or, she could somehow win the woman over to her side. Liu was a brilliant scientist who, Charlotte assumed, would one day have an original idea of her own. She would be better off with Charlotte as her mentor, not her enemy. She was smart enough to see the benefit of friendship.

She caught up with Liu in the hallway, on her way to the stairs, and walked down with her. They had the stairwell to themselves. "How about grabbing a light dinner with me?" Charlotte offered.

Betty Liu looked over at her, her dark eyes seeming to miss nothing. Charlotte had a minute to assess how beautiful the woman was, that cap of shining, black hair, her slender frame, those perfect lips. "You are seducing me?" Liu asked.

Charlotte threw her head back and laughed. "Yes, yes. I suppose I am."

Betty Liu put her briefcase down on the landing, took Charlotte's head in both her hands, and pulled her into a kiss that obliterated space and time. Later, as she was leaving Liu's apartment, Charlotte wondered who had seduced who and how the valence in the chemistry between them was now completely changed.

Chapter 23

March 31, 10 a.m.:

As before, William Dickerson answered his own phone. Lagarde was once again disconcerted. He briefly scolded himself for not being as modern as he should be. The old ways were more cordial, at least as he remembered them, gave a man time to gather his thoughts while the call was being transferred from a woman with a pleasant voice to the object of the call. Lagarde missed those small niceties. The world was moving too fast.

"Good afternoon, Dr. Dickerson," Lagarde began. "This is Detective Lagarde—"

"Yes, yes, Detective, I recognize your voice. Is there something new in Harold Munson's case?"

"Yes, in fact, there is." Lagarde, unseen by William Dickerson, leaned back in his chair and ran a hand over his head, wondering exactly how to tell the scientist what he suspected. "We were able to obtain a sample of Dr. Rolle's raw data from her cancer research and a few of her analyses from a thumb drive found at the crime scene."

"Oh, it would be invaluable for us to have that data, I'm sure. Thank you for contacting me. I think you can FedEx—"

"No, sir, I think you're misunderstanding me. We've had the data analyzed. It seems that Dr. Rolle has been… uh…overstating her research outcomes."

William Dickerson drew in his breath and was silent. Lagarde waited. In a few seconds, he would know if Dickerson was involved in deceiving the medical science community about the success of Charlotte's treatment.

"Ah," Dickerson said finally.

Then Lagarde remembered the letters J.D. after Dickerson's name. *Juris Doctor. In addition to his medical and scientific training, Dickerson has a law degree. Damn. He would be extremely careful about what he said from this point on.*

"How exactly did you determine this?"

So he's not immediately leaping to her defense. That's interesting. Did he suspect she was cheating? "A Dr. Harrison Norton at West Virginia University analyzed the data for us."

"Yes, Dr. Norton, well respected in the field of statistics. But not a medical researcher, certainly not a neuroscientist. I'd prefer to examine the data myself, of course, before I make any comments about it."

"I'm afraid we can't give you the thumb drive, sir. It's part of our evidence in the case."

"I don't understand. It's evidence of something in Harold's murder case?"

"Mr. Munson had a thumb drive with the data on him at the time of his death. Either he understood what was on it or he was going to find out. He and Dr. Rolle were in the middle of a bitter property dispute related to their divorce. The data gives Dr. Rolle a motive for wanting Mr.

Munson dead. Were you aware that Dr. Rolle was fudging her research?"

Dickerson gasped. Whether his shock was from the
assertion that his protégé would falsify her research results, or because someone had found out, or the assertion
that Charlotte might want to kill her husband, Lagarde
couldn't tell. He let the seconds tick off. Eventually,
Dickerson would fill in the gaps.

"I—I'm sorry, Detective, I have to talk with Dr.
Rolle before I say anything else to you. I have not seen
this material myself. For the protection of the institute,
you will need to talk to our attorney regarding this matter
in the future. Please do not call me directly again. I will
have my assistant call you with the attorney's contact information."

Lagarde nodded to himself. *Whatever we have found
on the thumb drive is serious business.* "Thank you, sir,
that's all for now."

He disconnected from the call and turned around to
Taylor. "Well, the data is a damn big deal, big enough for
Dr. Dickerson to lawyer up. We still don't know if Charlotte knew her husband had the goods on her or even if *he*
knew what he had. But I'll bet he wouldn't have kept the
thumb drive with him if he didn't understand it was valu-
able leverage in his fight with her. Let's go find out from
the doctor herself whether she knew about the thumb
drive."

Taylor patted his stomach. "Is there a rush? The
guy's already dead. How about lunch first?"

"Sure, fine. We've earned a decent lunch. Betty's in
Shepherdstown? I could eat a tuna sandwich on toasted
wheat, and the restaurant is less than ten minutes from
our Madame Curie wannabe's home."

"I'll drive," Taylor said, grabbed his jacket, and
headed for the door.

Chapter 24

March 31, 11 a.m.:

Charlotte, goaded by restlessness, paced her house. Spring rains had begun. Global climate chaos now caused the Eastern Panhandle to become a rain forest in the spring. There would be almost three months of rain where the temperature never climbed above fifty-four degrees. She shivered thinking about it.

The two rivers would rise, running swift and strong, threatening to overrun their banks across the hundred-year flood plain. A few novice kayakers who thought they could handle the raging water would drown. Every spring, helicopters flew close over the river, their blades whacking the air, sending sounds of desperation for miles as rescue crews looked for bodies.

To calm herself, Charlotte pulled out her yoga mat and began her customary practice with a long stretch into the tree pose. Sometimes she longed for the clarity of a California day or the baking heat of Dallas. Maybe, when this little kerfuffle about her data and the following big Phase III trials were complete, when she was a rich, famous scientist with a proven cure for brain cancer and a sufficient interest in the company that was manufacturing it, she would be invited to go back to Rockefeller University with a full professorship and a lab of her own. That would show her father.

It wasn't possible that Dickerson's concerns about her data would metastasize into anything serious. She could handle him. Her next paper, perhaps, would be a contrite resetting of expectations about her therapeutic approach and when the methodology could be expected to be mature enough for reliability. *After all, I am right about this, and I could prove it if people just got out of my way.*

Moving slowly into the warrior pose, Charlotte held the stretch until her thighs burned. When she wasn't working, she felt a little lost. A part of her constantly longed to be solving a deep puzzle. She turned and stretched out the other side of her body.

Her thoughts made a quarter turn and considered this idea about puzzle solving. *Certain brain chemicals emitted when a person successfully learns something new or completes a complicated task must be mildly addictive. The process would involve a neurotransmitter similar to dopamine or serotonin, perhaps an enzyme. If the trigger is replicable, if a synthetic cocktail could initiate a similar cascade that would make people feel successful...*

Her thoughts trailed off. Perhaps, after she had developed a cure for inoperable brain cancer, she might work on finding a bio-similar agent that gave people that ineffable sense of satisfaction they got from solving difficult problems, without the downside of hopeless addiction. It could be something as simple as dark chocolate without the refined sugar. She tucked the thought away and arranged her body into the downward-facing-dog position, inching into the stretch.

In the kitchen, her cell phone rang. Charlotte sank to

her knees in the child position, leaned over until her forehead touched the floor, felt the stretch from her fingertips to her knees, and held it for three more rings. It was probably that pesky detective wanting to ask her another set of stupid questions. She let the call go to voice mail.

Tomorrow was Harold's funeral. His parents had managed everything. She didn't quarrel with them when his mother told her they would handle the arrangements. Better them than her.

She had no interest in the formality of escorting her dead husband's coffin to the grave, but she would perform this last obligatory act. Now that he was dead, Harold didn't seem to be the complete creep she had told herself he was.

A twinge, a little guilt about not letting him have half the property they had amassed passed across her shoulders. She shook it off. *What have I been fighting him for? I don't need all those houses.* Charlotte sat in the lotus pose and hoped for calm and enlightenment. She stretched her neck and spine, lowered her shoulders, and leveled her chin. In the end, she had gotten everything she'd wanted. She was free of Harold, financially comfortable, and her work was gaining prominence. She was golden. She could afford to be pleasant to Harold's parents.

When the sweat from her workout had cooled on her face, Charlotte rose from the floor in one fluid movement, rolled up her mat, picked up her phone, and walked upstairs to take a shower.

She swiped the screen of her phone with her thumb and saw she had missed a call from Wiseman. She smiled. There *was* something she could do this afternoon that would trigger her own serotonin cascade.

∾∾∾

Mark was ready for her. He must have been counting down the minutes since she called him back. He met her at his front door, shirt unbuttoned, pants zipper down. It was obvious he'd been thinking about her. He pulled her sweater over her head before she was inside the house, his mouth was on her breast, his hands on her ass, and Charlotte's mind went away for a little while.

After the last shudder ran through her spine, she sighed and leaned her head on his shoulder. They were lying on the wool rug in the living room. She looked up at the golden pine of the vaulted ceiling. *It was quiet here.* She looked around at the room. *But maybe a little claustrophobic.*

Mark grinned at her. "Feels pretty good to be a free woman, doesn't it?"

Something in her froze. Was that a threat in his voice, a taunt, the suggestion that she owed him something? Her brain came back online. "Yes." Charlotte hoped her voice was noncommittal. Being free of Harold did change everything.

Mark caressed her buttocks. "We don't have to sneak around anymore."

She ran her finger along Mark's torso and played with the curly, silver hairs around his belly button. Was he asking for something specific or long-term? She didn't really know him well. He had been useful. Did he want more?

She leaned over, kissed his neck and flicked her tongue over his nipple. His hand on her hip tightened. It was still early in the day. She had plenty of time to get ready for dinner this evening with William. Why not go again? She rolled on top of him and sat up. "I've been thinking about a new position."

The man looked like he'd died and gone to heaven.

Chapter 25

December 15, 2015, 8 p.m.:

Way too late, Harold realized he should have married Randi Walker. He had everything in common with her. They dressed the same way. They thought the same way. They wanted the same things. He had to find a way to rectify this error in his judgment.

How had he not noticed before that he was sailing in circles without a rudder trying to find the right woman? He had a horrible memory of telling Randi she wasn't "the one" after he met Charlotte. They had gone for a drive to look at a new property. He had felt so noble, having the quiet conversation with her, in which he tried not to hurt her feelings, the "but we can still be friends" garbage just dribbling out of his mouth.

They got to the building and walked around taking photographs to get an idea of estimated market value that Randi would check against recent sales of similar properties before they listed it. The property owner babbled. Randi was silent, not even commenting about the space or location. Harold missed their usual amusing banter, but figured she was simply being business-like. When they were done, Randi stood in front of the building, looked straight at him and said, "I'll call a cab."

He had nodded and driven off, as if that was a completely acceptable way for friends to behave. What an idiot he was. He remembered the look of disbelief on her face. Something in his gut—a moment of clairvoyance or a memory—quivered.

Periodically, he would stand in the doorway of Randi's office, watching her on the phone working a client. She would flick a glance at him, swivel her chair to face the window, and go back to paying attention to the nuance in the client's voice. He loved her ability to concentrate on what was important at the moment. She was never at a loss for words, the right words at the right time. It was a talent he didn't have. Words often got stuck in his throat, particularly when he was afraid or angry. She completed him. They were great together. Of course, she knew that. He was the one who took too long to understand everything. He thought he could fix that.

As he recovered from his fury at Charlotte for initiating divorce proceedings against him—the insult of it, not the loss of someone he loved—he realized he had a new opportunity. He could marry Randi. His life could still be perfect. He hadn't counted on Randi being angry with him, angry to the point of almost sputtering when he suggested that they might get together on a more permanent basis.

They were celebrating their third big closing in three months, and he was close to persuading the Datapile folks to take the trip from the west coast to see the multi-million-dollar Wiltshire Road property. Harold was eating success with a spoon. The restaurant had already lowered its lights to the evening dimness the management seemed to think was romantic. Only a few patrons were at the bar with them. Harold leaned in close to Randi and ran the pads of his fingers lightly across her ass—a suggestion of sex to come. "Hey, girl, the whole future's ours for the taking."

She straightened her back in a way that pulled her away from him. "What do you mean?"

"I mean you and me together, world's our oyster, sky's the limit. You know what they say. Everything."

"Everything? Who says? You trite bastard. Now that I'm thirty-eight? We've been partners for ten years, and now you want us to have everything together?"

"You don't look at day older than thirty-five."

Randi gave him a look that would wither the balls on a man half his age and slid off the barstool. "You missed your shot. Long ago."

He grabbed her arm. "Wait. What do you mean? We're a great team. We play well together." He looked directly into her eyes in the way that normally made women swoon. "You can't walk away from this."

Randi laughed. "You're an idiot. You don't love me. Believe me, it's not hard to walk away from you."

He watched Randi leave the restaurant without a backward glance and felt he'd lost his best friend without understanding what he'd done wrong. He ordered another drink.

Chapter 26

March 31, 2 p.m.:

Lagarde knocked on Charlotte's door, then rang the door bell, and waited the polite amount of time for her to open it. When she didn't, he sent Taylor around to the back to check on whether she was on the patio and jimmied open the front door. Their warrant was still good, he told himself, and perhaps the forensics team had missed something in their initial search. Even if they couldn't question her about the data on the thumb drive, this didn't have to be a wasted trip.

Standing in the center hall, he took a few minutes to let all his assumptions settle and tried to look at the house without the debris from his guesses cluttering his perspective. Charlotte Rolle was a new widow. Her husband wasn't dead two full days. Confusion, sorrow, worry, and anger would be her normal responses to everything that happened around her. What he took as her cold condescension could be the way she dealt with grief.

"Dr. Rolle," he called out, in case she was upstairs. "It's Detective Lagarde and Corporal Taylor. We have a few questions for you."

No response came from upstairs, no footfalls reverberated across the wood floors. Lagarde looked into her office. She was neat, even though stacks of paper stood on either side of her laptop and in piles on a table behind her chair. She must have a method for poring through all that information. Was it possible for someone with that amount of concentration focused on her work to commit murder? Or did she do it because of her work? He should've asked Beverly these questions.

Charlotte had published two major papers a year for the last five years, and more than that before she came to NIH, according to an online search he did on PubMed. She was the first author on papers that appeared in top medical research journals. She was successful and known in her field, at the top of her game. Why would she risk that prominence to kill her husband over a property settlement? It didn't make sense, unless she thought poor Harold Munson was a threat to what she had achieved. He felt what could only be called a hot flash course through him. *What if we're looking in the wrong direction?*

"Hey, Sam," Taylor called out from the kitchen. "I think I found something."

Lagarde walked down the hall into the kitchen and saw Taylor standing over the desk. In his gloved hand was a piece of paper torn from a pad. Taylor handed it to Lagarde, who took it with the glove in his pocket. On the paper, Mark Wiseman's name, phone number, and home address were written. The handwriting, Lagarde recalled from the name and phone number she had written on the back of one of her cards, was Charlotte's. *Bingo.* His premonition wasn't far off the mark after all. The retired Baltimore cop captured in the photo Dave Weigle took in the middle of the night was someone Charlotte Rolle knew.

"Where was this note?"

Taylor pointed to the wall. "Tacked to the bulletin board, right there."

The small bulletin board was covered with overlapping notes, photos, and business cards. You could get a sense about what was important in a person's life by studying their kitchen bulletin board or refrigerator. "Humph." Lagarde pushed his hat back. "In plain sight. Of course, we missed it the first time around. Good eyes."

Taylor ducked his head in appreciation of the compliment.

"I think we should pay Mr. Wiseman another visit. Maybe he'll be there this time. And if not, we've already got the search warrant." Lagarde took a small evidence bag from his jacket pocket, slipped the note inside it, and tagged the bag. "Make sure this gets added to our evidence when we get back to headquarters."

Taylor took the baggie and headed out the front door, pulling off his gloves.

Chapter 27

March 31, 3 p.m.:

A car crash at the Y intersection of Flowing Springs Road and Shepherdstown Pike stopped traffic in all directions for miles. Still punctuated by large farms, Jefferson County's road system frequently offered only one official and round-about way to get from here to there, but anyone who lived in the county had memorized a map of back and sometimes unpaved roads that would get a vehicle where it needed to go in case of emergency.

Taylor made a U-turn and backtracked through Shepherdstown, then west on Kearneysville Road, past Charlotte's neighborhood, and south on Charles Town Road, driving right by the now boarded up wall in Weigle's Insurance office, through Charles Town toward the Shenandoah River.

They got to Wiseman's house at three p.m. A pickup truck was in the driveway, but Wiseman didn't respond to their knocks and Taylor's shout, "West Virginia State Police. Open the door. We've got a warrant to search the premises."

Lagarde looked around the property. Across the road, the river was high and fast. Maybe Wiseman was a kayaker out riding the white water. A single loon flew low over the river's surface. It was peaceful here, with no sign of people in the vicinity. Taylor discovered the back kitchen door was unlocked and they walked into the log cabin.

With the house arranged in an open plan without walls between designated kitchen, dining, and living room areas, Lagarde could take in the space in a few glances. There had been some kind of struggle in the living room. The wood coffee table was off kilter, and the woven wool area rug had been pushed out of the way. He walked closer. Blood, a dark pool of it, enough to nearly be someone's entire supply, seeped into the polished wide-plank oak floor. Someone had made a brief attempt to sop it up and then stopped. *Where's the body?*

"Get the crime scene guys here," Lagarde called out to Taylor, "watch where you step but make a visual check for a weapon. This much blood, it'll be a gun or a knife. I'll look down here."

Taylor practically tiptoed up the spiral stairs to the rooms that fanned off from a balcony that looked down into the living area. Lagarde wondered if Wiseman was already dead when they were at the house earlier in the day. *Maybe the blood isn't Wiseman's.*

The thought snapped him upright. No matter how fast they worked, it was never fast enough. In the end, they were only the cleanup crew. They were never going to prevent a death. *I should have already accepted that fact years ago,* he chided himself and felt the weight of all the crime scenes he had attended drag on his bones.

Lagarde walked back into the kitchen, pulled on his gloves, and began opening drawers and cabinets, searching through each one for something that would help him solve the mystery of how that pool of blood in the living room fit with the dead guy in a car in an insurance company parking lot.

Wiseman didn't have a lot of stuff: two plates, two glasses, two coffee mugs, two forks, two knives—he wasn't living fancy. Wiseman seemed to have envisioned a life in which only one other person might occasionally figure. Or was the extra place setting a show of optimism? He was obviously single and had been for a while.

A stab of recognition and fear cut through Lagarde. Without Beverly, this was *his* life. He opened the refrigerator—beer, sandwich meat, deli-made tuna fish, hot dogs. Wiseman was not a gourmet. He didn't seem to be a good fit for Charlotte. He was a good twenty years older, he wasn't rich, and he certainly didn't have years of academic education under his belt. Of course, neither did Harold, or Nick Waters for that matter. What did she see in Wiseman, or any of them? She must be attracted to her opposite—men who aren't smarter than she, and who won't belittle her, perhaps. *That's it. Beverly is my opposite. And she's the smart one.*

At the end of the counter, closest to what would be the dining area on the living room side, he spotted a wallet, loose change, a key ring with an assortment of house and vehicle keys, and a cell phone. A man didn't leave his home without his wallet and phone, on foot, unless he was under duress—or disposing of a body. *Did Mark Wiseman kill Charlotte Rolle?* The thought stopped him cold for a minute.

Lagarde flipped the wallet open, checked for ID and credit cards. The wallet, with eighty dollars in cash inside, belonged to Wiseman. The blood on the floor was not the result of a robbery interrupted. Then he noticed a second cell phone.

Lagarde picked up the phone and turned it on, relieved to see it wasn't password protected. Telling him-self, *start anywhere*, he touched the Photos icon. An im-age of Harold Munson, dead, face in the airbag in his car, front window splintered into a thousand cracks, zoomed up from the screen.

This photo was taken with the driver's door open. There was no window glare from a camera flash. Lagarde blinked. He pressed the "back" arrow. The photo was date stamped March thirtieth, one-fifty-nine a.m. *This photo was taken by the killer.* A chill ran through him at the coldness of a person who could kill and then photo-graph the results. But whose phone was it? Earlier, on March twenty-ninth, someone had taken a group shot of Harold with Randi Walker, Ed Milliken, and the Datapile clients time-stamped ten p.m. *Is this photo a selfie? Or is the person who killed Harold the same person who took the group shot?*

He clicked out of Photos and opened the text mes-saging app. The most recent text was the photo of a dead Harold Munson sent to Charlotte Rolle on March thirtieth at three minutes after two a.m. It had the feel of a "mis-sion accomplished" message.

Charlotte Rolle knew about her husband's death minutes after it happened. But the fact that someone texted her with the photo disproved Beverly's pet theory that Charlotte herself was the killer. *Was she being threatened? Was this murder a warning to her that if she didn't comply with some request, she would be next?*

The text before that, at twelve-fifteen a.m. to Charlotte said, *Great meeting. Don't need your damn money.*

Was Dr. Rolle as devious as Beverly thought she was, capable of killing her husband, taking this photo on her dead husband's phone, and sending it to herself in a text to establish an alibi? He shook his head. *God, I hope not.*

Lagarde backed up and ran through what he'd found again. This was Harold Munson's phone. It had to be. He scanned the other items on the counter. One of the car keys had the Lexus logo on it—*maybe for Harold Munson's car.* It took a few seconds for Lagarde to follow the logical path of these facts. Harold Munson's car key and personal phone were in Mark Wiseman's house. Fingerprints on the phone screen would prove whether Wiseman handled the phone. A log of texts received on Charlotte's phone and the number they were sent from would prove the incriminating text came from this phone. They already knew Wiseman was at the scene of Harold's murder from the photo Dave Weigle took. Ergo, Wiseman was Harold's killer.

And looking around at the new crime scene, he concluded that Wiseman was now dead.

But there was another possible investigative rabbit hole to fall down: someone other than Wiseman killed Harold, someone who knew Wiseman was a witness, and after he murdered Wiseman, the killer left Harold's car key and phone here, thinking they would incriminate Wiseman and lead the police in the wrong direction. That scenario would explain why the body wasn't here.

No, keep it simple, man, Lagarde cautioned himself. *This isn't some HBO special.*

Lagarde rolled his head around on his neck, squeezed his eyes shut to clear his vision, and opened the calendar app on the phone. He scrolled through the dates. The last scheduled event was Harold's meeting with the Datapile folks.

Lagarde heard Taylor clatter down the stairs, shouting "I found it!" and stopped following his thoughts.

Taylor raced into the kitchen, completely forgetting

about being careful where he put his big feet, skidding on the rim of the blood pool, dangling a tiny piece of purple lace that could only have been a woman's thong in one hand and a Colt .45 revolver in the other.

Before Lagarde could say "bag it," or wonder about how cozy Wiseman and Charlotte were that she left her clothes there, the crime lab crew were at the door, and his and Taylor's search of the premises stopped in the face of their more methodical collection of evidence.

Taylor handed the tech the underpants and gun and told her he'd found them in the drawer of the table next to Wiseman's bed. The tech shot Taylor an annoyed look, but he turned his face away from her and listened to what Lagarde was saying.

"The thong is probably a souvenir," Lagarde said. "It tells us something about Wiseman. Charlotte hasn't moved in, but he might be a little obsessed with her. The gun could be the weapon that killed Harold Munson and maybe Charlotte Rolle, if that's her blood, but maybe not. Ballistics will tell us."

Lagarde turned to the forensics tech, pointed to the wallet and two cell phones on the counter. "Hey, Anne, there's a key to a Lexus on that key ring. I'd like to know if it opens Harold Munson's car. I want to know whatever is on these phones, whose they are, and whose fingerprints are on them. And if there was a text from Charlotte Rolle's phone to Wiseman around the time of Munson's twelve-fifteen a.m. text to her."

Anne gave him a brief smile and went back to doing what she would have done anyway without direction. Lagarde reminded himself that all the crime lab folks had college degrees and knew what they were doing. He had to trust them.

Taylor shook his head. "Something's off." He snatched a look at Lagarde's face to see if it was okay to continue. Seeing no impending objection, he went on. "As far as Wiseman knows, nobody's aware of his involvement in Harold's murder. Why would he murder a second time? He's got a clean work record, never killed anyone in the line of duty. If Charlotte's refusing to pay him for killing her husband, or have sex with him, or whatever it is he wanted, why not just let it go? Unless he was worried she would implicate him in her husband's murder—now that might be a motive to kill her, particularly if he knows she can place him at the scene."

Lagarde grimaced, a look that could be taken for a smile by those who didn't know him. *The kid has entered the sorcerer's apprentice phase pretty quickly.* "Okay. Fair enough. We're both jumping way ahead of the evidence. Keep your scenario in mind as we find out more. See if the evidence matches your speculation."

Within a day or so, they'd know everything there was to know about Mark Wiseman and his connection to Charlotte Rolle. None of this evidence, however, solved the question of whose blood was on the floor, unless the DNA they would extract from it was in the FBI's database and matched someone's.

Lagarde's mind was spinning. "We still don't know where Harold was for two hours before he was killed. And, if Wiseman didn't murder Charlotte, then we might have two murderers—one who killed Harold and one who killed whoever's blood this was." He took off his hat and smoothed back what was left of his hair. "You drive," Lagarde told Taylor. "I need to think."

"What about this?" Taylor offered as he maneuvered the vehicle around the bend away from the river. "Munson's cell phone is the second piece of evidence that puts Wiseman at Harold's murder. It also puts Wiseman in the vehicle after Munson was dead, because how else would he have gotten the phone? Wiseman has to be the shooter.

The car doors were locked. No sign of a break-in. He had a key to the car that Charlotte must have given him. Wiseman took Harold's phone out of his pocket after he was dead and used it to take the photo and send the text to her to prove he completed the job."

Lagarde looked over at his apprentice, who was deep into the joy of inventing possible scenarios. He knew the pull of trying to corral random reality into a pen you could understand. "Yep. That's the most likely scenario. Charlotte hired Wiseman to kill her husband. But after he had done the deed, he wanted something more—more money, a relationship, or a lifetime of blackmail to subsidize his pleasant lifestyle? When Charlotte refused, he killed her and is off right now disposing of her body. That would make it her blood in the living room. Maybe he didn't intend to kill her, but things got out of hand. She fought him. Maybe he couldn't take that high-handed tone of hers."

Lagarde could imagine the conversation. He almost rolled his eyes in sympathy with Wiseman. "Whoever committed today's murder isn't a professional killer. Too much evidence was left lying around. The scene wasn't cleaned before he took off. He panicked and decided to dump the body first and then come back to get rid of other evidence. Bad planning. He miscalculated the time he had before anyone caught up to him. Maybe he didn't realize we were hot on his trail. It did take us a while to get there."

"You're saying 'he' now. You don't think Charlotte did it?" Taylor asked.

Lagarde looked out the car window at gathering clouds that threatened rain. "Right now, I don't know who the hell did it."

Twenty minutes later they were back in the office setting up a white board with all the facts in both crimes as they knew them. Lagarde felt he was putting together a three-dimensional, multi-colored puzzle of St. Basil's, the iconic Moscow cathedral with multiple onion-shaped domes. All the clues seemed to be in Cyrillic, upside down, backward, and hidden under layers of information that hadn't yet been revealed.

Chapter 28

The moment Harold caught a flash of understanding between Neal and Oliver he knew the sale was going to go through.

Standing in the center of the vast warehouse looking up at the venting of the HVAC system that ran above 150,000 square feet of open space, Neal smiled. "What are your winters like?"

"Cold, man," Edward said, "rain, snow, ice from November to March."

Oliver nodded, "No trouble keeping servers cool enough then. Lower electric bills. Of course, we'll put in solar panels and some wind turbines to offset long-term costs. That'll be okay with your zoning folks, right?"

Harold nodded. He knew then that Neal could see it, corridors of servers humming quietly, while staff had meals in the pleasant in-house café or took breaks in the lounge. Oliver had pointed out an area outside where a volley ball net could be set up. Neal liked the conference room, which still sported a twenty-foot-long table and comfortable chairs, and the staff locker room. There was even enough space, Ted noted, for a gym, a few tread-mills and stationary bikes, some free weights. Neal had a checklist on his phone he continually marked.

It looked to Harold that this space checked most of Ted's boxes. He worked to keep the glee that was fizzing up in his veins from showing. Harold didn't pretend to understand Datapile's business. *His* business was selling space, and they needed this amount of it. "Easy highway access to Maryland, Virginia, DC, and Pennsylvania. Fif-ty minutes to Dulles airport," he offered, although of course, they knew that. They wouldn't even be standing there without the asset of close proximity to power and transportation in place. He simply underlined the loca-tion's best qualities.

Tonight, his Datapile clients would meet local offi-cials, who would assure Neal, Oliver, and Ted that taxes in the state and county were low. They would wink and smile and backslap and add that if Datapile really created the two hundred high-paying, long-term jobs they prom-ised, there'd be other benefits as well, such as property tax forgiveness for the next five years. Visions of big payoffs from the eleven-million-dollar sale danced in everyone's heads.

The US Senator who had gotten his seat cozying up to coal barons would blanch slightly when Oliver reiter-ated the company's interest in adding alternative sources to feed an energy-voracious server farm, but then he im-agined the possibility of West Coast-sized campaign con-tributions to his PAC and smiled and nodded along with the others.

Harold wasn't modest about what this sale would do for him, personally. He looked forward to word getting out to other absentee property owners whose huge vacant warehouse spaces in the tri-state area had been empty for the last decade. He expected his phone to be ringing off the hook as they hurried to sign with him to sell their un-used buildings. Neal and Oliver would undoubtedly talk about what a deal they made. A path opened before Harold that led to the kind of success he'd always craved.

Randi looked over at Harold from behind Neal's shoulder. In that look, without her even smiling, he saw, "You did it. You brought them in. Congratulations."

Harold wanted to let out a glory whoop, do a little goal dance, and high five everyone on the spot, but he held in his triumph. There was still the dinner and the stack of paperwork to get through, not to mention the owner's agreement. Although how the owner could re-fuse a full-price offer with no contingencies, Harold didn't know. He could restrain his glee for another day and then, Charlotte or no Charlotte, he was going to have the celebration of his life.

Chapter 29

March 31, 5:00 p.m.:

When the door opened, Lagarde knew the blood in Wiseman's house wasn't Charlotte Rolle's. He felt an odd relief, even though she was glaring at him.

"What do you want now?"

She seemed to be dressed for a private party, a little too provocatively for a woman whose husband had died the day before, Lagarde thought, even if she had hated him. There was such a thing as propriety. "We need to ask you a few more questions, Dr. Rolle."

"Well?" She did not invite them into the house.

"It would be better if we could come inside." Lagarde took off his hat.

"All right." She sighed at the inconvenience, stepped back, and motioned for them both to enter the foyer. "I don't understand what you think you're accomplishing talking to me."

Lagarde smelled something delectable coming from the kitchen. "You're cooking."

"I'm heating. Bistro One Hundred Twelve cooked. I

picked up." She gave him a dazzling smile. "It's amazing where you can get take out these days."

There was no end to the woman's disregard for norms. She wasn't grieving at all. He nodded. "If you're going to eat alone, it might as well taste good."

"Who says I'm eating alone."

Taylor blushed. Lagarde stared at her. She turned her back on them and walked into the kitchen. *There is no bad view of this woman.* Lagarde mentally knuckle-rapped himself and followed. "We've been to Mark Wiseman's house." He waited to see her physical reaction. She had none, not a twitch or shiver.

"He's not in his house. There's a pool of blood on the living room floor."

She turned her face to him as she pulled two white dinner and salad plates down from the cabinet and placed them on the counter. "Blood? Hmm." She opened a drawer and removed two sterling silver forks, salad forks, knives, teaspoons from a soft, gray sack. From the next drawer over, she extracted perfectly ironed white cloth napkins. "That sounds ominous."

Do they learn this kind of detachment in medical school? Lagarde wondered. *Does she always set a fancy table for dinner?* "Is Nick Waters coming for dinner? He seems like a slice of pizza out of the box kind of guy."

No reaction from Charlotte.

Taylor flushed, his shoulders twitched. He had obviously had enough of her bullshit. "Do you know Mark Wiseman?"

She looked up at Taylor, noticing him the first time. She tossed her head and flipped her hair over her bare shoulder. She licked her lips. Lagarde worried for a second that she was planning to devour his sidekick. He could almost see his feet flailing as the last bit of his body was sucked into hers. *Did I read that in a novel?* Now he thought of it, Taylor did seem to be her type—young, handsome, fit.

"As a matter of fact, I do know him." She scrutinized Taylor's face. "But you already knew that."

Taylor nodded as if he was hypnotized. "How well do you know him?"

"You mean do I have sex with him?"

Lagarde observed that she obviously enjoyed taunting Taylor. *Was this her foreplay?*

Taylor found his normal voice. "Yes. How long have you known him, are you intimate, and when was the last time you saw him?"

"I've known him for a few months," she flipped her hair in the other direction, stacked up the dishes, napkins, and silverware, and carried them into the dining room. "I had sex with him this afternoon."

Taylor looked at Lagarde and made a note in his pad.

"What time?" Lagarde asked.

"I think I was there around one-thirty, or so."

"Did your husband, or Nick Waters, know you are having an affair with Wiseman?"

She came back into the kitchen, reached into the same cabinet and pulled out two deeply hued, red crystal wine glasses.

Is that Baccarat crystal? Lagarde wondered. *The woman's sparing no expense on this dinner. She's trying to impress someone.*

"Oh, I doubt that Harold knew. He was self-absorbed. If he did know, he wouldn't have cared. But I think Nick knows. He might be a little jealous of Wiseman." She let that idea trail off into the air as she placed the wine glasses on the table and put white candles in clear, cut-glass holders on the table on either side of a vase of fresh flowers. "Come to think of it, Nick does have a gun. He's a little hotheaded."

Lagarde looked at Taylor to say, *She's cold, giving up her lover like that. Or she's playing us.* He'd had enough of her controlling the interview. "Are you aware that Harold had a thumb drive with data from your clinical trials on it?"

She stopped setting the table and turned around to him. A slight flush infused her chest and neck. Lagarde could see her thinking about how to respond. Her careful silence was the same as an admission to him. He pushed. "Are you deliberately lying about the success of your cancer treatment?"

"I think," she said slowly, choosing her words, "the status of my research is outside the realm of your understanding or your inquiry. And from now on, I will not speak with you without the benefit of counsel." She put her lovely lips together in a flat line, walked to her front door, and indicated with her hand that they should leave.

Without enough evidence to get a warrant for her arrest, there was no point in trying to press the conversation.

Taylor got behind the wheel of their car and turned the key in the ignition. "There's something really infuriating about that woman, isn't there?"

Lagarde nodded. "Infuriating women make excellent murderers."

Pulling out of the driveway, Taylor chortled and aimed the vehicle toward headquarters. Lagarde was imagining a long, slow ride on Jake with Beverly by his side. He longed to look out over the view of the mountains at spring snapping to attention, a phenomenon he could understand.

Chapter 30

March 1, 8 p.m.:

Ever since their delicious interlude in January, Betty Liu had surreptitiously followed Charlotte after work, whenever she broke away from the lab at lunch, or went to the gym. She had become an expert at it.

But her definition of what Charlotte meant to her, what their relationship was, changed after the second time they made love. They had showered together after a workout and Charlotte kneaded Betty's sore muscles starting with her neck and shoulders and worked her way all the way down to her toes. Betty was in love, she understood that now, deliriously, walking-on-air in love. She couldn't eat. She couldn't sleep. She wanted only to suck the breath from Charlotte's mouth and sink into her skin. She was a walking cliché, and she didn't care.

When Charlotte stood behind her chair in staff meetings, Betty knew she was sending her a special affirmation of their love. Lab notes left on the white board with an arrow to her name in Charlotte's hand were secret love notes. If Charlotte smiled at her on the way to the bathroom, it was an invitation. Betty was most happy when they were standing side by side in the cafeteria lunch line to select their salads, and everyone could see how Charlotte doted on her, leaning over to commend her choice and tell her that walnuts not only provided protein but also Omega 3s.

By March, however, she was forced to admit, her love was more of an obsession. She could still exercise some scientific objectivity and, laying out the case for this love of hers, she saw the flaws in her logic. In the late hours of the night, she acknowledged she had lost her bearings a little. If she lost sight of Charlotte's car, or couldn't find her in a crowd, she panicked, her heart momentarily stopping and then pounding until she found her again. If Charlotte stopped to talk to someone in the lab, or put her hand on a colleague's shoulder, leaned over and looked into someone else's eyes, Betty paled. Jealousy rode high in her throat, ready at any moment to spill over into rageful words she had to control at all costs. The effort was exhausting her.

She needed to know as much as possible about any competition for Charlotte's time and affection. She needed to see Charlotte as often as possible, to watch her hair fall over her shoulder, to observe her looking up and listening intently to her words. She needed the bliss of having Charlotte's glance fall on her, knowing all that they shared. She caught herself humming love songs she hadn't even known she knew. She smiled at herself in mirrors. Her entire life had changed. She was more beautiful, taller even.

After a few weeks with Charlotte, she had formed the impression that Harold was barely more than a high-functioning animal. She could wait for them to be divorced. Then she would convince Charlotte to move to Bethesda, closer to her. She dreamed of deep, intellectual conversations over sushi, long bike rides, trips to art galleries, weekends spent wordless in the lab developing a ground-breaking cure for cancer. She dreamed of their minds in synch and countless small acts of kindness. Her dreams made her happy.

It was soon evident that it was impossible that a woman as brilliant and beautiful as Charlotte was trapped in a relationship with that ignorant brute of a husband. Harold barely qualified as Homo Sapiens. Betty couldn't stand the way he swaggered. His certainty about his right to claim Charlotte as his property and never let her go unless *he* wanted to made her writhe. She could barely sleep in her agony over the idea that he could put his hands on Charlotte whenever he desired. His mind was puny, full of self-aggrandizing affirmations. And, he carried that faint rotting-garbage smell of most meat-eaters.

Then she discovered that Charlotte was also having sex with that Orangutan, Nick Waters. Her heart constricted, Betty watched them through the uncovered back windows of Nick's townhouse. She had followed Charlotte there, wondering during the entire drive where on earth she was going. According to her GPS map, they were only sixty-five miles from Bethesda, but she might as well be on another planet in an earlier century. There weren't even any streetlights or shoulders to pull over on in case she missed a turn and got lost.

At one point, the road narrowed to a single lane under a covered bridge that hooked around a sharp bend. It was impossible to see if any cars were coming from the other direction. Drivers were instructed by a sign to honk before they crossed. Betty watched from half a mile away as Charlotte paused, honked her horn, drove her car onto the bridge and disappeared.

Her heart sank. *If I honk, Charlotte will know I'm here. But Charlotte already knows someone's car is be-*

hind her because of the headlights. She's not clairvoyant. She can't know it's me. Betty worried that if she didn't honk, she might be knocked off the road by an unseen vehicle and pushed into the creek below. But, she reminded herself, she and Charlotte had been the only two drivers on the road for the last fifteen minutes. Charlotte didn't know Betty was the driver in the car behind her. *Besides, it's not that far down. I'll survive the crash.* She held her breath and crossed without making a sound, exhaling only when she was again safely on a road the width of two cars. She stepped on the gas to catch up to Charlotte's receding taillights before her car turned into an unmarked lane and she lost her.

On her fourth spying expedition to Nick's, Betty walked through the unlocked back door from the deck. Charlotte and Nick were upstairs and, from the sounds—tortured animal groans that ricocheted off all the walls—she assumed it would be a while before they noticed their surroundings. She examined Nick's living and dining rooms, found nothing interesting, and moved on to the kitchen, opening every cabinet to see how he lived. Among an assortment of plastic bowls and glassware, she found Nick's gun in its neat holster.

She had no idea why she took the gun, but at the time, taking it seemed the only correct action. It felt good in her hand, useful. Its compact size and comfortable heft had a purpose she would eventually discover. Its weight in her purse made her feel safe, confident that she could hold her own in an encounter with a stranger in this odd backwater she wandered through alone at night.

Betty forgave Charlotte her affair with Nick. He lived closer to her than she did. He was more available and certainly less demanding. He seemed content with Charlotte coming to him in the middle of the night, exercising that part of her body her work couldn't satisfy, and leaving him, quietly closing the front door and slipping into her car. She understood Nick was a utility, emotionally unimportant. He was not a threat to her plans. She was capable of inventing a million excuses for Charlotte's behavior.

It was Mark Wiseman who infuriated her. Wiseman, she could tell the first time she watched him stride across his front porch and trot off along the river road, was a complete person. Betty didn't question her assumptions about him, which probably had more to do with his gray hair and a certain ease with which he moved than anything else. She had never had a conversation with him. She simply knew Wiseman was a threat. She could conceive of Charlotte choosing him instead of her after the divorce, at least for a while. She didn't want to leave that choice to chance.

Barely admitting that Charlotte had a flaw, Betty's heart was scalded the first time she watched Charlotte seduce Wiseman on the porch of his house in plain view of anyone who happened to be passing on the river road. She had followed Wiseman's truck after she saw Charlotte leap into it like a schoolgirl in the Bigmart parking lot. She held her breath on the turns as the road swooped around, then passed his house after he pulled into his driveway. She made a U-turn slightly beyond the house and drove back slowly, attempting to conceal her car next to an evergreen bush at the edge of his property.

Betty watched as Charlotte sauntered across the porch, unbuttoned her shirt, and leaned against the railing. She couldn't look away. The man seemed oblivious to anything but Charlotte. For a second, she thought Charlotte looked right at her. Her blood stopped. *She's doing this deliberately because I'm right here. It's a message. She's done with me. She doesn't look at me anymore when we're at work together. She seems annoyed when I'm near her. This man has taken her away from me.*

For a few weeks, Betty thought she had taken on too much. She couldn't adequately perform her research tasks and keep tabs on Charlotte and all her lovers. The vigil was exhausting her, and sleep deprivation made her irrational. She took a few nights off, staying home with her cat, but she couldn't sleep. She was driven by a desperate need to know what Charlotte was doing. She paced her apartment. She couldn't read. Nothing on television distracted her. Her need to know everything about Charlotte could only be satisfied by watching her. She could only breathe when she saw her, even if it was from a distance and with someone else.

Even on nights she told herself not to go, she found herself running down the steps to the parking lot, screaming *Stop, stop* in her head as she put the car key in the ignition. She had to follow Charlotte. If Charlotte took the train, Betty raced to get to the station in Duffields before Charlotte disembarked. If she was driving, Betty stayed two cars behind her, no matter which route Charlotte took home. Some nights, she thought Charlotte might know she was following and was glad of it. After all, who would not want to be loved like this?

Something had to be done. She would lose her mind if she kept up this vigil. And she couldn't leave anything to chance. She had to act.

Chapter 31

S omething for a woman whose husband has just died," William Dickerson told the florist over the phone. "No, don't deliver it. I'll pick it up in about forty minutes."

He had no idea what to bring a widow. He was hopelessly unsocial. It was his wife who understood what she called the social niceties—who should get flowers and who should get a bottle of expensive booze. William couldn't recall what people had brought him after his wife died. Maybe it really was the thought that counted.

Absorbed by his thoughts, he didn't realize he was lost until the GPS voice told him for the third time to turn around when possible. He'd never before driven to West Virginia's Eastern Panhandle—a place so geographically remote in his mind that he might as well be traveling to another planet. Surely, the GPS instructions were inaccurate. He suddenly discovered two rivers framed the panhandle separating the state from Maryland and Virginia. He felt like an explorer, seeing a new land for the first time. He had to admit, driving toward the mountains, the lights in the town twinkling, the view of Harpers Ferry along the banks of the river from the bridge over the Potomac took his breath away. Pages of time flipped backward until he was in a previous century. He could almost feel his blood pressure lower.

Then he inexplicably turned left onto Harpers Ferry Road going in the wrong direction and drove miles on an unlit, winding road into Virginia wine country while the GPS calmly instructed him first to turn around when possible and then, after recalculating, telling him to turn right onto Route 9. Driving along that highway toward Charles Town on a bridge that skimmed the tops of trees populating a vast, as yet undeveloped valley on either side of the Shenandoah River, William thought this area must be a developer's dream. *Maybe Charlotte isn't crazy to live this far away from her lab at NIH*, he thought. *Something peaceful about the place settles on you.*

When he finally stood at Charlotte's front door clutching the bouquet the florist had selected for him, his anxiety returned. He didn't even know the names of the flowers. Flowers had been his wife's area of expertise. He had a fleeting memory of Nancy arranging flowers on the hall table, light from the mullioned windows on each side of the front door reflecting from the mirror, throwing dashes of light across her face and hands. He smiled at the memory. The bouquet smelled good. That much, he could appreciate.

His hands were sweaty. He worried the white box that encased the glass vase for travel would be marked with his fingerprints when he handed the flowers to Charlotte. He looked around her suburban neighborhood and thought he might as well be in Chevy Chase, Maryland, except that these people had far more space around their large houses.

This area was as upscale as the Washington, DC,

suburbs but without the fancy wrought-iron gates and ridiculously high prices.

Charlotte opened her door. She was wearing a long black sweater that exposed one bare shoulder. A second later, he realized she wasn't wearing a bra. He gasped audibly and, then embarrassed, his hands shaking, pressed the flowers into her arms. His tongue swelled in his mouth, making it impossible for him to do more than mumble. His fingertips accidentally grazed her breast. His heart clutched, and he worried he might have a heart attack right there on the front step.

Charlotte smiled, took his arm, and led him into the house, chattering about the meal she had tried to prepare and what a disaster it was. She laughed, throwing back her hair. William gazed at her neck and suddenly understood why vampires went for the throat. It didn't matter what she served for dinner. He wouldn't be able to eat anything anyway.

She seated him in the living room and gave him Dewar's in a glass with two ice cubes. He made an effort to catch his breath, looking over into the dining room. The table was set for two with white porcelain dishes, silverware, and white candles. Charlotte removed the centerpiece she had on the table and put his flowers between the candlesticks. She lit the candles.

William realized he was the only one there with her. The drink shook in his hand, the ice cubes tinkling. He took a sip, then another, and put the glass down on the coffee table. The drink seemed to calm him. "Is it just us for dinner?"

"Yes. You're all I can handle today. I hope you don't mind."

"No. Not at all. I am surprised there aren't dozens of people here to help you, though."

"I told everyone I just wanted to be alone tonight."

She looked over at him and seemed to blush. "If that's okay with you."

William nodded and tried to make his face appear normal but his heart was dancing the Flamenco, and his pulse raced. He was completely tongue-tied. "No. Yes. It's fine, of course. So sorry about Harold." He flapped his hands in the air, horrified to see them moving through space as if they didn't belong to him, then placed them on his knees. Being alone with Charlotte was clearly impossible. He should have known better.

"I'll have dinner on the table in just a few seconds. I thought we could talk a little about my work. As you recall, my first review with the outside panel went fairly well."

"Yes," William managed to get out, "you were brilliant. We were all pleased."

"Although I don't have another three-day drill like that for a few years, I'm hoping that we can bring in another pharmaceutical partner now to give us additional funding as we prepare to enter Phase III trials. The funding will enable us to cast a broader net for subjects using several university medical facilities around the country. I'd like to recruit at least fifteen hundred subjects, maybe two thousand. With the extra funding, we'll be able to test my therapy against an existing chemotherapy treatment and a placebo as well as no treatment. We'll at least be able to say that my treatment extends life for twice as long as the standard treatment with a better quality of life for the patient."

William held up his hand. "I can see how eager you are to move forward, and I'm excited about your work. It has the potential to be groundbreaking, but we do need to talk about the data you already have first, Charlotte, and what it's actually telling us about dose, treatment efficacy, and patient outcomes. I'm not sure you're ready for…"

Charlotte took his hand in hers and pulled him to a stand. She placed her other hand on his chest, leaned forward, her body resting against him, and gave him a kiss on the cheek. "Let's have our dinner. We can talk data after dessert." She led him to the dining room table, indicated the chair he was to sit in, and walked into the kitchen.

William put the white linen napkin on his lap to cover an embarrassing erection that tented his pants. *It's a bad idea to be alone with her,* he chided himself.

When she walked back into the room carrying two plates of salad, he noticed her off-the-shoulder sweater seemed to have slipped farther down her arms so that her wonderful cleavage was revealed. Desire rose in his throat. He would not be able to eat. In the next second, as she leaned over him to put the plate down, he realized he had already surrendered to whatever she wanted.

Chapter 32

Male, Caucasian, six-foot-two, approximately sixty years old, two bullet holes in his chest, no ID, found in the Shenandoah River snagged on a branch by the dam southeast of Millville,'" Lagarde read from the text on his phone.

"Hey," he leaned toward Taylor who was deep in the online sergeant's course he was taking, his head down, shoulders hunched against possible failure. "Wiseman's body may have turned up. Looks like his killer dumped him in the river."

"Dumped in the river. Huh. Guess Dr. Rolle didn't do that herself. Even an Amazon can't carry twice her weight from that house to the river."

Lagarde leaned back in his chair. "Well, she could have used his truck, although we didn't find blood in the vehicle. Of course, you're right, she had help. Big help, lots of help. She has a pattern. She used Wiseman to kill her husband. She probably used someone else to kill Wiseman. Let's see what we've got."

He ticked off the evidence on his fingers. "We've got

Wiseman at the scene in Weigle's photo, the kill-shot photo on Munson's phone, which was in Wiseman's home, and the text to Charlotte with the deed-done photo. By now, the techs should have pulled his fingerprints from the mobile phone keypad."

Taylor leaned back in his chair. "So, Wiseman opened Munson's car with Charlotte's key but couldn't find what he was looking for—the thumb drive. She thought Wiseman had the thumb drive and was holding out on her in order to blackmail her. She got Nick to kill Wiseman and look for the thumb drive—remember, she practically lit up a neon sign over Nick's head that said, 'Look here, look here.'"

Lagarde nodded. "Right. But we've got the thumb drive, so she's frustrated. And by now, she knows that Dickerson knows about her lying and cheating on her research. God knows what she's got planned for him. Anyone who knows there's something wrong with her research is in her line of fire. Get on the phone to the medical examiner. See if we can ID the body in person, find out what kind of gun was used. We need evidence that proves not only who pulled the trigger but also Charlotte's intent to conspire to commit murder. I doubt any money changed hands and it's unlikely she communicated about her plans in email or text. That would be too easy. We need someone to spill as many beans as he has."

Taylor picked up his phone. "Do you think there's more information the forensics guys found that would help? I can check that also."

Lagarde grinned. *Jim Taylor was a go-getter. This day was looking better.* "Yes, go for it."

Half an hour later, they stood near the stainless steel table that held the remains of Mark Wiseman and officially identified him for the medical examiner from his driver's license photograph, which had been collected from his home with all other important artifacts about the man's existence the day before. The ME's office would also recover fingerprints from the corpse to match to the FBI's database and send out a blood sample for a DNA analysis to determine whether it matched the blood on the floor of his house, but Lagarde was now pretty sure it would.

Elaine Hartman, a medical examiner with a blonde ponytail, blue eyes, and multiple ear-piercings, was a looker, Lagarde had to admit, but not his type. She must have graduated from medical school when she was twelve. *If I'm honest, she's not my type because she's too young for me, and anyway, I have Beverly, what am I thinking?*

"The wounds were probably made by three-fifty-seven-caliber bullets," Elaine explained, "from the size of the initial impact, but water immersion in a dirty river for at least twelve hours distorted the wounds and makes time-of-death calculations a little muddy." She grinned at her own joke and looked at Lagarde, waiting for his corresponding amusement.

He was completely mystified about what she said that could be funny but smiled briefly to make her happy.

"It's a guess," she continued, "because body temp and decomp are completely whacked by being in cold water that long, but I put the time of death somewhere around two o'clock or three, yesterday afternoon."

"How many shots?" Taylor asked.

"Two, probably at close range, about two feet away. The shooter wasn't taking any chances. There are no defensive wounds, no abrasions around his wrists or ankles indicating he was tied up. I thought he might have been knocked out first, but there's no sign of pre-mortem contusions on his skull, no bruising on his neck. He was probably sleeping. The killer stood above him, arm extended toward the body. Your killer's not a pro, I'd say, or he would've put one in the head."

Lagarde turned his head away. "But effective enough." He didn't like the way the body count was climbing. "Thanks for your help. Appreciate it." He clapped Taylor on the shoulder, and they walked out of the morgue. "Did forensics mention anything else?"

"Oh, yeah, I forgot to tell you. I got a text saying they found three-fifty-seven bullets embedded in the living room wood floor under where the body had been and a Smith and Wesson thirty-eight special, the same make of gun that Nick Waters said had been stolen from his house, between the cushions on the sofa. The bullets match that gun, which is registered to Waters. Also, Nick's fingerprints are on the coffee table in the living room, the kitchen counter, back door handle, front door handle, and the gun."

Lagarde nodded. "Got it. We seem to have Nick Waters dead to rights in the shooting death of Mark Wiseman." He ran his hand over his face. "But who puts a murder weapon where it can be found almost immediately and then tries to hide the body? The guy's not that stupid."

Something about this evidence was off, but he had to go in the direction it was pointing. "Okay. Let's get an arrest warrant for Nick Waters and pick him up before *he* winds up dead."

Chapter 33

April 1, 9:30 a.m.:

William Dickerson was calmly drinking his second cup of coffee and scanning the *Washington Post*, the daily newspaper of the nation's capital. He was in a languorous mood this morning, and his reading was frequently interrupted by visceral flashes of his evening with Charlotte. The memory of her mouth on his usually flaccid penis—something his wife had never done—thickened the breath in his chest and made him groan out loud.

To recover his mind, he pondered the efficacy of increased blood flow during sex in relationship to neurogenesis.

Hadn't neuroscientist Sandrine Thuret said that sex increased the development of new brain cells in the hippocampus? He allowed his mind to explore the kinds of experiments he could devise to test this hypothesis with one human subject in particular.

His pulse-quickening fantasy was interrupted by Charlotte's post-doctoral fellow, the one Charlotte wanted transferred to another lab, who burst into his office waving a piece of paper and babbling so quickly he couldn't understand a single word she was saying.

"What, what? Please calm down Dr. Liu."

She waved the paper in his face. "You have to see this. It's all over Twitter and Facebook. I downloaded it and printed it out for you. I assume you don't have accounts for those apps—"

Dickerson batted her away. "Please. A little decorum. You're not in kindergarten." He took the page from her hand and read.

She waited, her nose in the air, sniffing him and determining he was malodorous.

"Ah, I see Dr. Norton has published something about Charlotte's data." He scanned the page. "He claims to have seen both the raw data from her small group study using an experimental immunological agent with human subjects and the statistical analyses related to that data and," his voice broke to barely a whisper as his eyes followed the words of the next sentence on the page, "and she's lying about the scientific significance of her results."

He closed his eyes and took a minute to compose himself. He looked up at a triumphant Dr. Liu. "Who has seen this?"

The young scientist's dark eyes flashed. "The whole world has seen it by now. The link on social media goes to his blog where he lays out his case." She rolled her eyes to say people over fifty should no longer be running important research centers. "She has destroyed all of our careers by association. Norton posted a video on YouTube where he explains his own analysis with slides. I suspected this was the case with her research. I thought she was fudging the results. At our staff meetings, I have repeatedly suggested that we go back to animal studies and re-establish our baseline. She—"

Dickerson held up his hand. "Thank you. I under-stand. I'll deal with it."

Dr. Liu gave him a look of incredulity and stomped out of the office.

By word of mouth alone, the entire institute and then the entire campus would soon know about his failure to adequately oversee Charlotte's research. That would be the kindly view. Anyone who ever envied him, who felt slighted by him or passed over, would put a nastier gloss on the news and gleefully rub their hands together over his fall from grace.

By the end of the day, the entire scientific communi-ty would have heard that Charlotte Rolle lied about her research. They would suspect he was complicit. They would call it fraud. It was a scandal of epic proportions. She would have to issue retractions for every paper that had been published on her research. She would have to write an apology.

If the center's ethics panel found she had cheated de-liberately, she could be censured and banned from any further research. Higher level investigations and excoria-tion would follow. No publisher worth the spit on a stamp would take a paper from her now.

His own career would suffer. His peers would call him a fool, or worse. He would have to retire—if they let him and didn't terminate him—losing the post he worked so hard to attain. His well-planned life was suddenly a shambles.

Thank God his wife was dead and not a witness to his ignominy. Of course, his sons would learn about it, the shame of it. He wouldn't be able to face them. He put his face in his hands and waited for some damage-control plan to occur to him, but all thought seemed to have fled.

ᘒᘓᘒ

An hour later, a few flights down from Dickerson's office in her NIH lab, Charlotte watched the screen of her computer load an email from the *Washington Post's* science writer asking for a comment in reference to Dr. Norton's assertions. She did not respond. His email was followed by one from the *New York Times* science reporter.

Charlotte had set up an alert for any social media posts with her name in them and for the next forty minutes, her mobile phone continually bleeped. The sound was driving her crazy. She put the phone on mute and read all of Norton's blog, watched the video, and scanned comments that popped up as she read. They were all negative. They infuriated her, these people, these morons, with no idea of what her work was about. Her blood boiled. This so-called statistician hadn't even bothered to consult with her. He didn't have access to the full data set. He wasn't even an M.D. It was absurd that he thought he was qualified to comment about her work, and in public forums, no less, where any idiot could read what he thought and comment on it. A virtual witch burning—that's what Norton had instigated.

She watched her in-box load one email after another from the editors of every journal in which she had ever published a paper about her novel cancer therapy. Every co-author on those papers, everyone who had been on any peer review group that vetted her work for publication, was sending her emails.

Subject line in the first email: *Geez, Charlotte.* In the second: *I regret to inform you.* It only got worse from there. The third email began: *How could you do this?* There was even an email from *Retraction Watch.* Charlotte almost laughed. She was suddenly infamous in a way she had never been famous. The only person who didn't try to contact her by email was Dickerson. His silence was telling. She couldn't wait for him to walk into her office. She couldn't face him. She was embarrassed, regretful, and furious all at once. None of them understood. *My work is true, my idea, my method—they're all right. Why does no one see this?*

She could hear her staff whispering together in the lab, conspiring against her. She heard the words "cited for research misconduct." Betty Liu walked past her door and glared at her. Those few nights and afternoons of delight hadn't done anything to quell Betty's animosity toward her. In fact, intimacy had made her rabid. Liu had gone completely off the tracks. Charlotte refrained from clutching her head. She wished she could disappear and reappear in another country on another planet. *Is there no way out of this mess?*

None of her research staff dared confront her directly, but she was sure they relished her complete mortification. She wouldn't give them the satisfaction of seeing her defeated. She checked her emails again. Ebulon Pharmaceuticals had sent her a message. She closed her eyes, pretending not seeing it would make it go away. She wouldn't open the email. What was the point? They were probably pulling their funding.

She had an answer for everyone, not that they would give her a chance to say it. So what if the numbers were a little fudged? So what if her treatment only worked once out of six tries? *I know I'm right, my work is on track, and a few decimal points plus or minus in one direction or another don't prove my hypothesis and approach are wrong.*

That wretched Norton would never understand that. There was nothing in his work but air—squiggles on a page, symbols for abstractions that someone claimed meant something. He might have been good at math, but his work was meaningless.

I'm doing something important and yet this *math—*

the arithmetic of position and status—makes me a minus.

Charlotte pulled down a box off the top shelf of her bookcase—the box in which she'd brought her books and diplomas to this office five years before—and methodically removed her framed diplomas, certificates, and awards from the walls of her office. She placed the objects that signified her early success in the box and scanned the room for what else she had to take with her right now. *Why should I let anyone else benefit from my thinking?* Her gathered her handwritten notebooks and stuffed them into the box. She looked around again. *I'm probably never coming back here.* The pink begonia on the window sill went into the box. She glanced at the photo of Harold in its small silver frame and left it on the desk. *I certainly don't need to keep that.* She felt a certain satisfaction in abandoning the photo to its inevitable fate.

Great work requires great sacrifices, she told herself as she walked down the corridor to the elevator, her heels clacking on the hard floor. *Subjects die during experiments. Their deaths are considered an acceptable loss in medical research if the greater good is served. Isn't that still true?* They could learn from every outcome. Perhaps she should have reported that most of her subjects died. No one would have blinked at that. Those patients were going to die anyway of inoperable brain cancer.

It's an experiment for God's sake! The important question is, what did we learn from the experiment? Why were all these so-called scientists suddenly infuriated about subject mortality? She wasn't flagrantly risking human lives. She hadn't tricked anyone into participating in her study without their informed consent. She wasn't selling slides of patients' brain tissue for a profit or maiming perfectly healthy people.

Charlotte paced in front of the elevator doors, waiting for them to open. *Isn't there anyone who understands me?* Her father's opprobrium floated into her mind. He would never forgive her for embarrassing him in this way. He might not ever speak to her again. He would take her failure as a deliberate attack on him. Her mother would be humiliated. She sucked in her breath.

Her mother had always been her biggest supporter, the person who told her over and over that she could do whatever she wanted as long as she was willing to work for it. Her mother's mantra had been the antidote for her father's verbal poison. She had worked hard, relentlessly, all her life. *Don't I get any credit for the work I've done? Can it all be swept away because of a few misreported numbers?*

The elevator doors opened, and Charlotte stepped inside, grateful the car was empty. Shifting the box to her hip, she hit the button for the first floor. For a moment, she felt a kind of remorse—that she hadn't succeeded in fooling them all a little longer, at least until she could say it was the pharmaceutical company that changed the methodology or scrimped on the infusion to increase profits and that's why her therapy didn't work. She shook off that feeling. *Be strong now, Charlotte,* she urged herself. *This is the time to show your true colors.*

She trudged through the lobby carrying the heavy box out to the parking lot. It certainly looked like Dickerson wasn't going to back her, and if he didn't, she'd have no future at the institute. She'd save them all the trouble and resign now, effective today. She could send him an email from home. She would feel safer at her own home, far away from DC and the backstabbing scientific class. She loaded the box of her belongings in her car and glanced around the campus. *I'll show you,* she thought, watching strangers walk purposefully by completely unaware of her. *I'll be back on top, and you'll still be ants.*

Good thing she'd driven into work this morning so

that she could make it back to the Panhandle in time for Harold's funeral this afternoon. Driving on automatic at seventy miles an hour along the Capital Beltway, she connected to I-270 until Frederick, her head buzzing, not noticing when she changed lanes, then exited onto I-70 and Route 340, and crossed the bridges into West Virginia. Sixty miles later, she was sure there was someone to blame for this mess, and she knew exactly who it was— that damned detective, Sam Lagarde.

Chapter 34

With the county prosecutor prepped and the arrest warrant for Nick Waters in hand, Lagarde and Taylor drove the thirty minutes from Charles Town to Nick's Inwood townhouse. He opened the door to their knock in shorts and a t-shirt, what Taylor now thought of as Nick's customary attire.

"Not the behavior of a guilty man," Lagarde said to Taylor, "but go ahead."

"Mr. Waters," Taylor read from the Miranda card in his hand, "we have a warrant for your arrest. You are being charged with the murder of Mark Wiseman. You have the right to remain silent. Anything you say can and will be used against you in court. You have the right to an attorney before making any statement and may have your attorney with you during questioning. If you cannot afford an attorney and desire one, the court will appoint one for you—"

"What? Stop. You're shitting me." Nick hopped from foot to foot, his agitation so great that his body couldn't contain the energy it generated. "I didn't kill anyone. What the hell are you talking about?"

Taylor continued his warning. "You may stop the questioning at any time by refusing to answer or by requesting to consult with your attorney. Do you understand each of these rights I have explained to you? With these rights in mind, do you wish to talk to us now?"

Nick's head rolled around on his shoulders, and his eyes bulged.

Lagarde leaned forward and took the man by his arm, looking directly into his eyes. "Mr. Waters, do you understand we are charging you with murder and arresting you? We have your gun at the scene of Mark Wiseman's shooting with your prints on it. The bullets that killed Mr. Wiseman came from your gun. Your prints are on the bullet casings and everywhere at the scene. Are you waiving your rights to have an attorney present when we question you?"

Nick looked around wildly for a way out that he simply had to think of it. Taylor grabbed his other arm and pulled out cuffs from his pocket. "Okay, okay," Nick yelled, "I'm coming." He slipped on the flip flops that sat on the floor next to the table in the hallway. "I can't grab my stuff unless you let go of me."

Lagarde nodded. Taylor released his grip. Nick yanked his arm away from Lagarde and dashed toward the back of his house. It took a second for them to realize what was happening. They heard the swish of a sliding glass door opening, and, in an instant, Nick was racing toward the tree line of the small woods behind the row of townhouses. Taylor sprinted after him, chasing him into the woods.

Lagarde walked out the front door, positioning himself where he could grab their suspect in case Nick abruptly changed his escape route and tried to get to his vehicle. From the side of the townhouse, he watched the chase. Ten feet into the woods, Taylor leaped forward and tackled Nick around the knees. Nick fell face down into leaf mold. Taylor pulled Nick's arms behind his back and cuffed him. Nick spit leaves, twigs, and dirt, shaking his head like a large dog to loosen the debris around his eyes. Taylor hauled the man to his feet and, keeping a firm grip on his arm, pushed Nick back toward the town-houses. His flip flops lost, Nick walked gingerly across sticks and stones that littered the ground and jabbed his bare feet.

When they came within earshot, Lagarde heard Taylor say, "It's stupid to run, man. That adds resisting arrest to the list of your crimes. Unless you've got a plausible story that pans out when we check it, we could charge you with murder one. You broke into the man's house, you brought a weapon with you, and shot him in cold blood while he was sleeping because he was having sex with your girlfriend. It's premeditated."

"No way. You've got it all wrong. I didn't kill that guy. I didn't even know him."

Lagarde briefly ruminated on Nick's notion that you had to know someone before you could kill him. Then he remembered all the senseless mass murders that seemed to occur every week and dismissed the idea.

Taylor held Nick by the nape, put him in the backseat of the police vehicle, and buckled the seat belt. Waters was still protesting. Lagarde murmured to Taylor, "Let him talk," and got into the passenger seat.

"But the Miranda warning."

"You gave him the warning, explained his rights. He heard you."

Taylor looked at Lagarde wide-eyed and then shrugged.

Lagarde turned around in his seat and looked at Nick. "But you *were* in Wiseman's house, right?"

"Yeah, I was there. But I didn't kill him. He was already dead." Nick's entire body jerked involuntarily as if a roach had just crawled across his knee. His face was briefly frozen in a look of revulsion. He shook his head vigorously, closed his mouth and looked out of the window as they drove back toward Charles Town.

Lagarde prodded. "So you got to the house, you walked in the back door, through the kitchen and saw what?"

"He was lying there on the floor, naked, a big pool of blood flowing out of him."

"And you didn't shoot him?"

"No. I told you. He was already dead. Why would I shoot him?"

"You were jealous that he was having sex with Charlotte Rolle."

Nick laughed. "Jealous? She pays me, man. I'm just her boy toy. I like her and all, but I don't love her."

Lagarde looked out the front window to gauge where they were and to avoid looking at Waters, for whom he had abruptly developed a deep disdain. They were on Leetown Road, farmland on either side of them, with the turn onto Route 51 just up the road. They would make it to county holding at the sheriff's office in Charles Town in fifteen minutes. He might have Waters' whole confession by then.

"So when you got there, you saw a dead guy on the floor and what else? Remember, we can charge you with obstruction if you keep any details from us."

Nick looked like he wanted to cry. His eyes darted back and forth between the car window and Lagarde's face. He was having trouble with his conscience. This was a guy who had been trained to save lives, Lagarde reminded himself. Killing might be difficult for him. Maybe he was telling the truth, and he didn't do it. They could still hold him for twenty-four hours while they checked out his statement.

"God, what a cluster fuck this is." Nick hung his head for a minute then looked up. "Okay, here it is. I'm gonna tell you the whole truth now."

Lagarde glanced over at Taylor. Whenever a suspect started talking about telling him the whole truth, he always expected a raft of shit to follow. The look on Taylor's face said he knew that also.

"I was at the clinic doing an eleven-to-seven shift—you can check that—and Charlotte called me all hysterical, crying and screaming, saying she was at this guy's house and he was dead, and there was blood everywhere, and she needed my help. I couldn't just let her handle that all by herself. I mean, hey, I'm human."

Lagarde nodded, giving Nick just enough encouragement to continue without leading him in any direction.

"So I clocked out of work and drove to the address she gave me. I'm driving so fast I get there in about fifteen minutes. I see her car and somebody's pickup truck in the driveway. She told me to go in the back door. I walk around to the back, turn the knob. The door's unlocked. I walk in. At first, I don't see anything because there's a kitchen counter that hides the floor in the living room when you walk in. Charlotte comes around the corner of the room, maybe she was in the bathroom. Her face is the color of skim milk. I see she's in a panic. Her pupils are dilated. I've never seen her in a panic before. She's always so controlled. Her shirt is wet, like she showered in it, and her hands, arms, and face are dripping with water. Even her hair is wet, like she dunked her head in the sink. She's dripping water everywhere. She's gagging every few seconds.

"She says, 'We have to move him. We have to get him out of the house.' She looks at me with those green eyes and you know, when you've fucked a woman every which way—" He shrugged. "—you know what goes through your head when you see her disheveled. Even so, I say we should call the police, because I don't get it at first. I thought she walked in and found him dead and maybe got blood on her from trying to save him and that's what she was washing off. I tell her, 'Let the police clean this mess up,' but she wasn't having any of it."

Nick stopped talking and looked out of the window. Lagarde waited. He looked down and saw that Taylor was recording Nick's confession on his cell phone. His eyes flicked to Taylor's face. Taylor smiled and kept his eyes on the road. Even if the prosecutor said this recording wasn't acceptable evidence in court, it could be used as leverage to get an official confession. Lagarde looked back at Nick.

"So anyway," Nick continued, "I get some towels from the bathroom and start to mop up the blood. But she's screaming, 'Never mind about that. Just get rid of the body.' Nothing she was saying really made a lot of sense. If she didn't do it, why get rid of the body? I don't think she knew what she was doing. There was no time to sort out anything. So, I take a sheet from his bed, roll him and the towels up in it, and hoist him onto my shoulder.

"She's yammering at me, 'Throw him in the river. The current's strong. It'll pull him into the Potomac. By the time they find him in Maryland, they'll have no way to know who he is. Maybe they'll never find him.' But I'm like, wait, what? I didn't even ask how he got those two bullet holes in him. And then she screams, 'Just do it, just do it!' So I did."

Nick looked down at his knees. Lagarde gave him a few minutes to think about what he'd told them. "Did you leave your gun at the house?"

"My gun? My gun is missing. Your side-kick here knows that. It was stolen."

"Did Charlotte help you roll him in the sheet?"

"No. She didn't want to go near the body."

"After you put the body in the river, what happened?"

"I had to poke him with a long stick to get the current to take him." He stopped talking for a second and shuddered. "I watched for a while, made sure he was moving downstream. The current was swift, and after he got going, there wasn't any trouble. When I turned around to walk back to the house, Charlotte's car was gone. I got in my car and went home." He moaned slightly and shook his head. "I had a bad feeling this was going to go wrong."

"What did you do with the clothes you were wearing?"

"Threw 'em in the washing machine."

"Did she call or text you?"

Nick paused for a long time. When he spoke, his voice was flat and cold. "She called me before I got home and said if anyone asked, I should say she wasn't at Wiseman's house."

Now he gets it, Lagarde thought, *the poor schmuck.* "We're going to have to charge you, Mr. Waters, whether that's for aiding and abetting or simply illegally disposing of a dead body depends on whether your story checks out. Meanwhile, we're going to hold you on suspicion of murder with a deadly weapon until we know."

Nick Waters was near tears, grimacing to hold them back. He was definitely having one of his worst days ever. Lagarde noticed they were five minutes outside of Charles Town. He had beaten his own guess of how long it would take the kid to tell him everything.

Chapter 35

April 1, 2 p.m.:

Lagarde and Taylor arrived at the cemetery at the tail end of Harold Munson's funeral. They had taken an official statement from Nick and put him in holding. He still hadn't secured the services of a lawyer. Either he was stupider than Lagarde thought, or he really believed in his own innocence. Not that innocence was any protection against being found guilty by a jury of your peers.

Lagarde strongly hinted to Waters that he should get a lawyer. If the kid didn't get legal assistance, he might just urge the prosecutor to let Nick go without even an arraignment. Nothing would be gained by charging him with a misdemeanor for illegally disposing of a body. The more Lagarde watched Nick, the surer he was that Nick did not kill Mark Wiseman. He wasn't even an accomplice in the murder. He was the hapless cleanup crew.

Taylor's first impression of the man was accurate. Murder was definitely outside Nick Waters' comfort zone. Would he get sucked into a domineering woman's scheme? Yes. But Waters wasn't capable of murdering anyone on his own. Unfortunately, that conclusion left Lagarde with two murders unsolved and no good suspects.

Standing twenty respectable paces from the assembled family and friends around the grave, he and Taylor watched the brief burial ceremony. The cemetery was small, immediately adjacent to an old brick church that sat right on Route 230. From where he was standing, Lagarde could see mountains holding vigil over the river. In the other direction, fields waited to be turned over for spring planting.

It was a quiet spot. Called Uvilla, the unincorporated area was marked by two almost identical looking churches on either side of the main road, one Methodist the other Lutheran—a doctrinal difference, as Lagarde understood it, of believing whether God's grace or individual good deeds saved you. If he was a betting man, and maybe he was, he'd prefer a church that gave you double the odds. He had often wondered during Sunday school classes at the Presbyterian Church his mother dragged him to when he was a child, whether you could actually do good deeds if God hadn't already marked you by grace. No one had ever been able to answer the question to his satisfaction. His work made him wonder if God bothered with such niceties anymore.

Lagarde watched Harold's parents, who he assumed were members of the church. They were of the generation that found their community at church suppers and picnics, people who would help a neighbor put up a new barn and reach out to strangers with an expectation of kindness in return—all values, Lagarde thought, that are quickly vanishing.

At some point in their long history, these small churches would have been filled to the brim with parishioners and their children. Now, ministers counted themselves blessed if twenty-five people showed up for service on a Sunday.

The preacher's prayers and words of solace wound around the quiet weeping of Harold's family and friends in a low hum. His removed position gave Lagarde an opportunity to observe how Charlotte and Harold's parents interacted. Coldly cordial was the only way to describe the Munson's behavior toward their daughter-in-law. She didn't partake of their grief. They stood an arm's length away from her, not touching, almost oblivious to her. Obviously, they knew she was divorcing Harold. That might account for their distance, but it seemed to Lagarde there was some other animosity between them. Did Charlotte's charming personality fail to bond them to her or did they think she killed their son?

It was possible they simply didn't like Charlotte even before she filed for divorce. Harold was their golden boy, their only child, and his wife had made him feel small and stupid. They wouldn't like her for that alone. Lagarde guessed Harold's mother had been glad her son was getting a divorce. She would have been relieved. "You'll find the right girl, now," he could imagine her saying to her son. "You'll find the one who thinks you walk on water."

That's what his own mother had said to him after his first divorce, the one that broke his heart and made him feel the world had split apart leaving devastation everywhere. Instead of finding the right girl, however, he had brought home every wrong one who said yes, in an odd, unspoken assertion to his first wife: "See, I'm still sexy. Women want me. Plenty of women are willing to live with me."

But their willingness wore off pretty quickly. His first divorce was only a warm-up for the marathon divorce series to come until he was immune to rejection, until he believed love was a word used only on greeting cards, and his seared ego sealed itself off from all human emotion. Until he met Beverly, that was. He wondered what his mother would have said about Beverly. Maybe she would have said, "Finally, you nitwit, you finally figured it out."

Harold's mother's gray head was bent, a tissue covered the bottom half of her face, and dark glasses concealed her eyes. Periodically she leaned her face against the chest of the older man next to her—Harold's father, Lagarde assumed—who gripped her shaking shoulder tenderly, more it seemed for his own comfort than hers. The man wore the blank mask of unbearable sorrow. Lagarde doubted they knew anything but that their wonderful son had been stripped off the face of the earth by a lunatic. He decided not to bother them unless they wanted to talk to him.

After the last flower was thrown into the grave and the formal service was finished, a tall, white-haired man in an expensive charcoal gray suit, white shirt, and gray and white striped tie walked up to Charlotte and Harold's parents. He shook hands with the parents, said a few quiet words, then turned and leaned over to say something in Charlotte's ear. She jerked her body away from him and turned in the other direction, walking briskly toward her car. He followed her, putting his hand on her shoulder.

Lagarde watched the man confront Charlotte again, backing her against the side of her Volvo. His cheeks were red, he was breathing erratically. His hands floundered, flapping the air around him. She was amazingly calm under the barrage of his words. She said something that made him take a step backward. Then she shook her head and yanked open her car door. From the driver's seat, she turned her head and glared at Lagarde before she drove out of the cemetery.

Lagarde and Taylor walked swiftly toward him and caught up to the man before he got into his car. "Sir," Lagarde called out, "can we have a minute?"

The man opened his car door but turned around to greet them. *Good manners, well ingrained,* Lagarde thought. He and Taylor produced their credentials and introduced themselves.

"Oh, yes, of course," the man said. "I'm William Dickerson. We've talked on the telephone."

Lagarde re-rolled his mental video of the encounter he'd just witnessed. There was obviously trouble in the scientific paradise the doctors Dickerson and Rolle occupied. "I have a few questions."

Dickerson nodded, looked longingly at the driver's seat of his car, and sighed.

"Did you see Dr. Rolle yesterday at any time?"

"Yes. I had dinner with her yesterday evening."

"What time was that?"

"I arrived a bit after six p.m. I got lost driving out here."

"Did Dr. Rolle seem—how should I say it—did she seem normal to you?"

Dickerson gave a laugh Lagarde classified as rueful. "Normal? That's not a word I would ever use to describe such a brilliant woman," Dickerson said. "She certainly seemed to be herself."

Lagarde watched a red flush creep up from beneath Dickerson's collar and spread across his face. *Something happened at dinner yesterday that had nothing to do with medical science.*

"And how long were you at her house?" He didn't really need to know, but he enjoyed watching Dickerson squirm a little. He told himself this kind of cruelty was part of his own dragon persona. *Was that something Beverly had said to him?*

"A few hours. I went home at nine-thirty."

"Was anyone else at the dinner party?"

"No. We were alone."

"Did she say anything about the murder of her husband?"

Dickerson blushed deeply. "No, nothing."

It was now clear to Lagarde that Charlotte didn't need to kill Dickerson. He was her pawn. "Did you discuss with her the fact that she's been lying about her research outcomes?"

The scientist turned pale. "I believe I told you on the telephone that if you want to talk about that issue, you need to talk with the institute's attorney. Did my assistant send you the phone number?"

Lagarde nodded. "What did Charlotte say to you just now after the funeral?"

Dickerson sighed. He suddenly looked old and sad. "She said she would not issue a retraction. There was nothing to apologize for. She said if I wasn't smart enough to understand her methods, then I should step aside and let science move into the twenty-first century. She said I was a dinosaur and worse than useless." He stepped unsteadily away from Lagarde, dropped into the driver's seat, and closed the door.

Lagarde knocked on the driver's window and waited. Dickerson started his car and rolled down the window. He looked up at Lagarde, completely depleted.

"Is that Dr. Liu that you said didn't like Charlotte here? I'd like to talk to her."

Dickerson pointed to a stunning young woman opening the passenger's side door of a silver Acura a few cars down the cemetery lane and drove off.

Her, Lagarde thought, remembering Beverly's scenario. He ran to the car Dickerson had indicated, flashed his credentials, while Taylor stopped the driver from taking off. Tapping on the passenger side window, Lagarde leaned down and spoke to a woman in a charcoal gray suit. *Charlotte was wearing charcoal gray also*, Lagarde thought. *Maybe that's their gang colors.*

The sharp toes of Dr. Liu's black pumps, he noted, pointed in exactly the same direction on the car floor. Lagarde had time to tell Liu that he wanted to interview her, watch her eye lids close in what he took to be assent, and then the driver took off, causing him and Taylor to jump back away from the car's rolling tires. *Guess folks from Maryland don't think they're subject to the laws of West Virginia.*

Walking back to his own car with Taylor, Lagarde wondered whether the precise positioning of the scientist's toes on the car floor indicated that Betty Liu was an obsessive-compulsive personality. *You might be losing it, buddy*, he cautioned himself.

Taylor looked around the cemetery. The rest of the Munson funeral party had departed. "What did Dickerson mean about a retraction?"

Lagarde took his hat off and rubbed the top of his head. "He means his professional reputation now has the same value as used toilet paper. I feel sorry for the guy, but there's nothing we can do about his problem. Let's get some lunch and then drive down to Bethesda and have a longer conversation with Dr. Liu. I think we're missing something obvious, and if we don't figure it out, someone else is going to die."

Chapter 36

April 1, 3:15 p.m.:

William Dickerson had made one stop on the drive to his office. Back on the research campus, he parked in his reserved spot, walked along the path he had taken for the last ten years, waved hello to the reception attendants in the lobby, and swiped his badge to enter the elevator. In the director's wing, he nodded to everyone somberly and proceeded immediately to his office. His staff, now silenced by the sense of impending doom since the morning's news, always respected his desire to be alone, which he signaled by closing his door.

He sat at his desk, looked around at the plaques and diplomas on the wall, the book-lined shelves, and the photo of his beloved wife on his desk. Turning on his computer, Dickerson opened his email and wrote a formal letter to all those estimable scientists above him in the institute's organizational hierarchy. He apologized for the errors in Charlotte Rolle's published papers, for his failure to ensure integrity in the research she conducted under his supervision, and for failing the excellent scien-

tists and researchers in his division who labored diligent-
ly and brilliantly to curtail human suffering. It was an el-
oquent letter. Rereading it, he felt a weight lift off his
heart.

Using his cell phone, Dickerson sent a text to his
sons. *I love and admire you. You are the best part of my
life, the only part that matters. I am honored to be your
father.*

Before his sons could text him back, and perhaps
knowing that they would consult each other first before
contacting him, given the oddity of his communication,
Dickerson put his cell phone down on his desk, picked up
the rope he had purchased at Home Depot, and climbed
the stairs of the new neuroscience building to the as-yet-
unoccupied sixth floor. He tested the railings for their
ability to hold weight; tied one end of the rope to the railing; tested its fastness; fashioned a noose with the other
end; put it over his head; climbed over the railing, feeling
a bit intrepid and proud of himself for his courage; and
jumped.

His neck snapped immediately.

One of the custodians, thinking he saw the shadow of
a large bird fluttering in the stairwell, climbed up the
stairs to find Dickerson's body hanging from the banister.
He dialed nine-one-one and called his boss. An hour later, everyone on campus knew that William Dickerson
had committed suicide.

Chapter 37

April 1, 3:30 p.m.:

S pring unfurled around the farm in slow motion. If Beverly was quiet, she could hear leaves opening. The world always seemed to be a lush Sibelius symphony in progress whenever she tuned into it. Her fingers yearned for a brush ladened with greens. She imagined the first mark she would lay down on canvas. This was a painting day. Color was calling to her in jubilant reveille.

For the moment, she stood at the rail communing with Jake, stroking the horse's nose. "What do you think, Jake? It's a beautiful day, right?"

Jake nodded his long head and allowed her to stroke his neck and ears. He nuzzled her cheek. Beverly understood why Sam loved the horse. He was a good companion. You could say anything to him—as long as he got his molasses-coated oats in the evening. Carrots worked also. Today he had walked up to her expecting a treat. *We're making headway.* She pulled another chunk of carrot out of her jacket pocket and held her palm up for Jake to nibble it out of her hand. His ears pricked up.

She was getting to know Jake and the other horses in the same way she was getting to know Sam. You could only really know people by living with them and seeing how they behaved when they were angry or sad. Good times didn't count. Anyone could be charming when they were happy. So far, she rated the man and his horses pretty highly, but she was like any other prey animal, ready to rear and bolt at the first sign of danger. She was far too old to put up with any nonsense from anyone, and anyone included Sam Lagarde.

The death of her husband four years before had taught her a few hard truths. She would always remember him, always love him, never stop missing him, or hearing his continual commentary about every damn thing he ever thought. A part of her mind and heart was reserved for him, and that would always be true. But she realized she deserved a life and couldn't wall herself up inside her house like the paramour of a dead pharaoh.

And if worst comes to worst, I can always go back to the townhouse and sit in my garden.

Unlike other couples—at least the ones in TV dramas—she and Sam never used the word love. In fact, they never talked about their relationship or their feelings. It wasn't a forbidden subject, but conversation about it was beside the point. Relationships were about doing something—action not words—at least in her estimation, even if that action was just bringing him a bowl of buttered, well-salted popcorn when he watched football on television.

It wasn't that they were too old for love, just the opposite, in fact. Love was the *only* reason to be together. All the other essentials of life they could cover on their own, without anyone. They weren't here out of need. They were together because they wanted to be, not in that youthful anything-is-possible way but in the way of old folks who had been there, done that. What survives death and betrayal—that pure substance left after fire subsides and ashes are strewn on the ground—that was love.

She delighted in Sam with all his idiosyncrasies, maybe *because* of his idiosyncrasies. She was old enough to admit to herself that she was fairly eccentric also. *Okay, maybe I'm very eccentric.* She was waiting to see if love was the word she would use for what she felt about him.

Jake stepped back from the fence and whinnied. *Does the horse know what I'm thinking?* Beverly turned her face away from Jake and now heard what he heard—vehicle tires crunching on the gravel lane toward the house. For a minute, she thought it might be Sam stopping by for a coffee and a kiss, but Jake's ears flattened back against his head, he tossed his mane and whinnied again. *Trouble coming—that's what the horse is telling me.*

Beverly watched over her shoulder as the gray Volvo stopped next to her own old Honda under the reddening branches of an old maple tree in the front yard. Jake wheeled and bolted to the far end of the paddock as a woman slid out of the vehicle—a woman with red hair, in jeans and a black cashmere hoodie, wearing black wool sneakers. *Those sneakers announce who she is beneath that every-woman camouflage,* Beverly thought.

The woman tossed her hair over her shoulder with a gesture Beverly had seen the horses perform, looked over at Beverly, and strode toward her across the grass. *This is not the Welcome Wagon woman.*

The woman held something close to her thigh. It was the tension in her arm and the fixed look in her green eyes that alerted Beverly to danger, although Jake had picked up the signal from the air. Beverly waited at the fence and ran through several scenarios in her mind—an old flame of Sam's who wanted to get some of her dignity back by chiding his current girl friend, a frustrated city woman lost in the country who needed directions out of here, a killer.

When her mind hit on this last version of possible realities, Beverly knew this was Charlotte Rolle. *What on earth is she doing here?*

"Is Detective Lagarde here?" Charlotte called out to her, still forty yards away but close enough now for Beverly to see that it was a gun she held in her hand.

Charlotte brandished the weapon, waving it in the air like a magic wand, seeming to say, "Abracadabra, I use this and all my troubles go away."

It was the way she was waving the gun that made Beverly nervous. It didn't appear Charlotte had ever taken a single gun-handling lesson.

"Nope," Beverly answered, trying to keep her voice even. "You missed him. He's out on a case."

Beverly backed away from the rail, mentally measuring the distance between the paddock and the house. "You should contact him at his office if you need to tell him something."

She sorted through her options. She didn't want the horses to be hit by a stray bullet, and she had no confidence this woman had enough control of herself to accurately fire that lethal weapon. She kept her face to the intruder and walked on an angle away from the woman and toward the safety of the house, telling herself, *Easy, easy. Don't exhibit panic.*

From what Sam had told her about the case, her initial hunch that Charlotte was the killer hadn't been confirmed by the evidence, but the woman turning up at the farm with a weapon wasn't going to do her any good. *It might not do me any good either.*

"Where did you get that gun?" she called out to

Charlotte across the hundred-foot distance between them, hoping she could somehow distract her with conversation.

Charlotte kept moving toward her in long strides, closing the gap. "At the new pawn shop in town, half an hour ago. It was ridiculously easy. No waiting. I left the store after I bought it and went back five minutes later and bought the bullets."

"Why did you do that?"

"A sign near the gun display rack said they wouldn't sell me the gun and the bullets at the same time."

Beverly nodded, not knowing what else to do, and continued walking backward in the direction of the house. Although Charlotte's explanation sounded rational, there was something deeply disturbing about what she said and how she said it.

When a crazy person thinks they're being rational, that might be the time to be really scared. Charlotte was thirty feet away now, and she kept coming. Even if she knew nothing about aiming the weapon, she might hit her mark.

Beverly's mind whirled with conflicting thoughts as she walked, keeping her eyes on Charlotte's face, her hands extended out from her body to catch herself in case she tripped on something and fell. *Don't fall, don't give her an additional advantage*, she coached herself. Each step generated another thought.

Charlotte was now twenty feet from her. Why would she risk coming to the detective's home brandishing a gun? Her mind must have snapped. She was a woman with nothing to lose. That's what made her dangerous.

Oh, God, stop thinking, get in the house, lock the door, call Sam.

Charlotte was within ten feet of her. Beverly lunged for the kitchen door, pulled the screen open, and had one foot in the house when a shot rang out. The bullet hit the door jamb. Wood exploded from the frame, flying at her face. That was close enough to focus her attention. *Maybe she does know how to use that thing.*

Her heart pounding, Beverly sprang inside the house and tried to push the solid wood door closed, leaning against it. *All the other ways Charlotte can get into the house. Do I have time to secure them all?* Her pulse thudded in her throat. Her breath came in gasps. *I might be too old for this.*

Charlotte ran at the door, slammed all her weight against it, and shoved. Stronger than Beverly, she was instantly inside the house, a hand's width away. She grabbed Beverly's arm.

Beverly reached for the gun but knew immediately the woman could overpower her. Height, youth, primed muscles—Charlotte would win any physical tussle with her.

Beverly stopped struggling. She stood still, trying to muster calm, trying to remember anything at all from courses she had taken in conflict management when she'd thought she wanted to be a social worker. Nothing useful came to her rescue.

Desperate, she tried conversation. "What do you want?"

"I want," Charlotte paused to catch her breath, "I want my damn life back the way it was before your husband, or whatever he is, started mucking around in it." She leveled the pistol at Beverly's chest.

"I can't help you with that. I have nothing to say about his work. Besides, your problems didn't start with Sam."

Charlotte ignored Beverly's last remark. "I think you can help me a lot." She looked around the kitchen, her eyes as wild as a horse's in flight. "I want you to call him and tell him I have you and that unless he stops this investigation, he'll never see you again."

"I'm pretty sure the state won't let him make a bargain like that."

Charlotte seemed to be inventing as she went. She had no clear plan. *Maybe I'll find an opening to defuse the situation*, Beverly thought, even as her knees began to buckle.

She tilted her head, a gesture she had learned from the horses. "Why don't you sit down? We'll have some tea. We'll talk through your crisis. You don't want to do this. If you're not guilty, why do something that will get you in trouble?"

Beverly stopped talking. *Too many words*, she said to herself. *The woman's not listening.*

A strange smile slid across Charlotte's lips. "You don't think you can outwit me, do you? I'm shortlisted for the Breakthrough Prize in Life Sciences. I'm going to cure brain cancer."

She cackled, near complete hysteria, then caught herself.

"You are, you are, what? A housewife? Lady, you can't even begin to be in my league." She threw back her head and laughed, but her gun was still pointed directly at Beverly's chest.

Beverly raised her chin, her voice suddenly strong and sure. "Beverly Wilson, I'm Beverly Wilson. Call me by my name. I'm no lady."

Charlotte raised her eyebrows, seeming momentarily impressed that Beverly had the kind of quiet courage it took to respond that way with a gun pointed at her. She shook her shoulders, and the gun twitched. "Call him."

"If you kill me, you just add one more body to your indictment."

"Please. Stop playing the heroine. There's not going

to be an indictment. I don't have anything to do with any other dead bodies. Call him."

She's a good liar, Beverly thought as she pulled her cell phone out of her back jeans pocket. Her hands shook. Exerting any remaining control she had over her extremities, Beverly woke her phone, found Sam's number and hit call. She had no idea where he was at this moment. She never asked for a blow-by-blow of his itinerary each day, knowing that, when he was on a case, he didn't know where he would be at any point in the day. He would likely not answer a call from her.

After four rings, Beverly said, "He's not picking up."

"Leave a message."

Beverly wondered how to let Sam know what was happening. *Is there a way to help him find me?* The call rolled over to voice mail.

"Sam." She tried to keep her voice calm and was embarrassed when it shook, ashamed she was so close to sobbing. She didn't want to break down in front of this lunatic. "Charlotte Rolle has me at gunpoint. At the farm. She says you need to stop investigating, or you will never see me again."

She looked up at Charlotte to see if she had complied with her wishes. Charlotte nodded.

"She's going to take me somewhere."

Charlotte nodded again.

"Will you tell him where to find me?" Beverly asked as voice mail continued to record.

"I'll contact him when it's clear he's stopped pursuing me and let him know where to find you. Whether you're alive or not depends on what he does. Tell him he's got one hour to call me and tell me he's calling off his investigation."

"One hour, Sam. You have to contact her in one hour. See you soon." Snugging the phone into her vest pocket without ending end the call, Beverly hoped voice mail would record long enough to give him some sense of where to look for her.

Gun muzzle against Beverly's neck, Charlotte pushed her toward the door. "Enough niceties. Out of the house. Get in my car. You're driving."

Beverly walked eighty feet across the yard to the car without faltering even though her heart banged away in her chest. She opened the Volvo's driver's door and slid into the seat. Sweat rolled down her cheek. *Get hold of yourself. You'll survive this.*

She knew the odds of getting away from Charlotte were not in her favor. *How long can a voice message run? How desperate is this woman?* She hoped voice mail continued to record at least until Charlotte slipped up and told her where they were going. Adjusting the driver's seat so her feet could reach the pedals, she looked over at the horses, alert and skittish, watching her. Jake broke from the rail and galloped the paddock perimeter, tossing his head, whinnying.

"Drive," Charlotte commanded. "I'll tell you where to turn."

Beverly turned the ignition key. The car purred to life. "Left or right at the end of the lane?"

"Left."

"Are we going into town?"

"Just turn where I tell you. You can't outwit me. Don't even try."

Chapter 38

April 1, 3:30 p.m.:

Just like Yoshiki Sasai," Dr. Betty Liu said to her colleagues the minute word reached them about Dickerson's suicide, "who hanged himself in his own research facility after Haruko Obokata destroyed his reputation."

Collectively they looked at her in shock and recoiled, moving away, gathering in a circle at the end of the lab to discuss what to do now. Betty's face mimicked sadness, but no one on Charlotte's research team was fooled. She was referring to a scientist whose brilliant career was brought down by a post-doctoral fellow doing stem cell research under his mentorship. Everyone knew the story. It was a cautionary tale. The drive to publish, to be first to declare victory on some ground-breaking discovery, had made some scientists careless with the truth, with sometimes devastating consequences.

"Obokata," Betty expounded in a loud voice in case any of her colleagues didn't know the story and were still listening, "in case you haven't been keeping up, still claims that she's right—any of the body's cells can be transformed into embryonic stem cells when subjected to extreme stress."

The staff shook their heads and moved out into the hallway, away from Liu. "How insensitive," Dr. Brown muttered. "First she attacks Charlotte for shoddy research methods, and now she's attacking Dr. Dickerson." Her colleagues nodded. They couldn't put enough distance between themselves and Liu.

Sanctimonious prude, Betty thought. She didn't care what they thought about her. She knew she was right. The scientific community had showered Obokata with praise for a breakthrough that promised cures for deadly or crippling illnesses without using embryonic stem cells, and then they turned on her, embarrassed because no one could replicate her results.

When the images and statistics in her papers were revealed to have been cribbed from other people's work, she was cooked. For Charlotte's research staff and colleagues, Betty's suggestion of research fraud struck too close to home. All their careers could be contaminated by such a charge. They could lose their jobs and never find another in their chosen field. They looked at Betty as if she was the carrier of a killer virus for which there was no cure.

Betty didn't care what the rest of the staff thought. They were dispensable. She walked back to her desk and sat in the swivel chair. She woke up her computer and stared at the screen. Something about that detective who tried to talk to her at the funeral today gave her misgivings. It was the way he looked at her as she was leaving the cemetery. She couldn't tell what he was thinking, but she felt judged and somehow diminished. She tried to dismiss him from her mind.

Within half an hour, the lab was empty. Most of her colleagues, aghast at Dickerson's suicide, had gone home. Their faces displayed shock and sorrow, lips quivering, pupils wide. Several had simply wept, standing in the corridor or seated at their desks, wherever they initially heard the news, his death seeming to portend their own.

The few left in their wing of the building, Dickerson's closest administrative staff, were waiting in the conference room to be questioned by Montgomery County Police. Betty found everyone's overwrought emotions discomforting. She had no need to be consoled or to share any stories about Dickerson with anyone. To her, he was a doddering old fool seduced by pheromones.

It would be several weeks, she thought, maybe months before the administration figured out what they wanted to do with Charlotte's project. Perhaps the team would be asked to attempt to replicate the results reported in Charlotte's latest paper. If they were successful, that would relieve the institute of any oversight culpability.

Unlikely they could reproduce Charlotte's results, though, Betty reminded herself. *I've been over those numbers. She lied.*

When the bureaucrats took over, everything would move in slow motion. Perhaps a new center director would have to be appointed even before decisions were made about Charlotte's research. There would be a full-scale review of work to date, maybe by an outside panel, and the inevitable jostling for position on the research ladder.

Betty sighed. *It's all to the good.* The research might improve under new leadership. For a moment, hope flickered. *Maybe Charlotte's hypothesis is right, and she just went about proving it the wrong way. Maybe we can still do it.*

Her brief optimism couldn't be maintained. She'd have to find another position, perhaps move to another state entirely, away from Charlotte. *I'm too involved with her. I should step back.*

The thought that she could take action to protect herself from Charlotte's pull made her feel in charge again. She wasn't a fly caught in a spider's web. She could free herself from all of this complicated foolishness. She wasn't a Summa graduate of Vassar for nothing.

Betty scrolled through several pages of text to give the impression she was working, just in case one of the institute's big shots walked by, but her mind was far away, four days before in what seemed to be another dimension, her own fanciful ripple in the space-time continuum.

She took a deep breath through her nose and exhaled through her mouth to cleanse herself. She had let her meditation practice slip. That was a mistake. She needed vast reserves of calm to call on. Events had gotten out of control. On the other hand, she had surprised even herself, discovering resources, strength, skills, and depths she never knew she had.

When she wasn't following Charlotte, because Charlotte had given her the slip or she simply couldn't bear to watch the woman for another minute—her heart scooped out and the great hollow in her chest aching—she followed Harold. She knew all his haunts, where he went for drinks after work, who he hung out with, all his moves. She had studied him the way she would one of her lab rats to establish a baseline before she injected him with an agent that would either cure or kill him. She didn't think of him as her enemy. He was an intriguing obstacle, one she had to surmount in any way possible.

Harold's behavior the night before he died was particularly repugnant. She had watched him from another table across the restaurant as he regaled his clients with his business and other exploits. It was clear he was having sex with the woman in the group from the way he frequently leaned over and touched her, brushing crumbs from her suit lapel or putting a stray hair behind her ear. The woman's tight smile betrayed annoyance, but Harold was tone deaf to her obvious non-verbal message.

He's marking his territory, Betty thought, fascinated by his ape-like behavior, *making sure the other men know she belongs to him. He's despicable*. After dinner, Betty followed them into the casino and watched Harold laugh as he lost hundreds of dollars at the roulette wheel. He was flying high. It was this new demonstration of his certainty about everything—and the fact that he smoked—that irked her, triggering a rising hate in her throat that made her gag.

When he left the party after their nightcap in the bar, she followed him again. She'd gotten good at following someone, staying back a few cars, keeping her eyes on where he turned. Harold never seemed to notice she was behind him.

He drove into the parking lot of a hotel and went into the bar, ordered a drink, and pulled out his cell phone. Feeling her pulse thrum at the base of her throat with the desperate courage of her gambit, she sat down on the bar stool next to him. He looked over at her. She unbuttoned the top of her blouse. She knew what he liked—the obvious gesture, the crassest invitation.

Harold ended his call and looked over at her. "Hey, I know you. You're in Charlotte's lab, right? I never forget a face." He glowed pink with drink and that certainty she despised.

"Yes," she extended her hand, "Betty Liu."

Harold took her hand, held it for too long, and took another sip of his drink. He swayed a little and leaned toward her until their shoulders touched. He reeked of alcohol. "What is a smart lady like you doing in a place like this?" He laughed raucously at his own words.

"Looking for you, obviously."

His eyes grew wide. She let him put his hand on her thigh. She leaned toward him to give him an eyeful of her cleavage. She was glad he didn't drool. After an excruciating half hour of increasingly vapid small talk, Betty said, "I took a room in the hotel up the road. Want to go?"

Harold grinned. "Of course! It's my night to celebrate."

"Why don't you follow me? I'm in the white Audi with the Maryland plates." She eased off the barstool. Harold paid their bill and followed her. It was all too easy.

Betty leaned back in her work chair and took another deep, cleansing breath. She hadn't expected to go as far as she did. She just wanted something to hold over Charlotte, something to taunt her with. But whatever happened next, she could handle it.

Chapter 39

April 1, 3:30 p.m.:

They grabbed lunch to go from the chicken place on Route 9 and were on their way to Bethesda, Maryland to interview Dr. Betty Liu on the NIH campus. The vehicle had taken on the fried chicken fat smell of their food. Lagarde lowered his window to clear the air and looked away from the endless traffic on I-270.

Taylor had gone surprisingly quiet and was staring fixedly at his phone screen.

"What is it?"

"There's a news alert from the *Washington Post*. 'Prominent medical researcher William Dickerson commits suicide by hanging at NIH.'"

Lagarde ran a hand over his head. "Whew. I didn't see that coming." He had an impulse to pull over to process the information but four lanes of nearly bumper-to-bumper cars speeding along at seventy-plus miles an hour deterred him. He stayed in the left lane and hoped his brain would do two things at once.

Taylor clicked on the story on the paper's website. "They don't have much yet. Apparently, he sent an email

to NIH directors taking personal responsibility for research misconduct at his center. That information is from
an anonymous source, so the email must have been
leaked to the paper. A janitor found him hanging from a
banister on the sixth floor."

He paused while he read further. "Wow, he really
had a lot of degrees. Do you think he killed himself because of Charlotte Rolle?"

Lagarde was speechless. He shook his head to clear
it and quickly ran a hand over his eyes to erase the image
the news sketched for him. Dickerson's suicide unexpectedly hollowed him out. It made no sense to him that an
intelligent man would take his own life because someone
he supervised screwed up. Obviously, he hadn't understood what was at stake.

"How do they know that it's suicide? There hasn't
even been an autopsy yet."

"I guess the note. Anyway, it's a news report. What
do they know beyond that he's dead? Everything else is
speculation and rumor. The photo of him hanging from
the banister might have come from someone's cell phone.
Kind of tasteless, if you ask me."

Taylor looked out of his window at all the other cars
and their determined drivers speeding down the highway.
When he spoke again, his voice was low. "Do you think
we're all in too much of a hurry to get nowhere? Look
how all that effort ends."

Lagarde grimaced. Taylor surprised him. He didn't
have the kid pegged as a philosopher. "Let's stick to what
we know. Maybe that will help us sort out this case."

He lowered the window, thinking that more wind on
his face would make his brain work better. "Harold Munson was killed by two bullets to the head through the
driver's side window of his car in the middle of the night
on March 30. Harold knew his wife was fudging her re-

search results. He and Charlotte were in the middle of a messy divorce. He knew that Charlotte had a man on the side. Even though they have money, property, and were successful in their work, they weren't happy, perhaps because they lost a child. Harold also had at least two ongoing extra-curricular affairs that we know about."

Taylor flipped through his notebook. "Right—no love left between them. All that gives Charlotte plenty of motive, doesn't it?"

"Maybe. If she's the jealous type, but I'm not sure she is. Charlotte regularly had sex with Nick Waters and also maybe Mark Wiseman. We know she'd at least met Wiseman from the note you found in her house. Waters thought she was having occasional sex with Wiseman. With all that extra-marital activity, I'm not sure she was jealous of her husband."

"Okay. So scratch the jealousy motive."

"So we move on to Wiseman who also was killed with two gun shots—maybe the killer's hallmark—this time to the chest at close range on March thirty-first, sometime in the early afternoon, one day after Munson was killed. The murders seem to be linked but only because they both knew Charlotte."

Taylor put small checkmarks against notes on his pad. "Waters told us Charlotte was at the house when Wiseman was killed, but that's still hearsay. Also, he might be her accomplice. Her prints are everywhere there, but that doesn't necessarily mean she was in the house when Wiseman was killed, or that she killed him. Nick's story could be a desperate fabrication to get out from under his crime."

Lagarde readjusted his posture in the seat. "We have two problems. The first is that Nick says he doesn't care who Charlotte sleeps with, and I believe him about that. So he has no real motive to kill Wiseman. Our second problem is, we don't have any evidence showing Charlotte did either killing, although possible motives point that way. Bodies are falling all around her. We need something that proves she's more than a casual beneficiary of all this death."

He took a quick look in all the car's mirrors, pulled into the right lane to pass the slower driver in front of him and then back into his previous lane. "With Dickerson's claim of responsibility for her research fraud and that statistician, Norton's assertions about how she screwed up her data analysis, Charlotte's professional life is going to take a detour through hell, but that still doesn't make her complicit in the deaths of two people. We don't have evidence of a conspiracy."

Taylor nodded. "Yeah, we've got plenty of breadcrumbs and no loaf." He grinned.

Lagarde hooted. *This kid might save my sanity.* He maneuvered into the left lane for the exit to Bethesda, then got into the right lane on Wisconsin Avenue. After being stopped at each of four red lights and noting there was more traffic on this one half-mile stretch in Bethesda than he would see in a year in Charles Town, he turned right into the NIH campus at the Visitor entrance. At the gate, Lagarde showed his credentials and asked the guard where the building he wanted was located and where he could park. The guard pointed to a six-story building where local police presence was obvious with four marked cars pulled up in front.

Inside the lobby, police tape barred access to one of the stairwells and crime scene unit personnel swarmed around the reception and stairwell area. Lagarde and Taylor stopped at the reception desk, showed their credentials, and asked to speak to Dr. Liu. In fifteen minutes they were escorted into a plain conference room on the reception level with gray venetian-blind-covered windows that looked out on several other buildings of various styles. They sat in the black Aeron swivel chairs and waited for Betty Liu.

When she entered the room, Lagarde was again surprised, not only by Liu but by his own thought. *I'm a rat in a maze being taught something new, but I can't figure out what it is or where the damn cheese is hidden.*

Liu had removed the jacket she wore to Harold's funeral and walked confidently into the room in a white silk blouse and straight gray skirt that stopped short of her knees. In the same black pumps as at Munson's funeral, small pearl earrings, her short nails unpolished, and her ID badge hung around her neck on a blue lanyard, she seemed to be half of Lagarde's idea of what a woman scientist would look like, except that on the side of her neck just under her right ear was a tiny dragon tattoo.

Does she breathe fire? Lagarde wondered.

Liu paused at the table for a second before she sat, giving them an opportunity to enjoy the perfect symmetry of her heart-shaped face and slender body. When she sat, she leaned back and folded her hands in her lap, in complete control of herself.

Lagarde leaned forward. "I'm sorry to bother you on the day of Mr. Munson's funeral..."

She waved her hand, not letting him finish his sentence. "No matter. We weren't friends. I went to the funeral as a courtesy to Dr. Rolle. I'm on her research team, as you know. We all work closely together."

Somehow, the world has grown a crop of brilliant, beautiful, self-possessed women who are now infiltrating every segment of society previously considered male enclaves. Lagarde felt a little anxious about this turn of events. Beverly would mock him endlessly for that thought if she knew. He would never tell her. But the fact was, Marie Curie was the only woman scientist he remembered, and Madame Curie didn't look anything like these women. *Maybe I was never taught about any others. Is it possible that was deliberate, that the history of science has always been written by men with an eye to taking all the credit?*

He shook off his failure to know anything about the scientific world with an almost visible twitch of his shoulders and tried another approach to knock Liu off her perch. "Sorry to hear the shocking news about Dr. Dickerson."

Liu shrugged and raised her fierce dark eyebrows. "And?"

Lagarde plowed forward, now realizing the woman might be unflappable. "I understand you think Dr. Rolle's cancer treatment isn't the success she claims it is."

Betty tilted her head and looked at him, squinting slightly, seeming to determine whether his brain was capable of understanding her. "I think Charlotte's concept is brilliant and potentially workable or I wouldn't be here. Several other research teams are working on similar ideas."

She paused to let her words sink in, appearing concerned he was slow on the uptake. "Molecular or immunological approaches to disease are the new frontier in medical science. This is the cutting edge. I'm here because I thought Charlotte's idea showed more promise for a radical cure sooner than any of the other approaches."

Lagarde thought he saw a slight blush begin at the base of her throat as she said Charlotte's name. *This woman doesn't have as much control of herself as she thinks.*

She cleared her throat and continued. "Dr. Rolle's approach is unique. But I don't think we have quite arrived at the correct method. We're missing something."

She paused for a second and allowed her eyes to

stray to Taylor, who was sitting across the table from her, his eyes glazed, trying without much success to understand what she was saying. She seemed to enjoy his confusion. "We need more testing with animals before we move on to human subjects. But I'm convinced we'll find the solution."

Taylor flipped to a new page in his notebook. "Let me get this straight. If Dr. Rolle isn't allowed to continue her research, her team would be able to go on with the work?"

"Of course. There are no patents in place. Although the research is applied, in the sense that we are looking to solve a specific human disease problem, it is still research based on a hypothesis, a hunch. If we find the miracle approach to curing brain cancer, other researchers will attempt to replicate our work to validate it."

Taylor ran the flat of his palm over his forehead, as if he were making room in his brain for new information. "I thought Rolle had backing from pharmaceutical companies. Didn't you all have to sign non-disclosure agreements?"

"Not yet. She has research grants, and we've been publishing openly. The approach isn't advanced enough for FDA approval or for a pharmaceutical company to have licensed it. If it doesn't work, we can go back to the whiteboard and think again. Although, I expect that Dr. Dickerson's email admitting research misconduct rolls the clock back a few years on Charlotte's approach becoming an effective treatment."

To Lagarde's eye, Liu's face betrayed a certain satisfaction with this outcome—a kind of "I told you so" attitude.

Liu turned her sharp chin toward Taylor, half-lowered her eyelids, and curled her lips in a disdainful smile that sent a jolt through Lagarde's spine. *Did Dr. Liu have a motive for derailing Charlotte's career? Was it possible this composed woman planned and executed two murders to discredit her colleague?*

Lagarde switched subjects. "Did you know Harold well?"

"I met him once at a party a few years ago when I first joined Charlotte's team. I wasn't impressed."

Taylor nearly choked. He looked down at his pad and took a breath. "Before today for Harold's funeral, when were you in Jefferson County?"

"Frankly, I don't know where we went today. That's why I rode with Allen."

That wasn't an answer to Taylor's question. *Two evasions, hiding some big lie,* Lagarde thought. "Where were you on March thirtieth at one-thirty a.m.?"

"Sleeping, in my apartment." The fingers on her right hand twitched briefly.

That was surely a lie, Lagarde thought. "Was anyone with you?"

She smiled slowly. "My cat, Ernest."

"Where's your apartment?"

"I can walk to it from here. It's off Pooks Hill Road."

Not much of an alibi. The cat can't talk. Lagarde liked his new favorite theory that Dr. Liu was the "She" that Beverly had said he should look for. It was a long shot, and he had to make sure she had a motive. "Do I understand this correctly? With Charlotte Rolle and William Dickerson out of the way, you get to take over her research?"

"Oh, no. Not me. Someone far more senior than I will be appointed to lead the work, if that's the decision of the research review board. I'll have to decide whether it's a good fit for me to stay here or if I need to find a new position elsewhere."

"You don't like Charlotte Rolle, do you?"

Betty looked up at the ceiling, down at the table, and dragged her eyes across the glamor photos of scientists at work on the wall opposite her to look at Lagarde. "I never said I didn't like her."

She's lying about something. Something big that matters. I'm wasting my time. She's just playing with us. He reminded himself they were interviewing Liu because Dickerson said she had issues with Charlotte. Would Dickerson have deliberately misled him? These people have their own agendas that have nothing to do with truth. *I need some daylight.*

"You're saying you had no motive to kill Harold Munson or to engineer Charlotte Rolle's professional demise."

Liu tilted her head and slowly formed words, her lips accentuating every syllable, making it clear she thought he was a simpleton and she had to explain again what she'd already said. For the first time in the interview, she leaned forward across the table, almost whispering. "That's correct, detective. I have no motive to kill Harold Munson, and I didn't engineer Charlotte's misconduct. She did that all by herself. She wasn't up to the task she set herself. She should've listened to her team. She's made a terrible mess for all of us."

Lagarde, suddenly incensed without understanding the reason, pushed back from the table and stood. "Sorry to have wasted your time." He nodded at Liu, put on his hat, and walked out of the conference room. Taylor was right on his heels.

Walking through the reception area, Taylor asked, "Do you believe her?"

"Not for a minute. Ostensibly, she has no motive, no reason to lie. And we've got zero evidence or cause to arrest her. But just to make sure, when we get back, run a background check on her. Find out where she got her degrees, where she was before here, and if she failed to get a license for her cat."

Lagarde reached into his jacket pocket for the car keys and found his phone. "Oh crap. Completely forgot about this thing." He looked up at Taylor's surprised face. "Guess that's not something your generation ever forgets, is it?"

He looked at the phone screen and noticed the voice mail icon had a tiny number one inside a red circle. He had a message. "Why didn't I hear the phone ring?" He turned the phone around in his hands. "Oh, yeah, I turned the sound off when we were at the cemetery."

Taylor rolled his eyes and Lagarde listened to his message. His jaw tightened, and his face paled. "It's Beverly. Charlotte's got her." He took a deep breath and replayed the message. "That was an hour ago." All his breath caught in his throat. He barreled down the front steps to the car with Taylor fast on his heels.

"I'll drive, sir," Taylor said.

Lagarde threw him the keys and listened to the message again. *Beverly is trying to tell me something more than that she's been abducted.*

Chapter 40

April 1, 5 p.m.:

In forty minutes, though it seemed longer, having raced at ninety miles an hour with the siren blaring north on I-270 and west on Route 340, Lagarde and Taylor were at Charlotte Rolle's door, banging, shouting, "Beverly, Beverly. Charlotte. Dr. Rolle."

While Taylor drove, Lagarde called in backup, using Charlotte's address as the location to assemble. "Abduction in progress," he explained, "hostage situation. Victim is a woman in her sixties. Perp has a weapon. Approach only on my say so."

That was as much as he could say for now. All the other words he might have used were jumbled in his throat, corked by fear.

Lagarde made no attempt to be stealthy. He ordered the troopers to break down the front door. "She knows I'm coming for her," he'd said through nearly closed lips as Taylor screeched the car to a halt in front of the house. "She asked for this."

Taylor and five troopers sprinted to the back of the house, found a way in through the French doors from the back patio, and ran through the house, top to bottom. No one was there.

Lagarde also ran through the house, his mouth dry, his face pinched. He wanted to yell at the top of his lungs, but he couldn't pull enough air into them to make a sound. The universe didn't have enough space in it for his fury and fear. Rage filled every iota of his body. He could have torn Charlotte to bits with his bare hands, with his teeth. Lagarde stopped himself, stood still and breathed deeply. *Calm, be calm*, he cautioned himself, *focus*.

Charlotte left no clues as to where she might have taken Beverly. Lagarde's mind raced through possibilities. They were endless. She could have taken Beverly anywhere. He listened to the voice mail again, on speaker so that Taylor could listen also. They had left his farm, navigated to the highway, and exited the highway in Charles Town.

Beverly's voice was clear, if shaky, in the recorded message. "Was that a left on One-Fifteen?" she asked Charlotte. The response was fuzzy, but the words could be made out. He turned up the sound volume. "Beverly's trying to tell me where to find her." He had only a second to relish the pride he felt at her courage before his fear and fury kicked in again.

"Yes, left on One-Fifteen then right on Millville," said the other voice Lagarde assumed was Charlotte's.

"A right on Millville? You're sure."

"Oh, no, a left."

"Okay. Make a left on Millville."

Charlotte seems disoriented, Lagarde thought. Perhaps that was a sign she was having a nervous breakdown rather than ramping up her killing spree. Kidnapping Beverly was certainly a complicated and dangerous way of getting even with him for exposing her research fraud. *Whatever her motive, the woman's gone over the edge.*

The sound of tires on less than perfect asphalt played on the recording, the car motor hum, some rustling sound and then, "There, turn left there."

"Is that Millville Road?" Beverly's voice again.

"Yes, whatever it is, turn left right..." The message ended.

The seconds ticked by while they scanned the maps in their minds. "The river," Taylor yelled, sprinting toward their car. "Charlotte's taking Beverly to the Shenandoah, near where Wiseman lives. It's nearly deserted there this time of year. Summer folks haven't moved in yet. The river's high."

Lagarde looked at him, felt his heart rate drop for a split second. Giving instructions to the rest of the troopers, he raced to the car. Taylor drove like a bat out of hell. Within a mile of Wiseman's place, Lagarde suddenly remembered to check his texts.

Charlotte had texted: *Stop investigating, or I'll kill Beverly. You have 1 hr to confirm.* The text was two hours old.

I'll never ignore this damn device again.

Lagarde read the text out loud to Taylor, who groaned. "Jesus. She's gone completely off the rails."

"Yes." Lagarde's face was a study in control. "And she's got two hours on us. Beverly could be dead already." All his will power was directed at keeping himself at maximum operating efficiency while his mind was screaming *No, No, No!* in a half-entreaty, half-command to the Almighty he rarely acknowledged.

He couldn't let himself be frightened by Charlotte's threat. *Okay*, he texted back, *consider the investigation over.*

It didn't matter what he said to a crazy person. This wasn't a contract negotiation. He'd say anything to get Beverly home safely. He didn't care about honor. He didn't have to keep his word. Anyway, Charlotte might well be past reading his response.

Taylor drove five more miles, five police cars blaring their sirens behind him, and then they rounded the last bend in the road on high alert for any movement outside of Wiseman's house, for the flash of a muzzle, or a sign this was an ambush. Charlotte's car was in the driveway.

They swarmed Wiseman's house. No one was in the house or in the immediate vicinity. They ran down the road and over to the river, scanning in both directions. "Spread out," Lagarde called

Police fanned out east and west along the river and up into the nearby unoccupied wooded lots. Lagarde and Taylor trudged through the underbrush at the edge of the river. Water rushed by them, at least five feet higher than normal, skimming the bank. Lagarde's eyes scanned everything that moved. He dreaded finding Beverly lying dead on the ground. He dreaded not finding her. Every step took him deeper into that dread. He couldn't run fast enough. He glanced over at Taylor. The guy was all steely resolve. He decided for sure that he liked Jim Taylor.

Suddenly, Taylor put his arm out and stopped their forward motion. "Look," he pointed, "over there, at the top of the dam. I see two people."

Lagarde stared. "It's them."

He could barely get enough breath to pass between his lips to make a sound. He took off, running beyond his own strength, beyond his own endurance. At thirty yards away the situation was clear. Charlotte was forcing Beverly to walk out into the river at gunpoint.

Beverly clung to the end of a long branch that reached out over the water from an old birch. If she lost her footing, if that branch snapped, she would be swept away by the rough water, over the dam to the rocks below.

Lagarde could see only Beverly, his friend, and companion, the woman he had thought he would never meet, standing in water rushing around her hips, pushing her legs downstream with it, her hands clinging to the branch, refusing to move any farther. Her white hair was blown into a halo around her head. He walked resolutely through the tall yellow grass at the river bank to where Charlotte could see him

He held his hands out from his body, palms toward her to demonstrate he wasn't holding a weapon. "Dr. Rolle," he called out in the calmest voice he could muster. "I'm here."

She turned her head and looked at him. For a moment, she seemed not to remember who he was. Her face was blank, her eyes wild. Lagarde kept moving toward her.

"I'm Detective Lagarde. You texted me. I'm here." Out of the corner of his eye, he saw Beverly get a better grip on the branch and begin inching back toward the shore. *She's okay, she's really okay,* he told himself.

Charlotte stared at him, her face still not registering recognition. The gun wavered in her hand, but she didn't lower her arm or change the direction of her aim. "You're too late," she screamed finally. "You waited too long. It's over now. I'm done with this."

Lagarde moved closer to Charlotte. "It's not too late," he yelled. "Beverly's okay. I can see from here she's unharmed. Lower your weapon, walk over to me."

"You don't understand anything. You messed up my life. Dickerson knows about my research. Everything is over. Nothing matters anymore."

"Drop the weapon. We can talk about it. Let Beverly go."

He kept talking, watching Charlotte's face as she considered what he was saying. He talked as Taylor moved stealthily toward her from behind. Taylor rushed her, grabbed her gun hand, and turned her away from Beverly. The gun waved in the air as Taylor struggled with her. A shot rang out, and then Taylor disarmed her, slamming her to the ground and cuffing her.

Lagarde ran out to Beverly, not worrying about his shoes or clothes, not concerned with anything except retrieving her, getting her to safety. He slipped twice on the muddy bottom, nearly falling into the rushing water, righted himself against the swift pull of the water, and reached her. He wrapped his arms around her and carried her out of the river to the bank.

Beverly pressed her face against his shoulder. "I knew you'd rescue me. I knew you'd come," she said between sobs.

Lagarde wanted to weep with her. He didn't tell her he hadn't been sure he would get to her in time. Her faith in him gave him back all the breath he needed. On the shore, she collapsed against him, and he held her for as long as it took for her sobs to subside.

"You're my brave girl," he said, and when she looked up at him, he corrected himself, "woman, my brave woman." He embraced her fiercely and kissed her mouth. "God, whatever you want me to call you, I'm proud of you, and I'm glad you're alive."

The ambulance, siren blaring, screeched to a stop at the river's edge. Emergency medical techs jumped out and ran to Lagarde and Beverly. Taylor corralled Charlotte in a semi-circle of state police and the county deputies. She wasn't getting away.

One arm wrapped around a still-shuddering Beverly, unconcerned with his own soaking clothes, Lagarde jerked his thumb toward Taylor and said to Sheriff Harbaugh. "Take our suspect, Charlotte Rolle, to the regional jail for holding prior to interrogation. Usual intake drill for a suspect apprehended during an abduction with a deadly weapon. But be gentle. She's a scientist."

While the EMTs gave Beverly the once over to make sure she was suffering from nothing more than shock and terror, Lagarde turned to Taylor. "Can you hop a ride with one of the troopers back to headquarters and start the paperwork? I'm going to take Beverly home."

The words home and Beverly belonged together, made a nest in his heart. He stifled the sob in his throat.

Taylor nodded. "Maybe we can't connect Charlotte to the murders but we sure as hell have her on kidnapping and attempted assault with a deadly weapon." His voice was calm, but his eyes burned, giving away the fierce fury in his gut.

⌇⌇⌇

They drove for ten minutes in silence. The image of Beverly standing in the river, clutching the branch, kept rising up in Lagarde's memory. *I can't lose her. I have to be more careful.*

Still wrapped in the silver blanket the EMTs gave her, she turned her pale face to him. "I was wrong. My theory of the crime was wrong. She's not your killer." Beverly's shivering had stopped, and her voice was back to its normal assured tone.

Lagarde thought he might lose his composure, but he held onto himself a little longer, one hand gripping the steering wheel, the other holding Beverly's icy hand. "Why do you say that?"

"If she was a killer, she would have killed me at the farm, or when we got to the river. She had a gun. She would have shot me, dumped me in the river, and run. A dead body is more of a warning to you than an attempt to kill me. Right? She's confused and desperate, but she's not a killer."

Lagarde looked at Beverly and then back at the road. "Wait. Just because she didn't kill you, doesn't mean she didn't kill her husband or Wiseman."

Beverly nodded. "I know there's no equivalency. But she knew that abducting me wasn't going to get her anything, certainly not out of the professional mess she's in. Forcing me to walk out into the river was an act of desperation. We waited over an hour on the porch of someone's house for you to respond to her text."

"She held you on Wiseman's porch? Wow, she is over the top."

"Oh, was that Wiseman's house? I wondered about the police tape. I think she was trying not to kill me. Walking me out to the river was a way of delaying what she had said she would do. She had doubts about it. She was waiting for you. She bought her gun today at a pawn shop, for God's sake. She didn't kill her husband or that Baltimore cop. I'm sure of it. She's clueless about how to commit any crime except lying about her research."

"You're certainly adamant about this for someone who was on the other side of that gun for two hours."

She smiled at him and squeezed his hand. "Then you should listen to me."

The world was immediately better as far as Lagarde was concerned.

Chapter 41

April 1, 7 p.m.:

Lagarde and Taylor walked into the windowless interview room together and took in its piss-yellow cinderblock walls, scarred stainless steel table marked by dried spittle and forehead-sized dents, the suspect chair bolted to the floor, the faint smell of bleach over vomit. Metal handcuffs were soldered to the table.

This, Lagarde thought, *is the last place Charlotte Rolle ever expected to be.* Oddly fragile looking in the prison jumpsuit, particularly wearing the required black, plastic sandals over white socks, Charlotte was appropriately miserable. She sat with her back hunched, her head lowered, completely cowed. Her glamour had been whisked away by jailhouse efficiency, reduced to anonymity, diminished to the number on her jumpsuit. *The only brains that matter in here*, Lagarde thought with a certain deep satisfaction, *are those you use to stay alive and out of trouble.*

He briefly wished Dickerson had seen Charlotte like this before he decided to take his own life. This scene alone might have dissuaded him from believing every-thing was his fault, or that her actions had anything to do with the value of his life. He might have, for a brief mo-ment, seen Charlotte as human and fallible.

"She doesn't need to be handcuffed," Lagarde told the attending uniformed guard.

The guard unlocked the cuffs, and Charlotte shook her arms loose. She shot him a look of gratitude and con-fusion. Exactly the result he wanted.

The county prosecutor and Charlotte's lawyer were in the room as well—the prosecutor to make sure Lagarde didn't slip up during questioning and throw away his case, the lawyer to protect his client from saying anything that would be held against her at trial. There had been a small tempest about whether Lagarde should in-terview Charlotte at all, given his close association with her latest victim, but he'd talked his way through that.

Charlotte folded her hands together on the table and waited. It was clear from her puffy eyes she'd been cry-ing. Not for her husband or Wiseman, or even for how she had terrified Beverly, of that, Lagarde was sure. She was crying for herself, her lost career, the complete dec-imation of any possibility for fame in that rarified envi-ronment in which she worked. Lagarde closed his eyes briefly and took a deep breath. He shouldn't get himself worked up. His anger would leak out in his questions.

He paced back and forth for a minute then stood at the end of the table to force her to turn her head and look in his direction. "Let's start at the beginning. You were arguing with your husband about the division of property during a divorce proceeding. Right?" It was a simple question, one she should say yes to—a way of getting her into a habit of complying.

Charlotte looked up at him and then looked away at something in the far distance in her mind. "Yes, although now I don't really know why I was fighting with him. Just reflex, I guess."

Her lawyer gave her a warning look and briefly put his hand on her arm, inclining his head toward hers to speak into her ear. "Only answer what you're asked."

"Harold discovered you were cheating on your research results and threatened to go to your boss with proof in order to get you to back off your demand for all the property you owned together. Is that right?"

"Yes."

Lagarde walked behind the prosecutor and stood directly in front of Charlotte. "And in the early morning hours of March thirtieth, after you did yoga, had dinner with friends, and went to your boyfriend's house—"

"Nick Waters isn't my boyfriend." Charlotte impatiently shook off her lawyer's restraining hand. She looked defiantly at Lagarde, daring him to push that point.

Lagarde nodded to acknowledge her response. "So, you had sex with Nick Waters, left his house, and then waited for Harold at one-thirty a.m. in the post office parking lot on Charles Town Road for him to drive by after his late night client meeting and you shot him. Is that correct?"

Lagarde already knew this scenario wasn't true. Stating it as fact was a maneuver to induce Charlotte to angrily rebut his statement and tell him the truth about what had happened.

This interrogation method sometimes made the suspect feel smarter than the detective and, if she took the bait, increased the likelihood she would slip up and incriminate herself.

"No. That's absurd. I didn't shoot him. I was still at Nick's house." Charlotte's lawyer leaned over and whispered into her ear. "I'm sorry, Detective," Charlotte added, "I didn't mean to say you are absurd, just your con-jecture."

Her lawyer's lips turned down at the corners. Lagarde thought the lawyer might be considering how difficult she would be to manage in court. Sam ignored the look of anxiety in the prosecutor's eyes and continued his questioning.

"You had previously hired Mark Wiseman to kill Harold. You gave Wiseman the key to Harold's car. After Harold texted you that his meeting was over, you told Wiseman where Harold would be in the early morning hours of March thirtieth, and *he* waited for Harold at the intersection and shot him."

"No. Of course, not." Charlotte tossed her head the way she used to, but somehow the gesture didn't have the same effect. "I did not hire Mark Wiseman to kill him. I asked Mark to follow him and keep me apprised of what Harold was up to, to get some advantage in the property dispute so that he wouldn't go to Dickerson with the little mistake he found in my data analysis. That's all. Mark wasn't supposed to shoot him."

"Do you think Mark shot him?"

"I don't know who shot him. Mark said he was fol-lowing Harold, but he had to pass him because when he came around the bend, he saw Harold had stopped his car in the middle of the road when the car in front of him stopped. Mark didn't want to risk being noticed. He said he drove up the road and turned around. By the time he got back to the intersection, Harold's car had gone through the wall of a building."

She paused for breath, her eyes closed, seeming to consult her memory. "Mark told me the car Harold slowed for drove away as he approached. He thought Harold was injured from the crash. He parked in the bank lot next to the post office and walked across the road.

Harold was already dead when he got to him. He used the key I gave him to search Harold's car for something incriminating, just in case I still needed it, and took a photo of Harold to show me he was dead. He texted the photo to me so I would know what happened, not to prove anything. He said he was debating whether to call nine-one-one when a man showed up at the insurance office. I believe him. I don't think he killed Harold. It doesn't make sense that he would kill him." She sighed. "I didn't need Harold dead."

"Were you paying Wiseman?"

Charlotte scowled, her eyebrows meeting in a V above her nose, her mouth twisted. "No. Of course, not."

"If Mark didn't kill Harold, do you think Nick killed him for you?"

Charlotte looked at Lagarde with disbelief, her eyebrows now rising—the wings of a hawk in flight. Lagarde resisted an impulse to shield his head with his arm.

"Why would Nick kill him for me?"

"That's what Nick said."

Charlotte didn't look surprised. She leaned back and took a deep breath, exhaling slowly.

Lagarde looked over at Taylor, read his face, and continued. "When Wiseman tried to blackmail you for the murder of your husband, you shot him and framed Nick Waters for that murder, thus cleaning up all your loose ends, except for Dickerson, who took care of himself. Is that how it went?"

"No. Dickerson? What do you mean?"

"You didn't hear on the news that William Dickerson committed suicide today?" Lagarde watched Charlotte's face pale. He drove the point home. "You're not aware he wrapped a rope around his neck and jumped from a banister in your research building?"

Charlotte swayed back in the chair and put her hand

over her mouth. She closed her eyes and shook her head. "Oh, God. This is impossible." Leaning forward, Charlotte picked at the orange fabric on her knee and looked up at him.

For the first time, Lagarde thought she might be having a normal human reaction to someone else's tragedy, and then she spoke.

"How is it none of you understand I didn't have anything to do with any of these deaths? I'm only doing my work. I'm saving lives, not taking them. My work is of vital importance to the entire world. I'm only a few years away from cracking it, and once I've done that, no brain cancer will ever kill anyone again. Millions of lives will be saved. Don't you understand how important it is? The rest of this is—"

Lagarde shifted to dead calm. "Let's go back to Mark Wiseman's murder. You were in the house when he was murdered?"

"Yes. We had sex. I was taking a shower. I heard two shots fired. The noise scared me. I had no idea what was going on. I jumped out of the shower, threw on my clothes, and ran into the living room. He was lying on the floor where I'd left him asleep. He had two bullet holes in his chest, and blood was seeping out of him, across the floor. I'm not good with blood. I—I lost it. I didn't know what to do. I couldn't think. I ran back into the bathroom and threw up and then I called Nick to help me."

"So your way of solving the problem of a dead body was to dispose of it? Why didn't you call the police if you didn't shoot him? Or call for medical help for him."

"I don't know. I wasn't thinking, as I said. I could see he was dead. There was no point in getting medical help. Nick said we should call the police, but I thought if the police found me there with him, they would think what you do—that I killed my husband and then Mark."

Lagarde nodded. "Yes. I see your problem. Did you hear a car pull away in the driveway or a door open and close before the shots?"

"No. I was in the shower. The water was running. The only thing I heard was bang, bang. I was terrified. I thought I would be next." Her face said clearly she thought he was an idiot.

Taylor looked briefly at Lagarde and asked, "So what's your theory about how your husband and Mark were killed?"

"I have no theory. None of it makes any sense. Someone is trying to destroy my life without actually murdering me. I don't know who hates me that much."

Lagarde stood straighter, his chin lifted, assessing all the messages carried on the air the way Jake did. Charlotte's narcissistic assertion that other people's deaths were an attempt to destroy *her* life aside, that was exactly the idea he had after they interviewed Dr. Liu. Someone was deliberately trying to destroy Charlotte's career. At any rate, it was a line of inquiry worth exploring.

"Is there a colleague, or a competitor, who wants to harm you or impede your research?"

"No one, really. I don't think. My true peers are all deeply engaged in their own work. I've had my little struggles with personnel on my research team, but I think they've all been resolved."

"There's no one who might feel you slighted him, or didn't give her the recognition she deserved? Someone whose work you plagiarized or whose idea you stole?" Lagarde knew he was being unkind, but he didn't care. He watched her cheeks burn red, with indignation perhaps. "Dr. Dickerson mentioned some kind of hassle with Dr. Betty Liu."

"Oh. Liu. Oh." Charlotte looked at her lawyer, who seemed dumbfounded. She hadn't told him everything.

She turned back to Lagarde, a new blush suffusing her lovely neck. "I had a fling with Betty, a brief one. She may have thought the relationship was more important than I did. She may have imagined we would be together when Harold and I divorced, but I'm fairly sure I didn't give her any reason to think so. I tried in a dozen not-so-subtle ways to let her know we were not lovers. She seems to have gone a little overboard about her passion for me, but she wouldn't kill anyone. She's a scientist."

Right, because all scientists are saints, and they only kill with their magic potions. In vivid detail, Lagarde suddenly saw Charlotte, her arm extended, gun pointed at Beverly, forcing her to walk out into the raging river. He saw the fear on Beverly's face, her fingers gripping the branch, the water rushing around her hips. He wanted to leap across the table and slap Charlotte until her eyes rattled in her imperious head, but he held onto his temper.

"One more thing, Ms. Rolle." Lagarde deliberately left off the honorific title of doctor. "You abducted Beverly Wilson, a person who had nothing to do with your life in any way, and you held her at gunpoint for more than two hours, forcing her into the Shenandoah River, possibly intending that she would drown. Is that accurate?"

Charlotte looked away from him. "I'm sorry about that. I briefly lost my mind and didn't know what to do. But in the end, I didn't kill her, did I?" Her eyes flashed at him.

Lagarde abruptly left the room. She had admitted the abduction. Her confession was recorded. The prosecutor and her lawyer, who was now counseling her to stop talking, were present. She wouldn't get off, no matter how she pleaded, and Taylor would follow through. There was enough firepower in the room to wrap up that case with a big bow and present it in court, if it came to that.

He didn't need to be there to see how they did it.

Even if she pleaded no contest to the abduction charges and threw herself on the mercy of the court, Charlotte would do a few years in an unscientific environment. That was enough. As far as he was concerned, he had his revenge.

Charlotte's life as she knew it was over. There wasn't any cure for the stigma of jail.

Chapter 42

March 30, 1:30 a.m.:

*T*his is a stroke of luck, Harold told himself. Just
what he needed—a little strange sex before he
went home to that cold fish who was still his wife.
He couldn't wait for that arrangement to be over. All the
blood in his body pulsed through his groin as he followed
Betty Liu over back roads onto Charles Town Road.

He wondered briefly how she knew where she was
going and then remembered that GPS made everyone na-
tives of everywhere. *She must be heading to the hotel by
the IRS complex in Kearneysville. How'd she ever find
that place?*

For a second, he had a moment's regret about standing Barbara up. He'd send her flowers tomorrow and
make some excuse. He could have Barbara anytime he
wanted, but he doubted he would have sex with this
woman from Charlotte's lab more than once. This would
be one more conquest he could gloat about if Charlotte
tried to belittle him. He had no qualms about the fact that
he hadn't a clue what brought Betty up to Charles Town
in the middle of the night.

I might be a little drunk, he admitted to himself.

In fact, the mystery of Betty Liu made this turn of events extra delectable. For another second, he thought he might have misunderstood her—his teen years of always being wrong, always saying the wrong thing, thinking the wrong thing flashed through his mind—but no, that was definitely a come-on she gave him in the bar.

A flash in his gut said *this might be dangerous*. He shook off the intuition. She had unbuttoned her blouse, leaned into him, and told him to follow her. He didn't misinterpret her signals. He wasn't the aggressor. That's what was so intriguing about her.

Harold automatically scanned properties along Charles Town Road, always on alert for fresh opportunities. The new highway had a devastating effect on the small businesses that had dotted this two-lane road between Charles Town and Martinsburg for as long as anyone could remember. The buildings were all closed up now and impossible to sell for commercial purposes because no customers would drive by here.

Even farm stands couldn't make it if no one impulsively stopped to buy tomatoes or apples. As much as he hoped the Datapile deal would come through and all those high-paid workers would move into the area bringing a demand for goods and new businesses, Harold missed the rural county where he grew up.

His parents missed it also, even though they settled into a comfortable retirement after selling their 500-acre farm for more than a million dollars to a developer.

"The new crop is houses," he had told his despairing father when he complained about impatient drivers honking at him to get his slow-moving combine off the road as he went from field to field or transplanted city folks who whined to the county commission about the smell of manure wafting over from the farm.

"Sell the land, take what would be fifty years in profits from crops, and buy a beautiful house for Mom. She deserves it."

His father did as he suggested. Now, when Harold drove by the subdivided property where a hundred roofs glinted in the sunshine, his heart broke a little. Last year, he couldn't even smell peaches on the air as he had every year in August since he was a small child and learned how to discern one smell from another.

He used to step out onto the porch on a sunny afternoon and inhale that special sweetness that meant peaches, delight cascading through his body as if his chin already dripped with juice. That week there would be a peach pie on the table for dessert. It was part of his mother's magic, he thought when he was little, that she knew what he hankered for, like strawberry-rhubarb pie, or blueberry pie with vanilla ice cream from the dairy up the road. All of that was gone in the name of progress. His mother now bought her pies at the farmer's market on Sunday mornings. They didn't taste the same.

Betty Liu slowed in front of him as they neared the light at the intersection of Charles Town Road and Kearneysville Pike. Harold had time to notice the car behind him came to a sudden stop fifty feet back and then passed him using the parking lot on his right and continued on through the intersection. When the passing car was gone, Betty's car screeched forward, made a looping U-turn and came back toward him.

He slowed to a stop, thinking Betty had changed her mind and now wanted to give him the brush off. That was really okay with him. He didn't need the sex. He scored when she invited him to follow her. He was happy to call it a day.

Harold watched Betty roll down her window. He saw her hand rise from her lap and thought she was indicating he should lower his window so they could talk. The gun barrel glinted in the moonlight.

Drive! his brain screamed. His body jerked away from Betty's car, foot slamming on the gas, hands pulling the steering wheel sharply to the right even before he heard the explosion that propelled the bullet out of the chamber.

Harold's car careened into the blue clapboard building on the other side of a small parking lot. He had forgotten how to stop it, his foot hovering between the gas and the brake, unsure of which to press. He saw the wood siding buckle then rip apart as the car slid through the wall like a knife through peach pie. The airbag exploded in his face, and he sighed, thinking he was all right, it was just an accident. She hadn't really shot at him. His tire had blown. He had misunderstood what he saw.

He rested a few seconds, then opened his eyes to start assessing the damage, and saw Betty Liu get out of her car, stomp over to him, and point a gun at his window. *Drive,* his brain screamed, *get away.* But he couldn't move a muscle. He closed his eyes.

Chapter 43

April 1, 8 p.m.:

On his way back to headquarters to check his emails and complete piles of paperwork, Lagarde phoned Beverly. "How're you doing?"

"I'm fine. Don't worry about me. I'm drinking tea, listening to music, and thinking. Any headway?"

"No. You were right, though. She's not the killer. We still don't know who killed Munson or Wiseman. The murder case is wide open. I'm thinking of just handing the whole thing over to Taylor and taking a break. A long break. Like maybe the length of a retirement break."

"Nope. You can't quit now. You have to see this through, particularly..." She didn't finish her thought out loud.

"You mean, particularly because Charlotte abducting you at gunpoint threw me, and if I don't get back on the horse now, I'll never ride again."

"Exactly."

"I love you," he said, his voice rough with unexpected emotion, and clicked off the call.

᎒Ꮄ᎒

One of Lagarde's emails was of particular interest. In addition to Nick's fingerprints on the thirty-eight special that killed Mark Wiseman, another partial set had been identified as Betty Liu's, who had been printed as a matter of course when she became a government employee at NIH.

The FBI's fingerprint database and analysis unit returned the result from millions of matched options in only a few hours. Of course, the eight-point marks on the trigger and stock were smudged and might be argued in court by a clever defense attorney. But, Lagarde reminded himself, no two fingerprints have ever been found identical in billions of human and automated computer comparisons. This was a truth learned early in detecting methods and routinely reiterated by experts and firmly believed by juries.

The email also told him the gun the crime scene crew found between the cushions of Wiseman's sofa matched the slugs they found embedded in the wood floor where the body had lain in Wiseman's house. Wiseman's gun, the one Taylor found in his nightstand drawer, was a match for the bullets that killed Harold Munson.

Oddly enough, Betty Liu's prints were on that gun as well. Of course, Liu's handling the guns and using them to kill anyone were two completely different actions, and the fingerprints didn't prove she shot Wiseman.

Lagarde ran a hand over his head. *But how the hell did this happen?* How did Liu, who until this moment he'd thought of as a bit player—maybe even an annoying distraction—in the Munson-Rolle drama, get access to the guns? Did she simply handle the weapons to see how they felt or did she take them? And if she stole the guns with intent to use them to murder anyone, why on earth didn't she use gloves or wipe off the gun after she shot Wiseman? How do smart people get to be so dumb?

For all Liu's intelligence, was it possible it never occurred to her that she could be traced through her fingerprints? Perhaps she didn't think she was doing anything illegal. On the other hand, maybe she thought no one was smart enough to catch her. Maybe she wasn't thinking at all. She stole two guns right out from under people's noses with intent to use them. And then she left the weapons where they could be found. *Is she taunting us? Or is she just plain crazy? Either way, I've got to follow down this lead because what else do I have?*

His distaste for Charlotte had metastasized into dislike for all scientists everywhere. He hoped he would recover from that cancer without medical meddling. Maybe someone had cooked up a T-cell soup, and a single infusion could restore naiveté. Lagarde pinched the top of his nose and shook his head. *I should long ago have realized that people are people, no matter how much education they have or what they do with their lives.*

Meanwhile, they needed a warrant to arrest Betty Liu on gun theft and possession charges. Prints alone wouldn't convict her of anything else, but she didn't know that. Maybe he could leverage her handling of the guns into a confession that would lead him to the killer. Perhaps she stole the guns and handed them off to a hired killer. *Nah. That's too convoluted. Keep it simple.*

Lagarde called the county prosecutor to expedite the warrant process and called Taylor to tell him to stop at the judge's home to ask him to sign the warrant on his way back from Regional jail.

Taylor had the warrant in hand when he arrived at the office. He called the Montgomery County Police, requesting they arrest Betty Liu on sight based on the warrant he was faxing them. Then he put out an all points bulletin for law enforcement in three states to be on the lookout for one Betty Liu, Ph.D., Asian-American, five-foot-five, approximately 120 pounds, short black hair, residing at 5348 Pooks Hill Road, Bethesda, MD. Current whereabouts unknown. He included her photo from the NIH personnel section of the institute's website.

"Is that a little over the top for theft?" Lagarde asked.

"Just in case she fled the area," Taylor explained.

Lagarde shrugged. "All the help we can get."

He was sure they'd find her. She had no idea they were interested in her. She wouldn't run. What he wasn't sure about was what she would tell them when they had her or whether it would matter to their murder case. An hour later, Montgomery County police called to say they had Dr. Betty Liu in custody. She hadn't even been trying to hide.

⚬⚬⚬

At ten p.m., Lagarde and Taylor arrived at Montgomery County Police headquarters in Gaithersburg, Maryland. To Lagarde's eye, the six-story modern building—graced by a courtyard fountain big enough to swim in—might have housed a suite of medical offices. There wasn't a whiff of formal police activities about the place except a back parking lot full of black and whites and the large fabric banner hanging above the entry that announced in English, Chinese, Japanese, Spanish and some other language he didn't recognize that they were recruiting police officer candidates and emergency dispatch specialists.

Lagarde and Taylor displayed their credentials at the reception desk and had a brief conversation with the officer, Sergeant Frederick, who executed their warrant.

"Yeah, I spotted her based on the BOLO photo. She

was just walking along Wilson Avenue—back to her apartment I guess—with a bag of Chinese food in take-home boxes from dinner she said she hadn't finished at the restaurant."

He scratched his head. "Looked like she had no-where to be in a hurry. Not like a perp who had some-thing to hide. She didn't give me any trouble when I ex-plained I was detaining her based on a warrant issued in West Virginia." He smiled slightly. "I looked through her bag to make sure she didn't have a weapon in there, and she just got into my vehicle without objection."

This woman is close to the murder of two people and maybe has deliberately destroyed someone's career and then takes herself out to dinner? Lagarde asked himself. *What kind of person is she? Or am I completely wrong about her?*

"She did keep saying she'd done nothing wrong," Sergeant Frederick reported.

Frederick asked to sit in on the interview. Lagarde said he could observe with Taylor. Lagarde was escorted to an interview room. Liu, unconstrained by cuffs and wearing jeans, a t-shirt, and a long gray sweater that came to her knees, was brought into the room by another of-ficer who remained standing by the door.

She glared at Lagarde. "How dare you have me ar-rested and mauled by the police. I was going home to feed my cat."

"Please sit down, Dr. Liu." Lagarde gestured to the chair, although he continued to stand. Taylor and Freder-ick watched from the adjacent room on the other side of the two-way glass. The interview room was set up for video recording with a control console embedded in the table top. The tape was rolling. *Nice to have money for police operations,* Lagarde thought, while he practiced the kind of silence that unnerved suspects.

Liu reluctantly took a seat and stared at the wall opposite her. Lagarde waited for her to look up at him.

"You have the right to have an attorney present," Lagarde began. "You should know that anything you say will be recorded. You have the right to refuse to answer questions—"

She waved her hand. "I don't need a lawyer, and I'm not afraid of your questions. What are you charging me with?"

That handles that. Lagarde plunged in. "Tell me how you acquired possession of Nick Waters's and Mark Wiseman's guns." This was a leap. He knew for a fact only that she'd handled the guns, not that she took them. He held his breath.

She shook her shoulders, a duck shaking off excess water from a brief dunk in a pond. "I took them."

Lagarde sat down and leaned back in his chair. *An admission of guilt on the first charge? That's too easy. Doesn't she know stealing is illegal?* "How did you come to take them?"

"I frequently followed Charlotte. When she was..." She looked around the room for the word she wanted to use. "...busy, I went into their houses and took the guns."

Was she stalking Charlotte? "How long have you been following Charlotte?"

"I don't know. A month? Two?"

"Why did you do that?"

She shrugged. "I don't really know. To see if I could? I suppose taking the guns made me feel powerful and in control. I've never had a gun."

"Do you realize that taking other people's property from their homes is considered burglary? That entering their homes without an invitation from them to do so is considered breaking and entering? These are felonies."

She looked at him blankly and shrugged. "The doors

were unlocked. They weren't using the guns. Anyway, they were involved with Charlotte."

This dumb routine is an act. There's more to this than just taking the guns. He changed tacks. "Tell me about your relationship with Charlotte."

"We're lovers." Her entire body quivered when she said it.

"She has lots of lovers. There must be more to it than that if you're following her. The others don't seem to care what she does when she's not with them."

Liu's face turned scarlet, then paled. She gripped the edge of the table. Her fingertips turned white. Keeping her teeth clenched, she said, "They don't love her." It took all her control to say nothing more. Her teeth chattered.

I need a way to break this woman. He thought about Beverly, how deeply she cared for the people she loved. "You're more than lovers, then," he said. "You love her."

Liu sighed, her shoulders relaxing—finally here was someone who understood her, who knew what she was going through. "Yes. I love her. More than anything."

"Would you do anything for her?"

"Yes. Anything. I can't exist without her."

"Would you kill for her?" It wasn't an innocent question. If he got the right answer, all the puzzle pieces might suddenly fall into place. He waited to see if the hook had sunk in and he could yank on the line.

Her eyes flashed. "Of course I would. Those men were fools. They soiled her with their sweat and saliva, their semen."

She clasped her cheeks with both hands and Lagarde thought for a minute that she would scream, but she went on with her rant.

"They're disgusting. The thought of them touching her..." She shuddered and looked up at him. "You understand. I couldn't bear it. I wanted her to come and live with me, to get away from them. I was just waiting until her divorce was final to invite her so that everything would be perfect."

"Did Charlotte know that?"

"Of course she did."

"Did she feel the same way about you?"

If Liu had feathers, she would have ruffled them. When she didn't answer his question, he nodded, indicating he understood her perfectly, and moved on. "But something happened, something went wrong with your plan."

"She didn't, she wasn't—" Liu's breath came fast, the pulse in her neck throbbed, and she broke into sobs, her words incoherent.

Lagarde waited. He handed her his handkerchief. She blotted her eyes and blew her nose. Lagarde prodded. "She didn't what?"

Tears streamed down Liu's cheeks. "She didn't want me." She groaned, sucked in her breath, covered her face with her hands and rocked herself. When she could speak again, her voice was harder. "Charlotte had no intention of making a life with me. I was a momentary fling. She used me." She turned her face away from him.

A lover scorned, why didn't I see that before? The motive is so much simpler than I imagined. Lagarde leaned forward.

"So what happened then?"

Liu's voice dropped an octave. "I couldn't bear that. She couldn't be allowed to do that to me. Not to me. I told Dickerson her research was a fraud and she didn't know what she was doing. I talked to everyone on the research team. Most of them, eventually, agreed with me. But still, Dickerson didn't set up a review of her work."

"He was moving too slowly for you, taking too much

time to consider what to do. She had seduced him, that old wind bag. So you, what? You took matters into your own hands." Lagarde found he was holding his breath again.

She nodded. "Yes. It was simple. I met Harold at a bar and suggested we have sex. He followed me out some dark, empty road that GPS took me on to the hotel where I'd told him I had a room, although I didn't. I was ahead of him. At an intersection in the middle of nowhere, I made a sharp U-turn, and he slowed to talk to me from the other side of the road. I tried to shoot him through the window of my car. But I hadn't correctly calculated the effect of a moving vehicle on the bullet trajectory, and I missed."

Lagarde nodded, encouraging her to go on, although his own mind was racing.

"Harold skidded into a parking lot and crashed into the building there. He was stupefied by the crash. I made another U-turn, pulled my car up next to his, got out, went over to his window and shot him in the head through the window. I shot twice to make sure he was dead." She raised her hands in the "nothing to it" gesture.

Lagarde's eyebrows went up, involuntarily. *This scenario is exactly what Beverly initially imagined. We've gone way beyond theft. She's the killer.* "So you shot Harold Munson."

Liu nodded.

"And then?"

"Then I went home and had the first good night's sleep I'd had in a long time."

"You didn't see anyone else there before or after you shot him?"

She shook her head. "There was nothing else. Blood rushed in my ears. My body quaked. Adrenalin coursed through me. My vision narrowed. I panted. I could only focus on one thing at a time. It's an interesting reaction, really, from a mind-body point of view. Harold opened his eyes. He seemed stunned from the crash. He saw me coming toward him with the gun. He blinked. He opened his mouth. He looked like a dying guppy in a fishbowl without water. After I was sure he was dead, all I thought of was getting away from there."

"And Wiseman? What happened with him?"

"I followed Charlotte to his house. I stood on the porch and watched them together. They were like animals. They made me sick. When she went to take a shower, I walked into his house. The door was open. He was lying on the floor naked and asleep. His obvious bliss was too much to take. I shot him."

"So you shot Harold with Wiseman's gun and then Wiseman with Nick's gun." This was a key element in the crime, the one that went to whether she knew what she was doing.

"Yes."

"Why did you do that—switch off which gun you used on which victim?"

She shrugged and smiled, as if they were conspirators discussing a secret plot together. "I thought it would throw the police off. It seemed to me you would think Wiseman killed Harold and Nick killed Wiseman."

Bingo. We've got her on means, opportunity, and motive. The murders were premeditated, probably obsessively. Lagarde suppressed his satisfaction and continued the interrogation. "Then you put Wiseman's gun back in his bedroom after you killed Harold?"

"Yes. I put it in the drawer next to his bed where he kept her panties." She made a face indicating disgust.

"You didn't see Charlotte after you shot Wiseman?"

She squeezed her lips together. "I heard her whimpering in the bathroom, but I didn't see her."

Whether she was disgusted because Wiseman kept Charlotte's panties or because Charlotte was whimpering at the sound of the gunshots, Lagarde couldn't tell. "And you put Nick's gun between the sofa cushions?"

"Yes."

"Why did you do that?"

"I had to get rid of it. I didn't need it anymore."

"You thought Wiseman saw you kill Harold, didn't you? You saw him in the car behind Harold. There was a witness to that murder. You couldn't take the chance that he would tell the police about you. He could have taken down your license plate number. You killed Wiseman because he was a witness, isn't that right?"

"No. Absolutely not. I told you. I killed that man because he was disgusting."

"But you didn't plan to kill Nick?"

Liu looked at him blankly. "What for?"

Lagarde switched tacks again. "Were you trying to frame Charlotte for their murders?"

"Oh, God, no. I wanted to free her from those men. Once they were gone, she would see that I was the only one who really loved her. Then we could be together." She inhaled deeply.

"But something else happened?"

"Well, then Dickerson went all crazy honorable on me. If he hadn't done that, I could have helped her clean up her research issues. We would have openly declared that we'd discovered problems with our data. We could have correctly reported the actual results, issued a retraction, and gone back to work. No harm done. But, no, Dickerson had to make a big production out of taking responsibility for research fraud. What a waste." She sighed.

This woman has no empathy for anyone—a natural born killer with advanced degrees. The world is a strange place. Lagarde stood up. He signaled to Taylor through the glass.

Taylor walked into the room trailed by Frederick, who was shaking his head and saying something about how you couldn't judge a book by its cover.

Taylor walked up to Liu and took her arm. "Dr. Betty Liu, I am charging you with the premeditated murders of Harold Munson and Mark Wiseman. We will escort you to West Virginia where these crimes occurred, and you will be arraigned there. I suggest you secure the services of an attorney."

Betty looked frantically around the room. "When do I get to see Charlotte? Are you taking me to where Charlotte is?"

Interesting, Lagarde thought. *She's back to her crazy act. Does she still think she can get away with murder after she's confessed to it?*

"That was amazing, sir," Frederick said. "I thought she was just some scientific type and that you had it all wrong."

Lagarde thanked Frederick for the use of the Montgomery County police premises and secured the original tape of the interview with Liu. The confession, even though she waived her Miranda rights, should hold up in court. They could call Sergeant Frederick as a witness if necessary.

Taylor looked over at Lagarde as he handcuffed Liu. "Maybe they'll be together after all," he muttered, "at least until their trials are completed. They'll be our own local Alex and Piper."

Lagarde shot him a look. "Our what?"

"*Orange Is…*" Taylor started to say, thought about who he was talking to, and stopped. "Never mind. Not important."

Liu was quiet all the way to the Eastern Panhandle's

regional jail in Martinsburg, for which Lagarde was deeply grateful.

Chapter 44

Lagarde worried that perhaps it was too early to call on Harold Munson's parents only a day after they buried their son but he had to get this duty out of the way. The obligation burned in his mind. He always dreaded these conversations with the bereaved.

He expected surgeons must feel this way when they had to tell families they'd lost a patient on the table. Except, this time anyway, he hadn't killed their son. That didn't matter though. He was the messenger, and all the turmoil they felt, their rage and helplessness might be directed at him. His training and experience had taught him to endure rage. He might have to use that training this morning.

Taylor rang the doorbell of the large Cape Cod clapboard and stone house that backed to the golf course in the upscale Cress Creek neighborhood off Shepherd Grade Road. Lagarde shrugged off his fatigue and looked around, out of habit and an instinct for fact gathering. The Munsons had retired well. Their only worry, before the death of their son, might have been a possible errant golf ball crashing through their den window. Silently chiding himself for callousness, Lagarde realized he desperately needed to get away from the job for a while.

The door was opened by Harold's father, a tall man with white hair, slightly stooped, his face haggard with grief he didn't try to hide. Lagarde removed his hat and introduced himself and Taylor. "Sorry for your loss, sir."

The man looked at them for a minute, forgetting what he was supposed to do next. Then he recovered himself, gestured to the interior and stepped aside. Lagarde walked into the large great room comfortably furnished with roomy chairs and sofas. Light from the windows played on the wood floor. Harold's mother, who seemed to have shrunk since the funeral the day before, was sitting in a chair, her head back against the cushion, staring into space. Her gray hair was unwashed, her clothes looked slept in. She didn't acknowledge anyone was in the room with her.

"Alice," Mr. Munson said in the gentlest possible voice, "we have company."

Alice looked over at her husband, seeming to wake from a dream. "Oh, Jeremy, that's nice." She turned her head and went back into her memories.

Jeremy spread his large hands out from his sides. "I don't know what to do."

Lagarde nodded. He held his hat in his hands. "We won't stay long, Mr. Munson. I just wanted to let you know we have arrested your son's killer. She's confessed."

Alice gasped, suddenly wide awake and looked at Lagarde sharply. She pushed herself to a standing position and pressed her hands flat against her heart. "Was it Charlotte? Did she do this to him? I always hated her. She, she—"

Alice put her hand over her mouth. Jeremy walked

over to her and wrapped his arms around his wife. She sobbed into his chest as if the whole world had collapsed in a sudden earthquake and all the children in it had died.

For her, it has, Lagarde reminded himself.

"Charlotte didn't kill him, ma'am," Lagarde continued, knowing it almost didn't matter what the truth was but wanting them to know what had transpired before they saw news reports on television or were blindsided by a careless visitor's comment. "The killer was a colleague of hers at work, Dr. Betty Liu."

Jeremy looked at Lagarde over his wife's head, his eyes blank. "You mean a complete stranger killed my boy?" He shook his head. The world made no sense anymore. "Why? Why would this Liu person kill my son?"

"Jealousy, sir."

"What? What are you saying?"

"She was in love with Charlotte, she says."

Lagarde stopped talking. Telling them anymore about the case against Liu wouldn't make it better, wouldn't make their grief go away, or make their son's death understandable. And the thing they wanted most—to have their son back, alive, touching them, talking to them—no explanation or assignment of guilt would ever make that happen. The fact was, no violent death was understandable. Every murder left people gasping, repeating over and over, "Why, how is this possible?" Lagarde had no answer for anyone.

"A woman? In love with Charlotte?" Harold's father was completely still, reaching deep into his memory of his daughter-in-law. Finally, he whispered, "How could anyone love her?" He went back to stroking his wife's head, his eyes closed.

Lagarde looked over at Taylor, who nodded. "We'll let ourselves out, sir."

As they went out of the door, Jeremy Munson was

consoling his wife, weeping quietly, saying, "We loved him so much, didn't we Alice, we loved him. He was our golden boy."

Chapter 45

A few days later, all paperwork was filed, interviews with the prosecutor were complete, and a court date was set for Liu's trial which should, with her recorded confession, be a slam dunk unless her lawyer pleaded her not guilty by reason of mental defect—a defense that might work if she could fool the state's psychiatrist. Lagarde had never understood the caveat of the mental defect defense. In his estimation, all murderers were insane, but that didn't mean the state shouldn't hold them responsible for crimes they committed.

Lagarde had dragged himself through this final part of the routine required of him. Fatigue had won. Everything about the office and his duties made him angry and sad at the same time. He was losing it. When his computer crashed just as he was completing the final report, he nearly picked up the ancient behemoth and threw it against the wall.

Only Taylor's quiet, "Hey, old man, I can recover it. No worries," got him to calm down.

There was only one solution. Lagarde walked into his captain's office and without any small-talk prelude said, "I'm taking vacation leave. I deserve it, and I need it, and that's that."

His boss looked up from the pile of paperwork on her desk and removed her reading glasses. "Sam?"

"It's all in the prosecutor's hands now. I've done my job. The state has its vengeance for Harold Munson's and Mark Wiseman's murders. Liu will be locked up somewhere, and Charlotte Rolle is pleading no contest to the abduction charge in return for a reduced sentence."

"Getting too old for this line of work, Sam?"

Maybe it was supposed to be a joke, but Lagarde didn't smile. "Could be. But I've got six weeks of vacation saved, and I'm going to take every damn day of it. Starting now."

She raised her eyebrows. He gave her a half-hearted salute and went to tell Taylor that he would be catching the next big murder on his own.

Taylor leaned back in his chair and shook his head. "I don't think so."

"You're ready, Jim. No worries. Just trust the forensics team and the crime lab. Ask the captain for backup. You'll be fine."

Taylor shook his head again, shrugged, and then smiled, realizing that Lagarde had given him an unexpected compliment. "Well, have a good vacation, then. See you back here in six weeks, old man."

Lagarde grinned. His mind was already at the farm, walking through the barn, breathing in the sweet smell of hay and animals, talking to Jake.

Two hours later, he and Beverly stood in the aisleway of the barn grooming their horses in preparation for a ride. Beverly ran the brush in a long, steady glide across the horse's back. The mare's coat gleamed.

"Let's go somewhere new, Sam."

Lagarde looked up from his task. "You mean take a different route today from our normal one? Where do you want to go?"

"Iceland."

It took him a minute. She didn't mean somewhere new they might ride to on the horses today. She meant a real trip on planes or boats to strange places he had never been. He let the idea roll around in his mind. Iceland was way out of his comfort zone.

"Isn't it cold there?" It was a test-the-waters kind of question, not a real objection. Frankly, he would do anything she asked. She had withstood the terror of being kidnapped at gunpoint by a murder suspect who was crazy-angry at him and never blamed him for a second.

"Who cares if it's cold. We have warm clothes. Besides, there are these natural hot springs there and a volcano. Let's do something different, something that wipes away the horror you see in your work. I want to put something else in its place, something beautiful and eternal—Northern Lights, deep oceans, primeval lands, and kind people."

Lagarde could see Beverly was passionate about this trip. He stroked Jake's nose and asked his horse, "What do you think of this idea, Jake?"

The horse nodded his head, raised his left foot and put it down. He nickered.

Lagarde grinned at Beverly. "I guess that's a yes."

They layered on pads and saddles, cinched girths, and swapped out halters for bridles with medium bits. He watched Beverly walk her horse out of the barn and mount. A woman mounting a horse might be one of the sexiest things he'd ever seen.

It was a beautiful day with clear skies and still cool enough to wear a jacket. They would ride out across the fields listening to leathers creaking, and, when they got home, they would plan to go somewhere they had never been before. Somehow, that all made sense.

He mounted and brought Jake up side by side with Beverly's horse, leaned over in his saddle, and kissed Beverly's cheek. "You are the beautiful, eternal something that wipes away the horror."

He closed his eyes for a second, opened them, and looked directly into hers. "In case you didn't know that."

She smiled at him. "Walk on," she said to her horse and moved on down the path through the greening grass.

THE END

About the Author

Ginny Fite is an award-winning journalist who has covered crime, politics, government, healthcare, art, and all things human. She has been a spokesperson for a governor, a member of congress, a few colleges and universities, and a robotics R&D company. She has degrees from Rutgers University and Johns Hopkins University and studied at the School for Women Healers and the Maryland Poetry Therapy Institute. She is the author of *I Should Be Dead by Now*, a collection of humorous lamentations about aging; three books of poetry, *The Last Thousand Years*, *The Pearl Fisher*, and *Throwing Caution*; a short story collection, *What Goes Around*; as well as two previous Detective Sam Lagarde mysteries: *Cromwell's Folly* and *No Good Deed Left Undone*. She resides in Harper's Ferry, West Virginia.

CPSIA information can be obtained
at www.ICGtesting.com
Printed in the USA
FSOW02n1845070218
44307FS